Murder of a Mermaid

A Redmond and Haze Mystery

Book 11

By Irina Shapiro

Copyright

Table of Contents

Prologue

The morning was cold but clear, the rising sun setting the deep gray waters of the Thames aflame and wrapping the still-dark buildings in a mantle of crimson light. It was a sight that took one's breath away, and Dick Hawley got to enjoy it nearly every day.

He sucked the last few drops of gin from his dented tin flask and pulled his knitted cap lower, but it would take a lot more than that to warm him up. He was near frozen, and his joints ached mercilessly, reminding him of his advancing years. But he wasn't ready to quit yet. What would he do with his time if he did, and who'd look after him once he got too old to work the oars?

There were few boats on the river, but Dick liked having the river to himself, if only for a short time. When asked, he said he was a ferryman, and he was, for a few daylight hours, but it was his nighttime activities that kept him fed and watered. He went out nearly every night, making sure to pass close to the bridges and listening intently for the telltale splash that often preceded a fortuitous find. What was it with people throwing themselves off bridges? he wondered as he rowed along hour after hour, hoping to spot a floater. Surely there were easier ways to die if one had a mind to end it all. But if they'd chosen to drown their sorrows permanently, or if someone had given them a helping hand, there was always something to find on a fresh corpse.

At best, the poor sod still had his purse and valuables on him. At worst, the coat and shoes could be sold to a rag and bone shop once they dried. Sometimes there was even a fancy waistcoat or a snuffbox still full of tobacco. Even now, Dick's pockets held a pretty timepiece and the purse he'd lifted off some posh cove he'd spotted not two hours ago. The silly bugger was hardly more than a boy, and there were sure to be parents and possibly some young woman who was about to learn she was now a widow. Shame that, but it would have been a waste had the valuables been lost to the murky waters of the river, or worse yet, picked by another boatman.

Dick peered into the shimmering sunrise, surprised to see another boat. He hadn't noticed it before, but it must have been there for some time. It was drifting slowly, leisurely, the prow nosing its way toward him. Dick shielded his eyes with a hand clad in a worn fingerless glove and fixed his gaze on the dinghy. At first, he took it to be empty. It might have come untied and drifted away from its hapless owner. But then he spotted a mass of copper curls, the tresses glinting like a freshly minted coin in the rays of the rising sun. Gripping his oars tighter, Dick rowed toward the tiny craft, his mouth opening in shock once he could see inside.

A woman lay in the bottom of the boat, her face serene, her eyes closed, her breasts bare beneath the thick tendrils of glorious hair that had been adorned with flowers. Dick leaned forward, craning his neck to get a better look at the rest of her. Her bottom half was wrapped in silky blue fabric, making her legs look like the tail of a mermaid. The woman was breathtaking, but her beauty was nothing more than a momentary illusion, for death was already her master, and it had started about its ugly work.

Despite the cold, Dick pulled off his hat and held it to his chest in a moment of silent acknowledgement of the person she had been only a few hours before. Then, he reached for the hook he used to harpoon the floaters and pulled the boat closer, tying it to his own so he could tow it to shore. He'd summon a constable once he tied up. He owed her that much, he decided, for she was his very own mermaid.

It was only when he'd pulled the dingy onto the thick mud of the bank that he noticed the gold band on her finger. It glinted in the sun, taunting him with its promise. Well, he'd be hurting no one if he took a little souvenir, Dick reasoned. This lovely no longer had any use for it, did she? Dick slid the ring off the woman's finger, then yelled, "Oi!" when he noticed a ragamuffin child hovering in the shadow of the bridge.

"Come 'ere, boy. I's got a job for ye," Dick cried, and held up a sixpence.

Chapter 1

Thursday, February 11, 1869

The morning was pleasant, the sun that shone benignly from a pale blue sky having burned off the soupy fog of the night before. The river wound into the distance, a shimmering ribbon speckled with vessels of various shapes and sizes. Boatmen called out greetings to each other as they rowed past, and there was the usual cacophony of noise from traffic along the embankment: carriages, dray wagons, carts, and hansoms all vying for space on the too-narrow road, and street vendors calling out to passersby as they tried to hawk everything from fresh buns to morning papers.

Jason Redmond and Daniel Haze alighted from a cab near the New London Bridge and made their way down the stone steps that led to the riverbank. Sergeant Meadows, who'd come to summon them not half an hour ago and had been forced to sit squeezed between the two men, led the way. Despite the time of year, the air was heavy with the reek of wet mud, rotting fish, and various other organic matter that Jason chose not to dwell on as his feet sank into the slippery muck. The Thames looked picturesque from a safe distance, but up close, the turbid water and awful smell were testament to centuries of abuse. The river swelled with sewage and corpses—human and otherwise—and everything from broken furniture to capsized boats littered the riverbed. Occasionally the river gave up its revolting contents after a particularly bad storm that left the banks strewn with debris.

Sergeant Meadows, who was tall and lean, jumped from one bit of flotsam to another like a mountain goat, managing to keep his feet dry and his helmet from sliding into his eyes, while Daniel moved gingerly, having only just recovered from major surgery. This was to be his first case since the stabbing that had robbed him of a kidney last December, and although eager to get back to work, he was understandably nervous.

Constable Napier, who was stocky, fair-haired, and at the moment pink-cheeked from the cold, stood on a chunk of board. The hems of his trousers were muddy and wet, and he looked miserable, but the young man straightened his shoulders as soon as he spotted the approaching group and smiled, obviously relieved that his watch was nearly over.

"There she is," Sergeant Meadows said unnecessarily, pointing to the weathered dingy that had been pulled up onto the bank.

"Where's the boatman who found her?" Daniel asked, since there were no other people in the immediate vicinity, although a small crowd had gathered along the embankment, the onlookers gawking at the odd scene on the riverbank.

"He went off," Constable Napier complained as he made an expansive gesture toward the opposite bank. "Said he was too tired to hang about and that he had nothing more to add."

"What did he say, exactly?" Jason asked.

"Why, nothing much, sir," Constable Napier replied. "Just that he saw a dinghy drifting toward him and rowed over to investigate. Once he realized the woman was dead, he towed her to shore and found a street urchin to go fetch a constable."

"That's very civic-minded of him," Daniel said sarcastically. "Had he taken anything off her?"

"The old geezer swore he never touched her," Constable Napier replied. "If he had, he would have taken the shawl. Pure silk and sure to fetch a few bob."

"Did you take his name and address?" Daniel pressed the constable.

"He wouldn't give it, sir."

"I wager his pockets were filled with ill-gotten gains," Daniel muttered, his lip curling with disgust. "Robbing the dead is a lucrative occupation."

"Keeps him in gin," Constable Napier agreed. "The old boy reeked of spirits."

Daniel sighed in obvious frustration. "Has Mr. Gillespie been summoned?" he asked, turning to Sergeant Meadows. It wouldn't do to move the body before the police photographer took photos.

As if on cue, a man Jason had never met hurried toward them, the tripod in his hand and the bulky boxed camera slung from his shoulder identifying him as a photographer. He wore a felt-top hat, a navy wool pea coat, and dickersons to keep his feet dry. Jason thought he might be from a newspaper that had got whiff of the story, but Sergeant Meadows raised a hand in greeting and addressed him by name.

"Good afternoon, Mr. Braithwaite. She's over here," he said again, as if the man could possibly miss the body. "Mr. Gillespie was unavailable," Sergeant Meadows explained to Daniel and Jason, and performed the introductions.

Jason ignored Mr. Braithwaite's obvious surprise when the two men were introduced. People were frequently confused by his noble rank, American accent, and inexplicable willingness to perform pro bono work for the police, but Jason felt no need to explain himself. He had grown accustomed to his newfound station, relished his work at the hospital, and was happy to offer his services to Scotland Yard, particularly on cases that were assigned to Daniel Haze. In return, Daniel encouraged Jason to participate in the investigations and treated him as a partner rather than the bored aristocrat his peers regularly assumed he was. It was a happy outcome for all concerned.

Once the social niceties were out of the way, everyone got to work, each member of the group intent on his own grim task. Jason sat back on his haunches and studied the woman before him.

She was laid out in the dingy, her head resting against the prow. Dark red hair was spread about her shoulders, the curls shimmering in the sunlight. She was one of the most beautiful women Jason had ever seen, her skin like porcelain, her features perfectly drawn. Her eyes were closed, the lashes as thick and red as fox fur.

The woman's torso was bare, her breasts full and tipped with rosy nipples. A silky peacock-blue shawl was wrapped around her lower body, hiding her pelvis and legs, and giving her legs the appearance of a fishtail. No wonder the old boatman who found her had thought she resembled a mermaid. Several colorful blooms were tucked into her hair, and a few more were scattered across her chest and stomach. There were no marks on the alabaster skin or any obvious signs of violence, but there was no doubt in Jason's mind that this woman had not died a natural death.

"She's beautiful," Constable Napier whispered on a sad sigh. "What a waste of a young life."

"She is that," Sergeant Meadows agreed as Mr. Braithwaite set up his tripod and mounted the camera.

Jason stepped aside, then carefully turned the woman over once Mr. Braithwaite had taken the initial photos. The hair on the back of the woman's head was matted, the strands glued to the skull with dried blood. Mr. Braithwaite took two more photographs before closing the camera and packing it away in its case. No one spoke.

At last, Daniel asked, "What do you think, Jason?"

"I think someone has a good imagination," Jason replied.

"Is that what killed her?" Daniel inquired, his gaze on the bloodied contusion on the back of the woman's head.

"I won't know for certain until I open her up and determine the cause of death. Let's get her to the mortuary."

Daniel turned to Sergeant Meadows. "Have you sent for the police wagon?"

"Should be here any minute, guv," Sergeant Meadows replied. "We'll get her there safe and sound. Don't you worry."

Jason sighed. This young woman would never be safe and sound again. He turned away and retraced his steps, wishing only to get away from the sight of that haunting face.

Chapter 2

Once at Scotland Yard, Jason and Daniel parted ways. Daniel didn't have the stomach to observe a postmortem, so he took himself off to catch up with the colleagues he hadn't seen since December and find a cup of tea. Jason made his way to the basement mortuary, where The Mermaid, as she was already being referred to by the men, was laid out on the slab, her tresses sliding off the table in corkscrew curls. Jason hung up his coat and hat, set his Gladstone bag on a nearby chair, put on the leather apron he wore to protect his clothes, and tucked his hair into a linen cap to keep it from falling into his eyes.

He began by unwrapping the shawl from around the woman's legs and turned it over in his hands, looking for any identifying marks. There was nothing, but Constable Napier had been correct in his assessment. The silk was fine, the shawl fairly new, the fringe not yet frayed. Jason folded the garment and set it aside, ready to turn his attention to the body.

Lying there, the woman looked perfect. Her skin was supple and smooth, her hair lustrous, and her nails clean and unbroken. This was a woman from a well-to-do family, someone who had not only enjoyed a plentiful and varied diet but had been waited on hand and foot. These were not the hands of a servant or a sempstress. They were the hands of a genteel woman, a wife, Jason thought when he noticed the slight indentation on the fourth finger of her left hand. Her ring had either been stolen at the time of death, or afterward by the boatman who'd brought her ashore. And it had probably been pure gold.

Jason lifted each hand in turn and examined every finger closely before leaning over until he was almost nose to nose with the deceased. He sniffed experimentally, then pushed his fingers into the mouth and probed before removing his hand. The teeth were intact, and there was nothing lodged inside the mouth. Jason smelled his fingers to be certain the woman had not vomited before death. She hadn't.

After wiping his hand on a linen towel, Jason lifted the eyelids to examine the woman's eyes, which were a vivid blue, the irises almost an exact match to the color of the shawl. Nodding to himself, he turned her over. Her back and thighs were unblemished except for an indentation where the bare back had pressed against the rowing bench, and the skin just over the left temple where the head had rested against the prow. The feet were soft and clean, the nails carefully buffed.

Jason parted the hair at the back of the head and examined the wound closely, noting its shape, size, and severity. He then turned the body back over and pushed apart the milky white thighs. It would be negligent not to check for sexual assault. Satisfied with his initial findings, Jason reached for a scalpel. He was ready to begin but couldn't seem to bring himself to make the first cut. He didn't normally get emotional about the cadavers he worked on, but something about this woman made him question the ethics of taking her apart and destroying something that until mere hours ago had been nearly perfect. Annoyed with himself for giving in to this uncharacteristic sentimentality, Jason pressed the scalpel into the cool flesh and sliced, making the Y incision that would open her chest and allow him a glimpse into the inner workings of her body.

Three hours later, Jason emerged from the mortuary. He found Daniel, and together they made their way to Superintendent Ransome's office. Jason hadn't seen Ransome since they'd made the arrests in the case that had nearly claimed Daniel's life, and found that he was actually glad to see the man. John Ransome had his flaws—he was arrogant and unapologetically ambitious, eager for the power that climbing the chain of command would bring— but he cared deeply about his men and about justice and was a good man to have in your corner in times of trouble. It wasn't widely known, but Superintendent Ransome had insisted that Daniel be paid a full wage during his convalescence as he had been hurt in the line of duty.

John Ransome pushed to his feet and reached across the desk to shake Jason's hand. "Pleased to see you again, Lord Redmond. I've already had the pleasure of welcoming Inspector Haze back to the fold," he said, settling back in his chair. "Gentlemen." He indicated the guest chairs.

Jason hung up his coat and hat on the rack in the corner, set down his bag, and settled in the proffered chair.

"So, what have we got?" Ransome asked, directing his question to Jason.

"The victim is a woman in her early to mid-twenties. Rigor is well established, so she's been dead for more than twelve hours. Of course, given that the body was left out in the open, it's difficult to say for certain. I think it's safe to say that she died sometime last night. She came from a well-to-do household, and I believe she was married. A ring was taken off her hand either by her attacker or by the boatman who found her this morning. She was in fairly good health but suffered from endometriosis."

"Which is?" Ransome interrupted.

"It's a condition in which extraneous tissue begins to grow on the outside of the womb. This can lead to infertility or complications if the woman does become pregnant."

"Is this condition relevant to her death?" Daniel asked.

"No."

"So, what killed her?" Ransome demanded.

"There's a fracture on the back of her head that corresponds to the subgaleal hemorrhage over the left parietal bone. The contusion is about six centimeters in diameter and is circular. The victim was struck on the back of the head with a blunt object. It could have been a cudgel or possibly a round stone. The impact would have almost certainly stunned her and possibly rendered her unconscious."

"Is that the official cause of death?" Ransome asked.

"I think it's safe to say that the victim died of a subdural hemorrhage caused by the blow to the head, but it's possible that she was still alive when she went in the boat. There was a thick fog last night, and it was cold and damp, more so on the river. Had she still been alive, the hypothermia would have almost certainly killed her, since no one would have noticed her until the fog lifted this morning."

"Could she have been saved?" Daniel asked, clearly thinking back to his own recent brush with death.

Jason considered the question. "Perhaps, if she was brought to a hospital immediately and the attending physician was able to alleviate the pressure on the brain caused by the hemorrhage, which wasn't as severe as one would expect given the size of the contusion."

"Meaning?" Ransome asked.

"I don't believe she was hit with great force," Jason speculated.

"What does that tell us about her killer?"

"Perhaps the person couldn't achieve a favorable angle, or the weapon was too heavy, or they didn't mean to kill, only to incapacitate."

"Well that last theory doesn't stand up, does it?" Ransome scoffed. "If they didn't mean to kill, then why take off her clothes and leave her floating on the river?"

"Perhaps they thought they had killed her and needed to dispose of the body. How the victim was displayed says a lot more about the killer than the method of the murder. I would hazard to guess that the victim either knew her attacker or was taken by surprise."

"What makes you say that?" Daniel asked, giving Jason a sidelong glance.

"I found no evidence of a struggle. There are no defensive wounds, no bruising on the wrists, and no particles of skin beneath the fingernails. She never saw it coming."

"The poor woman," Ransome said with a heartfelt sigh. "I hear she was quite beautiful."

"She was," Jason said. "A woman like that will always attract unwelcome attention."

"Is that it, then?" Daniel asked, clearly disappointed. "That's not much to go on."

"No," Jason agreed. "But I did find something else that might be of interest."

"Tell us, man," Ransome invited, leaning forward in his eagerness.

"There is bruising and tearing to the vagina and evidence of recent sexual intercourse. I also found twin bruises on her hip bones that would correspond to thumbs. It would appear that someone had gripped her hips with considerable force."

"So, she was raped," Daniel concluded. "Perhaps after she was knocked unconscious, which would explain the lack of defensive wounds."

"The amount of semen present would indicate that she either had sexual relations with one man several times within a short period or she was used by several men, either before or after the head trauma was inflicted."

"Perhaps she was a streetwalker who had taken several clients within a short time," Ransome speculated.

"If she was a prostitute, she was very new to the profession," Jason replied. "There are no visible signs of the abuse such a lifestyle takes on the body. Her skin is supple, her hair lustrous, her teeth in excellent condition, and there's not a mark on her, except for the contusion on her head. Prostitutes rarely have such well-tended and unblemished bodies."

"But there is the tearing to the quim," Ransome pointed out.

"Which might have been the result of ardent sexual intercourse, possibly with her husband."

Ransome nodded and averted his eyes, his lean cheeks turning the telltale pink of someone who was embarrassed. Perhaps he was recalling an ardent experience of his own. Jason had never met Mrs. Ransome but had heard she was a force to be reckoned with, much like her husband. Two such strong personalities often led to strong feeling, and passionate lovemaking.

Unlike Ransome, who seemed a bit hot under the collar, Daniel's expression was pained.

John Ransome cleared his throat. "And the presentation of the body?" he asked, moving from the physical to the abstract. "I do declare, the killers in this city are becoming more creative by the day."

"The only thing I can state with any certainty is that the shawl was relatively new and of good quality. The flowers were still fresh, so probably purchased shortly before the murder."

"So, what sort of individual are we looking for?"

"I really couldn't say," Jason replied. "But the victim was laid out with obvious care. Perhaps it was someone who'd admired her in life."

"Was there anything on the shawl to give us an inkling of who she was?" Daniel asked.

"No."

Ransome nodded. "Right. I will send runners to the other divisions to check if anyone fitting the woman's description has been reported missing. If she died last night, then surely by now someone will have realized that she's not come back. With any luck, we'll have a name for her before long. In the meantime, I will wish you gentlemen a good day. I have a meeting with the commissioner, and I will be late if I don't leave now." He grinned, the smile lighting his dark eyes. "Good to have you back, Haze. Try to keep from getting stabbed this time, eh?"

Daniel gave the man a tight smile. "I will do my best, sir."

Jason and Daniel retrieved their things and left, heading directly out into the street.

"That's all we can reasonably do for today," Daniel said. He looked tired and pale after spending the last six weeks mostly indoors.

"Get some rest, Daniel. Perhaps we'll have more information tomorrow."

"Perhaps," Daniel agreed. He pulled on his gloves, tipped his bowler, and melted into the gathering dusk of the winter afternoon.

Chapter 3

When Jason arrived at his home, Katherine was in the drawing room, mending the family's linen. She might be a noblewoman by marriage, but she was still a vicar's daughter at heart and felt she shouldn't be idle if there was work to be done. Katherine put aside one of Lily's baby gowns and rose to her feet, coming to meet Jason.

"I was beginning to worry," she said, looking at Jason anxiously. "You've been gone for hours. Is Daniel all right?"

"Daniel is absolutely fine," Jason replied as he kissed her tenderly. He then led her over to the settee she'd just vacated and settled in next to her. "We were called out on a case."

"But Daniel wasn't due back at work until next week," Katherine protested.

"It seems there was no one else available, and this case promises to be a corker."

"Tell me," Katherine urged.

She liked hearing about the cases Jason worked on and often held forth, not only on the victim but on the investigation. Normally, Jason was more than happy to listen. His wife was one of the most astute, practical women he'd ever met, and her insights often led to unexpected breakthroughs, but he hated sharing the more gruesome details with her, especially when the victim was either a woman or a child. But if he tried to spare her any unpleasantness, she'd accuse him of treating her like a feeble-minded woman who'd get the vapors at the mere mention of violence. He sighed in resignation and plunged in.

"A young woman was found on the river, her body arranged in a dinghy. She was nude, except for a silk shawl wrapped around her hips and legs. There were flowers in her hair, which is a glorious red, and petals were scattered across her stomach."

"Was she murdered?" Katherine asked, clearly shocked by Jason's description.

"I'm afraid so."

"How did she die?"

"She was struck on the back of the head. If she didn't die of the head injury, she would most certainly have died of exposure to the elements," Jason replied.

"And you say she was drifting along, adorned with flowers?" Katherine asked.

"Yes. Why?"

"It makes me think of Ophelia."

"From *Hamlet*?"

"Yes, but I'm referring to the painting by John Millais. Did you ever see it?"

"Can't say I've had the pleasure. Did you?"

Katherine shook her head. "I was only six when the painting was exhibited at the Royal Academy, but my mother had seen it and told us all about it. She said it was beautiful, but very sad and dark."

"Tell me about it," Jason invited.

"Well, you know Ophelia drowns in the play," Katherine reminded him. "One is never really sure if her death is intentional or accidental. In the painting, Ophelia is depicted lying half submerged in the water, her face serene, her body adorned with flowers. And her hair is red," Katherine added. "But she's fully clothed."

"And you think there's a connection?"

"Not an obvious one, but a young, redheaded woman floating along and decorated with flowers is not so very different, is it?"

Jason considered this for a moment. Katherine was right. There was something serene and beautiful in the way the woman had been displayed, as if whoever had laid her in that boat had tried to create a work of art out of death.

"Why do you think someone would want to put her on display like that?" Jason asked, hoping for more insights.

"I think it was a tribute. They wanted to show the world how beautiful she was, and possibly make her immortal."

"How so?"

"Did the police photographer not take photographs?"

"He did."

"Well, there you have it. Tomorrow these photographs will be in the papers, and everyone will see this *artwork*. Perhaps it will even be archived, so future generations might refer to the case."

Jason looked away for a moment. "Her legs were bound with the shawl," he said quietly. "So it's not all beauty and serenity."

"Perhaps the bondage is a symbolism of sorts," Katherine said.

"Symbolism for what?" Jason asked, wondering if Katherine was reading too much into an act of barbarism.

"The role of women in society," Katherine said without missing a beat. "Women are bound from the moment of birth, by their fathers, their husbands, the limitations society sets on them, the lack of rights over their life, property, and even the physical body and offspring. Should I go on?" she demanded hotly.

"Do you feel bound by me?" Jason asked. He felt irrationally wounded by his wife's anger, even though he didn't think it was directed at him.

"No, but I am bound *to* you. By choice," she added, smiling sweetly at him. "But not all women marry the man of their dreams, or if they do, he often turns out to be not quite what they expected and asserts his rights as soon as he has control over their finances and person."

Jason nodded. Katherine was right, of course, in everything she'd just said. "That's an intriguing theory, Katie. I hadn't considered it."

"Will you explore it?" Katherine asked, giving him the gimlet eye.

"I will share it with Daniel and see what he thinks. But we must follow the evidence, first and foremost."

"Do you have any evidence?"

"Not a shred," Jason confessed.

"I will be more than happy to consult on this case," Katherine offered playfully. "I might even charge you a fee."

"Oh, really? What's your price, Lady Redmond?"

Katherine leaned forward and kissed him. "Your complete surrender, Yank."

"Ooh, I like this game," Jason purred, and was about to show Katherine just how much when Fanny appeared at the door with a tea tray, putting an end to their negotiations.

Chapter 4

Friday, February 12

Jason had just finished a routine appendectomy and was removing the smock he wore over his clothes during surgery when Nurse Pritchard knocked on the partially open door of the doctors' lounge.

"You have a visitor, Dr. Redmond," she said. "It's Inspector Haze."

"Thank you, Nurse."

Jason grabbed his coat, hat, gloves, and walking stick, and headed downstairs, where he found Daniel waiting for him in the vestibule. Daniel stood with his back to the staircase, his hands clasped behind his back as he studied the bleak scene outside the window. The mellow sunshine of yesterday had passed, leaving behind a dreary day that made one want to sit by the fire with a large brandy and a good book.

"Daniel," Jason called out softly so as not to startle him.

Daniel turned and smiled in greeting. "I hope I didn't come at a bad time."

"You didn't. Any news?"

Daniel nodded. "The other divisions weren't able to shed any light, but the story ran in the *Daily London Post* and the *Daily Telegraph* this morning. Ransome had furnished the publications with one of the less alarming photographs. We have a name," he announced triumphantly. "Eliza Bennington."

"Who recognized her?"

"Her husband, Alan Bennington. The poor man was distraught."

"Or acting the part," Jason replied.

"Or acting the part," Daniel agreed. "In fact, he was so overcome with grief after identifying the body that Ransome sent him home. I'm on my way to speak to him now and thought you might like to join me."

"I would indeed." Jason pulled on his coat and plopped his shiny topper on his head before pulling on his gloves. "Let's go, then."

The Benningtons lived on Frances Street, just off Vauxhall Road in Lambeth. The street was lined with redbrick houses, the area masquerading as genteel but decidedly equivocal, with shops, private residences, and factories all intermingling in a somewhat haphazard fashion. Number twenty-six had a black-painted door with a brass knocker and crisp lace curtains in the windows of the front room. The step was cleanly swept, and the windows of the upper story grimly reflected the dense clouds hovering above the houses. Despite the chill, the chimney pots of twenty-six were the only ones in the row of identical houses not to belch coal smoke into the overcast sky, nor were the lamps lit against the preternatural darkness of the gloomy afternoon.

A girl of about fourteen opened the door. She had mousy brown hair tucked into a linen cap, wide amber eyes, and round cheeks, the right one smudged with soot. She wore a gray serge dress and a less-than-clean apron tied around her middle. But her smile was naturally friendly and spoke of a trusting nature.

"How can I 'elp ye, sirs?" she asked, eyeing the strangers with curiosity rather than unease.

Daniel showed her his warrant card and introduced them. "We're here to speak to Mr. Bennington," he explained.

The girl nodded mutely and let them in. "'E's just through there," she said, pointing toward the front room but not bothering

25

to announce them or take their things. Instead, she disappeared down the dim passage, presumably to return to her chores.

"Mr. Bennington," Daniel called as he advanced into the room.

The man was sitting before an unlit hearth, sucking on a pipe that had either gone out or had never been lit. The room was dispiriting, the cold damp and penetrating. Alan Bennington had dark blond hair, eyes that appeared to be dark brown in the gloom of the parlor, and a cleanly shaved, aristocratic face. He was in his shirtsleeves, the collar of his shirt open, the waistcoat unbuttoned. His disheveled appearance conveyed indifference, or distress, or just slovenliness. It was hard to tell at first glance.

The room was well appointed, with a gilt mirror above the mantel and matching walnut sofas and chairs with green velvet upholstery. A thick carpet in shades of green and cream covered the polished boards of the floor, and several occasional tables displayed various knickknacks and several framed photographs. A halfway decent painting depicting a hunting scene occupied the wall above the sofa and the green velvet curtains that were tied back with braided tassels had not yet faded from years of exposure to sunlight.

"I-I'm sorry," Mr. Bennington muttered as he staggered to his feet. He was tall and very thin. "Please, come in. I wasn't expecting you to come so soon."

He peered into the gloom of the corridor, presumably searching for the maid, then gave up and went to turn on the gas lamps before shifting his attention to lighting a fire. Within moments, the room was filled with warmth and light, making it appear more welcoming. Alan Bennington folded himself back into the chair he'd vacated and stared morosely into the flames, completely ignoring his visitors.

"Mr. Bennington, you identified the woman discovered yesterday as your wife, Mrs. Eliza Bennington," Daniel began.

The man nodded, his gaze going to the photograph on the mantel. Since he didn't seem about to rouse himself for a second time, Daniel walked over to the fireplace and reached for the photograph, passing it to Jason once he was done looking at it.

"It's her," Jason confirmed.

In the photograph, Eliza was seated, her husband standing behind her. She was looking into the camera, her eyes open wide as if in wonder, and a small smile tugged at the corners of her mouth. Her hair was elaborately styled, and she wore a fashionable gown adorned with a lace fichu. Her husband wore a somber suit and a dark-colored puff tie. Unlike his wife, he wasn't looking at the camera but at her, his expression one of such tenderness, it was impossible to believe that something awful could befall this handsome, happy couple.

"That was taken on our wedding day," Mr. Bennington said, his voice flat and emotionless. "We were so happy."

"When was this, Mr. Bennington?" Daniel inquired.

"Three years this March."

"Do you have any children?" Jason asked, wondering if the endometriosis that had disfigured Eliza's womb had affected their plans for a family.

"No. We wanted a child very badly, but Eliza wasn't able to conceive. We were still hopeful before..." His voice trailed off, and he looked like he was about to cry.

"Mr. Bennington," Daniel said, keeping his voice low and casual, "when was the last time you saw your wife?"

"Wednesday morning. We breakfasted together, as we always do...eh, did," he corrected himself, "and then I went to work."

"What do you do?" Daniel asked.

"I own a bookshop in the Strand."

"What happened then?"

Alan Bennington shrugged, as if the details no longer mattered. "I closed up at six and came home. The house was dark. Eliza wasn't here."

"What about your maid?" Jason asked.

"Nell takes her half day on Wednesdays. She'd gone to visit her mother."

"Did you look for Mrs. Bennington?" Daniel asked.

"Of course. I walked the streets, searching for her. I even walked toward Westminster Bridge. I thought perhaps she'd gone to the shops on Oxford Street and was running late."

"What did you do when she didn't come home?" Jason asked.

"I questioned Nell as soon as she returned. She said Eliza was in fine spirits when Nell left and had not mentioned any plans for the afternoon. I stayed up all night, looking out the window, waiting for her. I didn't know what to do."

"But you didn't report her missing," Daniel said.

"No."

"Why?"

"I was afraid, I suppose. Reporting her missing to the police would be admitting that she was really gone. I did scour the papers, though. I thought maybe there'd been an accident. And then I saw the photograph."

Alan Bennington buried his face in his hands and began to cry, his shoulders quaking with grief. "I don't understand," he moaned. "What was she doing in that boat? Who put her there?"

"Mr. Bennington," Daniel began once the man had calmed down somewhat, "did Eliza have any family, friends? How did she spend her time while you were working?"

"Eliza has a father and an older brother. They live in Mornington Crescent, in Camden. Eliza's father is the vicar of St. Pancras Old Church, and her brother, Alastair, works for the railways."

"How did you two meet?" Jason asked.

"Eliza used to come into my shop whenever she was in the area. She loved books."

"Did she come alone?"

"No, she came with her sister-in-law. They made a day of it once a month or so. They'd go shopping in Oxford Street, then come to the bookshop. Once, I arrived at the Willow—that's a tearoom near the shop—and found Eliza and Janet having tea. They invited me to join them," Alan explained shyly. "It was Janet's idea. She was matchmaking, you see."

"Her efforts paid off," Daniel remarked.

"Yes. Eliza and I were married three months later, with her father's blessing," Alan added.

"Are you on good terms with Eliza's relations?"

"Yes. Yes, of course."

"Did your wife behave normally in the days leading up to her death? Was she afraid of anything, or anyone?" Daniel inquired.

"She seemed absolutely fine."

"Mr. Bennington, when was the last time you and your wife were intimate?" Jason asked.

Alan Bennington's pale cheeks flared, his words coming in a torrent of indignation. "How dare you, sir? How dare you ask such an impertinent question when my beloved Eliza lies dead in that horrid mortuary, her mortal remains desecrated, her privacy violated by some faceless butcher who took it upon himself to perform a postmortem? Without my permission, I might add. What gives you the right?" he bellowed.

"Mr. Bennington, I was the one to perform the postmortem on your wife," Jason said.

"And who are you, exactly? What is your role here, *my lord*?" Bennington mocked angrily.

"I am a trained surgeon, and I work with the police. I did not ask the question out of morbid curiosity. There was evidence of recent sexual activity, and I had hoped to rule out one possible avenue of inquiry," Jason explained patiently. He could understand the man's anger, and his frustration at having the woman he loved probed and dissected by indifferent hands. "Your wife's remains were treated with the utmost respect," he added quietly.

Alan Bennington nodded. "Eliza and I had not..." His voice trailed off. "Not in the past few days," he added, nearly choking on the words. "When can I bury her?"

"As soon as you make the arrangements for the body to be collected by an undertaker," Daniel said.

"Thank you," Alan said, even though he had little to thank them for. "You will find whoever did this, won't you?" His gaze was so earnest and hopeful, Jason hoped Daniel would reassure him, but Daniel was noncommittal.

"We will do everything in our power to apprehend the killer, Mr. Bennington. Now, we'd like to speak to Nell, if we may."

"Of course. I'll ask her to come in."

Alan Bennington left the room, closing the door softly behind him.

Chapter 5

Nell looked uncertain as she entered the room and stood as far from Jason and Daniel as the space permitted. She'd cleaned her face and washed her hands, but her hair was still trying to escape from beneath the cap, and her apron was stained. Daniel wasn't sure how much she knew of what had befallen her mistress, but it was only natural that she would feel intimidated at the prospect of being interviewed by the police.

"Sit down, Nell," Daniel said gently, and pointed toward the sofa. Nell perched on the edge, clasping her hands in her lap.

"Nell, are you aware of what happened to Mrs. Bennington?"

Nell nodded. "I know she were found dead, sir."

"Do you know the circumstances that surround the discovery of the body?"

"No, sir. Mr. Bennington didn't see fit to tell me, and I were too afraid to ask."

That sounded reasonable enough. Why would Alan Bennington tell his teenage maidservant that her mistress had been found nude and floating down the Thames with a crown of flowers? That would be wholly inappropriate.

"Nell, was your mistress frightened or upset these last few days?" Jason asked.

Nell shook her head almost violently. "No, sir. She were just as always."

"And how was she, always?"

"Kind, understanding. She were a gentle person," Nell added, her face crumpling. "I ain't very good at me job, but she never scolded me."

Jason extracted his handkerchief and handed it to her, but Nell balked at taking it. "Thank ye, sir. I've got me own." She sniffled and pulled out a plain square of cotton.

"Nell, did Mrs. Bennington have any friends? Did she receive any callers or pay calls of her own while Mr. Bennington was at work?" Jason asked.

"Mrs. Reynolds came to call. Mrs. Bennington's sister-in-law," Nell explained tearfully. "She used to come more often, but she's had a baby, so Mrs. Bennington usually went to see 'er instead. Reverend Reynolds were 'ere only last week. 'E came to dine at least once a month. And Mrs. Henchy came to tea on Thursdays."

"And who's Mrs. Henchy?" Daniel asked.

"She lives just down the street, sir. Mrs. Henchy and Mrs. Bennington were friends, of sorts."

"What do you mean by 'of sorts'?"

"Mrs. Bennington weren't one to gossip, sir. She liked to talk about books and art."

"What sort of art did she like?" Jason asked.

"I don't rightly know, sir, but she liked to visit the museums."

"Was she friendly with any other neighbors?" Daniel asked.

"There's the old bag across the street," Nell said with obvious disdain. "She were always trying to chat up Mrs. Bennington, but the mistress didn't like 'er. Said she weren't the right sort."

"Nell, did Mrs. Bennington ever mention mermaids?" Daniel asked, feeling silly. He expected Nell to stare at him, dumbfounded, but Nell nodded eagerly, happy to help.

"Yes, sir. She loved *The Little Mermaid*. That's a fairytale," Nell added for their benefit. "It were 'er favorite, and she even read it to me once. Mrs. Bennington bought a storybook for when she 'ad a child of 'er own. A beautiful thing it were too," she said wistfully. "Never 'ad a storybook when I were a young 'un."

"What happened to it?" Jason asked.

"She gave it to Mrs. Reynolds. Said she 'ad no use for it." Nell sighed. "Oh, and there's a mermaid on the dressing table," she rushed to add. "I were ever so careful dusting it."

"May we see it, Nell?"

"Yes, sir."

Nell left the room and returned with a porcelain figurine of a mermaid seated on a rock. The mermaid had long, flowing red hair that artfully covered her bare breasts, and a peacock-blue fishtail. A wreath of fresh flowers adorned her head, and she gazed off into the distance, her blue eyes wide with wonder and a secret little smile playing about the pink-painted lips.

"Where did Mrs. Bennington get this?" Daniel asked.

"Mr. Bennington gave it to 'er on their first wedding anniversary. She treasured it, the mistress did, 'specially since the master said the mermaid looked just like her. Beautiful and mysterious," Nell said with a deep sigh.

"Nell, who else knew about this figurine?"

"I don't know, sir. It were on the mistress's dressing table, and no one went into the bedroom save Mr. Bennington. And meself, o' course."

"Thank you, Nell. And which house is Mrs. Henchy's?" Daniel asked as an afterthought.

"Twenty-two, sir."

Jason and Daniel took their leave but stopped just outside, on the pavement before the house. "Let's speak to Mrs. Henchy," Daniel said. "If she's a gossip, as Nell implied, she might know something of the Benningtons."

"Yes, I—" Jason began just as the door of the house across the street opened and a young maidservant stepped out, heading toward them.

"Are you from the police, sirs?" she asked shyly.

"Yes. I'm Inspector Haze of Scotland Yard, and this is my associate, Dr. Redmond."

There were times when Jason's rank came in handy when interviewing potential suspects, but it was usually a detriment when speaking to common folk, who tended to clam up in the presence of nobility and would have more faith in a doctor than in a privileged nobleman. Jason didn't mind and actually encouraged Daniel to introduce him as just plain Mr. Redmond, as British surgeons were referred to, or Dr. Redmond, since unlike British surgeons Jason was university educated.

"Please, sir. My mistress would like a word."

The maidservant's speech was more cultured than Nell's, and Daniel briefly wondered if that was a reflection of her mistress's standards or just the fact that the young woman might have had some education prior to going into service.

Once inside, she showed them into a fussy parlor. The room was so overstuffed with furniture, ornaments, and domed bird displays that Daniel found it difficult to breathe, his chest constricting with an unfamiliar anxiety. His gaze fell on the yellow glass eyeballs of a stuffed fox that stood on its hind legs, its teeth bared, the paws raised. Daniel felt the bile rise in his throat, his heart going out to these creatures that were suspended between life and death and used as decorations for individuals who perceived their remains as objects of beauty.

A woman in her fifties sat in a wingchair by the window, her slipper-clad feet propped up on a velvet footstool. She was dressed in a gown of red and green tartan, the lace ruffles on her bosom and puffed sleeves making her appear even wider than she actually was beneath all that fabric. She wore a lace cap over dark hair that was gently threaded with silver, and a thick velvet ribbon decorated with a cameo brooch around her neck. Daniel thought the ribbon might be more to hide her aging neck than to display the cameo. The woman's lashes and eyebrows were surprisingly dark for someone of her age, and there was a delicate blush on her still-smooth cheeks. She must have been very beautiful once and was obviously still vain, since her appearance had to be enhanced by the use of cosmetics.

Daniel produced his warrant card and introduced himself and Jason. The woman nodded and smiled graciously, obviously pleased they had come.

"Orchid Bloom," she announced proudly. Daniel bit the inside of his lip to keep from laughing at the silly name. "Do sit down, gentlemen," she said. Her voice was unexpectedly husky and her tone almost playful.

Having settled on a moth-eaten sofa, Daniel faced the woman. "You wished to speak to us, Mrs. Bloom?"

"It's Miss Bloom, actually," she purred. "I never married because I wanted to keep the name, you see. Orchid Bloom is so pretty, don't you think? It was my mother's idea. My father wanted to call me Imogen, but Imogen Bloom doesn't sound quite as lovely. My name was well known once, and I was much admired," she added wistfully.

"It's a very beautiful name," Jason agreed, clearly amused by the woman.

"Have you never heard of me?" Miss Bloom asked, her lips pouting like those of a young girl.

"Should we have?" Daniel asked.

"I was quite famous in my day," Miss Bloom said, a self-satisfied smile playing about her lips. "It was said I was the most beautiful flower to adorn Drury Lane."

"You were an actress?" Jason asked.

Miss Bloom smiled wider, a faraway look in her eyes. "I was. Until I was pushed out by younger women, but that's the way of it. No one lasts long upon the stage. I held on longer than most. But I was smart," she announced, the smile becoming almost predatory. "Unlike other actresses who fall on hard times as soon as the parts dry up, I made sure I had something to fall back on."

Everything this woman owned had probably been paid for by past admirers, Daniel decided as he studied her. She had practically ignored him but clearly found Jason to her liking and was appraising him openly.

"It's always wise to plan ahead," Jason agreed, smiling at her as if she were still the beautiful young woman of her memories. "Did you know Mrs. Bennington, Miss Bloom?"

"I did, yes. She called on me from time to time. Out of Christian duty, I expect," she added bitterly. "She was a pretty young thing, I'll give her that. Had she been of noble birth, she could have done very well for herself. But she seemed content with her lot. Loved her husband."

"Did she tell you that?" Daniel asked.

"Not outright, no. But when you've acted out as many romantic entanglements as I have, you can always spot such things. I often saw them from the window, and there was genuine affection between them."

"Miss Bloom, when was the last time you saw Eliza Bennington?"

"Wednesday afternoon. She left the house a few minutes after Nell. Nell is always off like a shot at noon on Wednesday. It's her half day."

"And which way did Mrs. Bennington go?" Daniel asked.

"To the right. I expect she was heading toward the bridge. She went that way every Wednesday."

"Do you know where she went?"

"No, she never shared that with me, but she was in a hurry. Her step was brisk, and she looked determined."

"When did she normally come back?" Jason asked.

"She usually returned around five. And she didn't have anything with her, no parcels or packages. Only her reticule."

"How did she seem when she got back?"

"Furtive," Miss Bloom replied coyly, clearly enjoying the attention.

"Do you have a theory you'd like to share with us?" Jason prompted.

Orchid Bloom beamed at him as if he were one of her admirers. "She had a lover," Miss Bloom announced.

"What makes you say that?" Daniel asked.

Miss Bloom looked at him as if he were the daftest man she'd ever laid eyes on. "Well, Inspector, you tell me why a woman would only go out after her maid has left and return, empty-handed, I might add, before her husband is due back from work. She wanted to make sure no one saw her come and go, and she obviously had a standing appointment with someone, didn't she?"

"Have you ever seen a man who might fit the bill call on Mrs. Bennington at home?" Jason asked.

"The only two men who ever called on her were her father and brother."

"Did anyone else come to call while Mr. Bennington was at work?"

"Mrs. Henchy called once a week. She's a real busybody, that one," Miss Bloom said, completely missing the irony of that statement.

"Does Mrs. Henchy call on you as well?" Daniel asked.

"No," Miss Bloom replied, clearly offended. "She doesn't have a high opinion of women who must earn their living. She has a mighty high opinion of Mrs. Reynolds, though. Always tries to stop in when that woman calls, probably in the hope that she'll be invited to stay to tea. She'd love nothing more than to further the acquaintance."

"And had she managed to secure an invitation to tea while Mrs. Reynolds was visiting?"

Orchid Bloom nodded curtly. "Eliza Bennington was too polite a creature to chuck her out, but little does Mrs. Henchy know that the company she seeks is not as exalted as she might imagine."

"How do you mean, Miss Bloom?" Jason asked.

"That Janet Reynolds. She is married now and has a fine house, from what I hear, but it wasn't so long ago that I saw her at Drury Lane. Janet Brody, she was then. A chorus girl," Miss Bloom spat out. "Didn't even have enough gumption to try for a speaking part. Still, it worked out well for her. Snagged a wealthy husband so she can play at being respectable. I wonder if the Reverend Reynolds knows the truth of her background. Not very likely, I say! A man of God would never stand for such a thing."

Daniel tried to bite back his impatience. The woman oozed bitterness and probably hadn't wished either young woman well, jealous that they had youth and the male companionship that Miss Bloom clearly lacked.

"So, Mrs. Bennington went out on Wednesday afternoon, as was her habit, and never returned?" Daniel asked, eager to bring the conversation back to the victim.

"Isn't that what I said? She went out as soon as Nell skedaddled, and never came back. I saw that husband of hers looking out the window, then going out. I suppose he went to search for her."

"What time did he return?"

Miss Bloom shrugged. "I retire at nine, Inspector, so it had to be after that. I saw him again the following day. He left just after I had my breakfast and didn't come back until about noon. He looked dreadful. Scared out of his wits. I didn't know Eliza was dead then, but I suspected something was terribly wrong. And then Polly brought me the papers." She shook her head in disbelief. "What a way to go. Wish I had seen that with my own eyes. Did you see the headline in the *Daily Telegraph*?" she asked, clearly relishing the moment. "*Death of a Mermaid*. Imagine that."

Daniel pushed to his feet. He didn't think Miss Bloom had anything more to tell them, and the obvious pleasure she took in someone else's tragedy was setting his teeth on edge. "Thank you for the information, Miss Bloom. You are a very observant witness," he added for good measure.

"Thank you, Inspector. Had I been born a man, I would have considered a career in the Police Service myself. My skills would have been invaluable, I think."

"Undoubtedly," Jason agreed.

Miss Bloom preened with the praise, and the men took their leave, inhaling deeply once they were outside to clear away the fetid smell of Miss Bloom's parlor and the tang of bitterness that had hung in the air. They then made their way toward the Henchy residence.

Despite being labeled a busybody, Mrs. Henchy had nothing useful to add. She had no idea Mrs. Bennington was dead, since Mr. Henchy did not approve of respectable women reading the papers, nor did she know of anything or anyone who might have wished to hurt her neighbor. She became hysterical when the details were revealed to her and had to retire to her bedroom, cutting the interview short.

Frustrated with the lack of progress, Daniel and Jason returned to Westminster and adjourned to a chophouse Daniel favored. Discussing a case over a meal was always more pleasant than comparing ideas out in the street or in Daniel's cramped office at Scotland Yard, and since they had nothing of great import to share with Superintendent Ransome, there was no rush to get back.

Chapter 6

Daniel ordered mutton chops with boiled potatoes while Jason decided on a fillet of beef served with mashed potatoes and peas. There were times when he missed American food, especially some of the spicy and flavorful Creole dishes he'd tried in New Orleans before the American Civil War, and the Thanksgiving feast his mother had put on every year before life had been so irrevocably changed. Mrs. Dodson had tried to recreate a Thanksgiving dinner last November, and although Jason was grateful for her effort, it had neither tasted nor felt the same. But a beef steak was something he could always appreciate, and he looked forward to the meal.

They didn't speak about the case until the waiter brought their drinks, beer for Daniel and red wine for Jason, and a basket of warm bread, and departed. Daniel reached for a piece of bread and spread it with butter, taking a bite and chewing thoughtfully.

"We know more than we did yesterday," he said, "but not enough to draw any conclusions."

"On the contrary," Jason replied. "We know that Eliza Bennington had a fondness for mermaids, a fact that her husband was well aware of. We also know that she went somewhere on Wednesdays, leaving immediately after Nell to keep her appointment private."

Daniel nodded. "For all we know, she went for a walk or to visit the British Museum. Do you think someone presented her as a mermaid to point a finger at her husband?"

"Or perhaps it *was* the husband," Jason replied. "If Miss Bloom is correct in her assumption that Eliza Bennington had a lover, it's possible that her husband killed her to assuage his wounded pride."

"But why do it in such a public way?" Daniel mused. "Surely there are easier ways to dispose of an errant wife."

"Perhaps he never expected her to be found."

The waiter reappeared and set the steaming plates before them, looking from one man to the other for approval.

"Thank you," Daniel said, dismissing the man.

"We know that Eliza Bennington was last seen around noon on Wednesday," he said to Jason. "Her body was discovered by Dick Hawley just after sunrise on Thursday, and rigor was well established by the time you first saw the remains, so it's safe to assume that she was killed on Wednesday evening. So," he went on, punctuating this thought with his fork, "if we can determine the speed and the direction of the current, we can perhaps estimate where the boat went into the water. Perhaps we can find witnesses or discover if the victim had some connection to the area."

"That's an excellent idea," Jason replied.

"It's the only one I have," Daniel said moodily.

"Katherine had a theory, as it happens."

"Oh?"

"The way the body was displayed reminded her of a painting by John Millais. *Ophelia*."

Daniel shrugged. "Never seen it. Was Ophelia naked?"

"No, but she was in the water, adorned with flowers. She was portrayed as beautiful and ethereal in death."

"Is the painting currently on display?" Daniel asked, his expression thoughtful.

"I don't believe so. Katherine mentioned that her mother had seen it at the Academy when Katherine was a child."

Daniel shook his head, clearly unimpressed with the tenuous link. "So, unless the killer is an avid patron of the arts who happened to see the painting when it was on display years ago, chances are they wouldn't be aware of it. Please thank Katherine for her suggestion, but I think we need to stick to the facts, scant though they might be."

"All right," Jason said. He agreed it was a far-fetched theory, but he'd felt he owed it to Katie to at least mention it.

"We know that the way the body was displayed was intended to make a statement, and we can also assume that the killer was aware of Eliza Bennington's affinity for mermaids. The man had to have known her quite well," Daniel concluded.

"Are we sure the killer is a man?"

Daniel's eyebrows lifted in surprise. "You said there was evidence of recent sexual congress and Alan Bennington clearly stated that it wasn't with him."

"Yes, but what if Eliza was murdered by her lover's wife?" Jason suggested.

Daniel stopped chewing, the idea having apparently never occurred to him. "That is a viable possibility. Which would also explain the shocking display. She might have wanted her husband's mistress to be humiliated in death, her photograph in the papers, the lurid details discussed in drawing rooms and taverns."

"We need to discover who Eliza Bennington's lover was. If she had one," Jason added.

"She must have had," Daniel replied. "It's the only theory that truly makes sense. An illicit love affair would give several people a motive for murder. Her husband, the wronged wife, as well as the lover himself, if Eliza had crossed the line in some way or had decided to end the affair."

"She seems to have been close to her sister-in-law," Jason said. "Perhaps she confided in Mrs. Reynolds."

"I think it's time I spoke to Eliza's family."

"If you can wait until tomorrow, I'll come with you. I'm giving a lecture later today on the benefits of maintaining a hygienic environment in the operating theater. I will probably get laughed out of the auditorium," Jason said with a shake of the head. He was forever advocating the cleaning of surgical instruments between procedures and advising his fellow doctors to wash their hands, but his suggestions fell on deaf ears. Some of his fellow surgeons actually thought he was quite deluded and weren't shy about saying so. Jason pulled out his pocket watch and checked the time. "In fact, I really must be going."

"Tomorrow will be fine. In the meantime, I will see what I can discover about the currents," Daniel said.

"That sounds like an excellent plan."

The two men paid for their meal, said their goodbyes, and headed in opposite directions.

Chapter 7

By the time Daniel arrived at home, he was both physically and mentally exhausted. After luncheon, he had returned to Scotland Yard to consult with Superintendent Ransome on whom best to approach regarding the tides and currents theory he had formulated. Ransome had directed him to the Admiralty to speak with the head of the HM Coast Guard. A sprightly septuagenarian by the name of Admiral Arthur Skelton occupied a spacious office decorated with maps, antiquated nautical equipment, and several models of warships, executed in minute detail and protected from the elements by glass cases.

Admiral Skelton, who had puffed on a foul-smelling cigar the entire time Daniel had spent in his office, went on at great length about the incoming and outgoing tides, locks and weirs, islands, tributaries, currents, and strong winds from the North Sea that could lead to flooding. He also pored over a map, poking his stubby, tobacco-stained finger at various points along the river, but when all was said and done, he had no inkling where the boat might have gone in.

"Execution Dock," he announced in his phlegmy voice. "That's where I would do it. If only because the location has such a lyrical sense of poetry. It has seen the deaths of hundreds of pirates, smugglers, and mutineers. Oh, you should have seen it, Inspector Haze. Those were the days. I witnessed my first execution when I was just eight. My father was a sea captain and wanted to make certain I fully understood the gravity of committing a crime at sea. He took out a rowboat so that we could watch the hanging from the river. It was a sight to behold," the admiral said, his eyes clouded with what was obviously a cherished memory.

"The procession from Marshalsea Prison was led by the High Court Marshal and his deputy, who carried a silver oar. The condemned—there were three that day—rattled behind them in a cart, the chaplain riding with them in case they wished to make a last-minute confession. The youngest prisoner was no more than twelve, and he looked terrified, but in those days, a twelve-year-old was considered a man and tried like one."

They still are, Daniel thought, but didn't dare interrupt.

"If lucky, they died quickly, but there was a special punishment reserved for pirates and smugglers. The shortened rope," he announced with relish. "The drop wasn't long enough to break the neck, so they died by slow strangulation, their limbs jerking as they suffocated. The Marshal's Dance, it was called. You should have heard the laughter from the crowds as they watched the three convicts perform their pantomime. Even my father permitted himself a smile, although it was a solemn occasion."

"Were the families permitted to claim their loved ones' remains?" Daniel asked.

"After the body was submerged by three tides," Admiral Skelton replied. "Fitting, wouldn't you say?"

Daniel thought the whole thing was barbaric in the extreme but decided not to engage in a debate with a man who obviously missed the "good old days" of public torture. "The young woman was not hanged," Daniel reminded him instead.

The admiral shrugged. "I'd ask around Wapping if I were you," he said. "Perhaps someone saw something."

"I will. Thank you, Admiral."

"Always happy to assist Scotland Yard," Admiral Skelton said, puffing furiously on his cigar. "Hope you got what you came for."

Daniel hadn't, but he wasn't about to say so. He thanked the admiral again and left, gulping fresh air once he was outside.

At home, Daniel found Charlotte in the kitchen with Grace, sitting in the highchair that had been a present from her grandmother. The chair kept Charlotte from falling out and even had a small tray to hold a plate and a cup. Charlotte was currently enjoying slices of dried apple while Grace deftly diced beef into small cubes.

"Papa," Charlotte chirped happily.

"Good afternoon, my darling," Daniel said, smiling at the child.

Charlotte held out a piece of apple, and he accepted it and popped it in his mouth, making her laugh.

"Where's Miss Grainger?" Daniel asked Grace, who wielded the sharp knife like a trained assassin.

Grace shrugged. "Said she had an errand to run, sir."

"Has she been gone long?"

"'Bout an hour now."

Daniel nodded and lifted Charlotte out of the chair.

"Story," Charlotte demanded.

Daniel took Charlotte up to the nursery and settled in the window seat. After she had selected *The Rose and the Ring* by William Makepeace Thackeray and climbed into his lap, Daniel read the story, but his mind wasn't on fairytales, at least not those with happy endings. He couldn't get Eliza Bennington off his mind.

Murder was commonplace. In a metropolis the size of London, countless people died every week through acts of violence, but the method of the murder, as well as the motive, was usually obvious. Tavern brawls that ended badly, stabbings or shootings during a robbery, gang-related violence that was becoming more frequent, and the usual crimes of passion that were easy enough to explain away. The police didn't always cuff the culprit, but they understood the nature of the crime and had a fairly clear idea of the sort of person who'd perpetrated it. But the case of Eliza Bennington was wholly different.

Few killers bothered with the details once the act was done, all their thoughts directed toward avoiding repercussions. Most victims were left where they fell or were dumped in the river or a ditch, their killers long gone by the time the body was discovered. Whoever had killed Eliza Bennington had taken the time to remove her clothes, wrap her in the shawl, and sprinkle flowers over the body. That would have taken a quarter hour at the very least, during which time they could have got as far away as possible from the scene of the crime. Why had it been so important for the killer to arrange the body just so? Was it an act of love? A desire to humiliate the victim? An attempt to attract the sort of attention that would get all of London talking? The presentation of the body was key, but a key to what?

It was early days yet, but Eliza had been described as a kind, gentle young woman who was devoted to her husband and close with her family. The suggestion that Eliza had been involved in an adulterous affair was not to be ignored, but Daniel had to consider the source, and Miss Orchid Bloom did not fill him with confidence. She seemed a bitter woman who would be murderously jealous of someone as young and beautiful as Eliza Bennington; however, until he could discover where Eliza had gone on Wednesday afternoons, he could hardly discount her suggestion.

Daniel sighed and closed the book, glad Charlotte had dozed off. Her dark head rested against his chest, her breathing even in sleep. Daniel kissed the top of her head, then pulled out his pocket watch and checked the time. It was nearly five. Where was Rebecca? It was growing dark outside, and he was concerned for her safety. And eager to see her.

Daniel was grateful to be alive after the last case had nearly cost him his life and left him with only one kidney, but the timing couldn't have been worse. He had just declared himself to Charlotte's governess, and she had given him cautious permission to court her when he'd found himself in the hospital, fighting for his very survival. Rebecca had been there waiting for him when he finally came home and had even kissed him in a moment of joyful relief at their reunion, but their romance had stalled, Rebecca's role going from that of a young woman respectfully courted by her employer to nursemaid to said employer in his hour of need.

There had been moments when Rebecca seemed more wife than governess and others when Daniel was overcome with embarrassment, mortified that the woman he'd come to hold in such high regard should see him at his most vulnerable and unkempt. Even though he was fully recovered, Daniel couldn't get over the insecurity the past few months had seeded in him. And it seemed Rebecca felt the same. She had cooled toward him, and had been undertaking more unexplained errands of late, disappearing for hours on end.

Daniel longed to ask her where she went but felt he would be overstepping his authority. He had no right to question her, and she had every right to step out for an hour if she needed to. Grace was always happy to look after Charlotte, and Charlotte was happiest in the kitchen, eating a bit of fruit or a leftover biscuit as she watched Grace go about her chores.

Daniel peered out the window, watching the darkening street for Rebecca's silhouette. What if Eliza Bennington had been a victim of some madman, and what if Rebecca unwittingly came across the same man? He knew it was unlikely, but Rebecca worked for the very man who was investigating the case. What if that made her a target?

Daniel breathed a sigh of relief when he heard the front door and Rebecca's cheerful voice downstairs. She must have come from the other direction. After a few moments, he heard her light step on the stairs and then she was standing in the doorway, illuminated by the light from the lamp in the corridor, a warm smile on her face. Charlotte lifted her head and smiled back, happy to see the woman she had come to see as her mother. Some days, Daniel wondered if Charlotte could even remember Sarah, who had died more than six months ago now.

Rebecca lifted Charlotte out of Daniel's arms and held the little girl close, stroking her hair until she was fully awake. It was time for nursery tea, so Daniel unfolded himself from the window seat and left Rebecca to it, going downstairs to pour himself a drink. Perhaps once Rebecca had put Charlotte to bed, they'd have dinner and then sit companionably by the fire and discuss the case, as he had done with Sarah in the days when she'd still cared to speak to him. Rebecca was clever. She might offer some insight into the life of the victim, who'd been around her own age.

But Rebecca never came down for dinner. She pleaded a headache and retired to her room, leaving Daniel alone with his thoughts.

Chapter 8

Saturday, February 13

Saturday morning found Daniel and Jason in Camden Town. They decided to start with the Reverend Reynolds and headed directly to St. Pancras Old Church on Pancras Road. Despite the name, the church looked practically new, having been restored only about twenty years ago. It was a lovely building, inside and out, the interior spacious and light.

Their footsteps echoed inside the nearly empty building, but the man who sat in the front pew, staring mournfully at the beautiful triptych behind the altar, didn't turn at first. His shoulders were hunched, his hands clasped as his lips moved in silent prayer. When he finally shifted his gaze and faced the two visitors, lines of despair were etched into his lean face. He looked to be in his fifties, with thick salt-and-pepper hair, elegant eyebrows, and an aquiline nose, his eyes the same blue as his daughter's.

"Reverend Reynolds?" Daniel asked softly, sorry to have disturbed the man in what had clearly been a private moment.

"Yes." The reverend did not stand or offer words of greeting. He simply sat there, probably hoping they would leave him in peace.

"I'm Inspector Haze of Scotland Yard, and this is my associate, Lord Redmond. May we ask you a few questions about your daughter?"

Reverend Reynolds nodded and pointed to the pews directly across the nave. Daniel and Jason sat, taking the end seats of the two adjacent pews, their hats in their hands as a sign of respect for both the house of God and the man across from them.

"What do you want to know?" the reverend asked. His voice was flat, his gaze guarded.

"What sort of woman was Eliza?" Daniel asked.

"Passionate. Headstrong."

"Did you approve of her choice of husband?" Daniel asked, assuming that the character traits mentioned reflected on her marriage.

The reverend sighed. "Alan Bennington is a good man, but he is…" He never finished the sentence, allowing the silence to lengthen.

"He is what?" Jason prompted.

"Ineffectual," the reverend replied with obvious reluctance. "Men and woman have their roles, and Alan wasn't adhering to the script." The man made it sound as if the members of his family were actors in a play rather than real people, but perhaps it made it easier for him to express his feelings on the subject.

"How do you mean, Reverend?" Jason inquired, asking the question that was on Daniel's lips.

"Alan acquired the bookshop some years ago. Since then, he's made no improvements, has cultivated no new custom, and has run up a debt. It's his role as a man, the head of his family, to support those dependent on him. He has failed to do that."

"Did Eliza tell you that?" Daniel asked. The Benningtons didn't reside at a fashionable address, but the house was comfortable and tastefully furnished, and they had a servant, albeit a rather inexperienced one. Perhaps the reverend was judging his son-in-law too harshly.

"She didn't have to," the reverend replied. "Alan came to Alastair, my son, a year ago, begging for a loan. Alastair is an ambitious man, and a successful one. He sees to his family's comfort and financial security."

"And did Alastair give Alan Bennington a loan?" Jason asked.

"He did, for the sake of his sister. The terms of the loan were a year with ten percent interest."

"Was the loan repaid?"

"No. Alastair has not seen a farthing."

"What were the funds for?" Daniel asked.

"To pay off Alan's debts, I presume. My daughter hadn't had a new gown in a year, nor could she afford a proper cook. They have that girl, Nell. She's hardly more than a child and is expected to do the work of several people. Alastair had offered to hire a cook for Eliza, but she refused. She was concerned with wounding her husband's pride," the reverend said bitterly.

"Reverend, did Eliza have any enemies, or anyone who may have wished to hurt her?"

"You mean do I know of anyone who would murder my daughter, strip her naked, wrap her in a flimsy shawl, and send her corpse floating down the river? No, I do not, Inspector."

"The manner of her death suggests that it was someone she knew," Jason pointed out.

The reverend shook his head in dismay. "I honestly have no idea what Eliza got up to these last few years. Alan was at the shop all day, reading mostly, instead of working to bring in new business. I doubt the man even knows what's on his shelves these days. Eliza was left to her own devices, and with no child to care for…" A pained look crossed the reverend's face, as if he blamed his son-in-law for the lack of offspring and Eliza's empty days.

"Did your daughter ever visit you on Wednesdays?" Daniel asked.

"No. When they did visit, Eliza and Alan came for Sunday lunch."

"Did they visit less often?" Jason asked.

The reverend pursed his lips, as if he didn't want to acknowledge a possible rift. "Only recently. Before, they joined us every Sunday."

"Did something happen to precipitate the change?"

"Not with Eliza, but I think Alan was embarrassed about defaulting on the loan and wished to avoid Alastair."

"Thank you, Reverend Reynolds," Daniel said, pushing to his feet.

The reverend really looked at Daniel for the first time, his blue gaze boring into Daniel's face. "Find whoever did this, Inspector. Please. Allow me to lay my daughter to rest knowing that she got justice."

"I will do everything in my power to find Eliza's killer," Daniel promised.

Daniel and Jason left the church and climbed into Jason's waiting brougham after instructing Joe to take them to thirty-nine, Mornington Crescent. The address was fairly new, the crescent built less than fifty years ago when London's exploding population spawned extensive expansion into hitherto commercially undeveloped areas. The handsome terraced houses were generously proportioned and nearly identical, each with a shiny black front door and wrought-iron railings. Alastair Reynolds had to be doing well for himself to afford such a large house and probably looked down his nose at his ne'er-do-well brother-in-law, who couldn't afford anything more prestigious than a much smaller and shabbier house in Lambeth.

The men were admitted by a uniformed maid of middle years who wouldn't have seemed out of place in a regiment of foot soldiers. She practically saluted when Daniel asked to see Mrs. Reynolds and marched them to the drawing room after taking their coats and hats. She announced them with such aplomb, one would think they were visiting a duchess, or a countess at the very least. Annoyed by the maid's militant demeanor, Daniel decided she must be frightfully efficient and promised himself never to hire anyone even remotely as irritating as the woman who stood watching them with a gimlet eye as they approached her mistress.

Despite the black crape that covered the mirror and the clock that stood silent on the marble mantel, the room was beautifully decorated in shades of cream and peach. It was spacious and bright, the feeling of airiness further achieved with a vase of hothouse flowers and a lovely landscape executed in delicate pastels hanging above the mantel. All the furniture was crafted of a light-colored wood, unlike the oppressive, dark furniture that had been so popular in the earlier half of the century.

Janet Reynolds was no older than twenty-five, a lovely young woman with golden ringlets, wide blue-green eyes, and a generous mouth. Her handsome features were further enhanced by high cheekbones and a stubborn chin that gave her a slightly elfish appearance. Despite the delicately shaped face, she was rather plump, but she wore the extra weight well, her curves voluptuous rather than portly. She was dressed in a gown of black taffeta and a matching lace cap, as was fitting for a woman in mourning, but the gown was cut in the latest style, and the jet beads of the earrings and necklace were set in filigreed gold.

If Mrs. Reynolds had ever been on the stage, as Miss Bloom had intimated, there was no trace of the actress now, the woman before them a genteel mistress of a rather fine house. Perhaps Miss Bloom was mistaken and had confused Janet Reynolds with someone who happened to bear a passing resemblance to the woman before them.

"Please, sit down, gentlemen," Mrs. Reynolds said. "Can I offer you some coffee or tea? Investigating a murder must be thirsty work."

"It is," Daniel admitted. "And cold."

"Sit closer to the fire, then," Mrs. Reynolds invited. There was a warmth in her that Daniel rarely found in individuals he interviewed. They normally treated him as an interloper, someone to hide the truth from, but Janet Reynolds seemed eager to speak to them, and Daniel meant to capitalize on her openness.

Once Mrs. Reynolds had called for tea, she turned back to them and smiled sadly. "I just can't believe Eliza is gone. Only this morning, I thought of something I would have liked to tell her and then suddenly remembered that I could no longer share anything with her. At that moment, it felt like losing her all over again. I can't tell you what a void her death has left in all our lives."

"How long had you known Eliza?" Jason asked.

"Four years. We met when Alastair—my husband—first introduced me to his family. I am an only child, you see, and I lost my mother at a young age, so I was always lonely and starved for female companionship. My father, although loving, wasn't much of a conversationalist. I don't suppose he knew what to talk to a young girl about, and my governess was rather stern, not the sort of person to offer comfort. When I met Eliza, I knew right away that we would be like sisters. And we were," she added, her eyes welling. She turned away and dabbed at her tears.

"Did you spend a lot of time together?" Jason continued once Janet Reynolds had recovered herself.

"Not as much of late. Alastair and I have recently welcomed our first child. A boy," she added proudly. "We have a nursemaid, of course, but I do so hate to leave him. He's such a joy. Spending time with him is like a balm to the soul. Do you have children?" she asked, looking from Jason to Daniel.

"A little girl," Daniel replied.

"Same," Jason said.

"So you understand," Janet Reynolds said, smiling dreamily. "It's an entirely different sort of love, isn't it?"

"It is," Jason agreed. "Our children make us vulnerable."

"Yes, that's exactly what I mean. Suddenly, the world seems full of danger." Having realized what she'd just said, she looked toward the window, her eyes shimmering with tears. "And it really is," she whispered.

A different, less combative maid brought in a tea tray laden with all the essentials plus a heavenly smelling cake and a plate of tea sandwiches. Having collected herself, Janet Reynolds tucked her handkerchief into her sleeve and poured out before cutting into the cake and handing each man a generous slice. She didn't take one for herself.

"Thank you," Daniel said, eager to sample the treat.

"My dear late mother's recipe. I have Cook bake it at least once a week, in case there are callers."

"This is hardly a social call," Daniel reminded her gently.

"No, but you're here to help us, so you're doubly deserving of cake."

Daniel smiled at that. Janet Reynolds really was the perfect hostess.

"Was Eliza happy in her marriage?" Jason asked. He hadn't touched his cake and set the plate on the low table before him.

"Oh, yes. She adored Alan. My father-in-law, the Reverend Reynolds, thinks Alan is a layabout and doesn't—didn't—keep Eliza in the style she was accustomed to, but he simply didn't understand how much they loved each other. No money can buy that kind of devotion."

"So, their marriage was perfect?" Daniel asked, leading Janet Reynolds in the hope that she would reveal something relevant.

"No marriage is perfect, Inspector, but theirs was a true union of heart and mind."

"Was there anything Eliza might have been unhappy about?"

Mrs. Reynolds sighed, averting her gaze for a moment, as if the subject were too delicate to discuss. "Eliza desperately wanted a child," she said at last. "I tried to comfort her. These things don't always happen right away, do they, but it was difficult for her when our Jack was born. She was determined to be a doting aunt, but I could see the despair in her eyes every time she looked at the baby. I urged her not to give in to her melancholy, but that's not the sort of thing one wants to hear."

"Did Mrs. Bennington seek medical advice?" Jason asked.

Janet shook her head. "Not that I know of. Her father had advised her to put her faith in God, I do know that."

"And did she find this advice reassuring?"

"I really don't know. Eliza would no longer confide in me once she discovered I was expecting. It was as if I had betrayed her somehow," Janet added miserably.

"Did Eliza ever call on you on Wednesday afternoons?" Daniel asked.

"Not on Wednesdays, no. Eliza and Alan usually came to Sunday lunch, so I saw her then."

"But you did meet from time to time. Just the two of you."

"We preferred to see each other away from the house," Janet confessed. "It was nice to get away for a few hours. We went shopping, or for a walk in Hyde Park. We even went to the zoological gardens once," she added wistfully.

"Any idea where Eliza might have gone on Wednesdays?" Jason asked. "Her neighbor, Miss Bloom, saw her leaving the house on Wednesdays, shortly after Nell left for her half day."

Janet scrunched up her nose in distaste at the mention of Miss Bloom. "That nasty old baggage," she said with feeling.

"Always watching and asking prying questions. Eliza didn't much care for her."

"Nevertheless, she saw Eliza leaving the house on Wednesday afternoon," Daniel persisted. "Where might she have gone?"

"I think she probably just went for a walk," Janet said. "She didn't like to be in the house by herself. It gets lonely when there's no one to talk to, not that Nell can offer much in the way of conversation, but she's company of sorts."

"Mrs. Reynolds, can you think of anyone who might have wished Eliza harm?" Daniel asked, desperate for a lead. Surely someone must have disliked the woman.

"Nancy Pruitt," Janet Reynolds announced triumphantly.

"And who is Nancy Pruitt?"

"Nancy and Alan had formed an attachment when they were quite young, but Alan stopped seeing her when he met Eliza. Nancy never forgave Eliza for coming between them."

"Did Miss Pruitt ever threaten Eliza?" Jason asked.

"Not threaten, exactly, but she did say Eliza would get her just deserts one day."

"Where can we find Nancy Pruitt?" Daniel inquired.

"I don't have her address, but I'm sure Alan can point you in the right direction."

"Mrs. Reynolds, is your husband at home?"

Janet shook her head. "Alastair is in Manchester on business. The reverend has cabled him with the sad news. I'm sure he'll come home as soon as he's able."

"Thank you for your time, and the tea," Daniel said, and stood. Jason stood as well. "Just one more question, Mrs. Reynolds. Did Eliza have a particular fondness for mermaids?"

"Oh, yes. She liked stories of mythical creatures. Eliza had a very vivid imagination."

"Thank you, Mrs. Reynolds," Jason said, and bowed gallantly over her hand. "And please accept our sincerest condolences."

"You're very kind, my lord," Janet said, and watched them take their leave.

Chapter 9

Jason had to call in at the hospital to check on a patient, so Daniel found a hansom and made his way to Alan Bennington's shop. The bookshop was closed, the windows dark. Although the shop was situated in a desirable location, it had a somewhat ramshackle appearance, the windows dusty, the sign above the door faded, and the paint peeling slightly at the edges. The window displays were uninspired, the titles months out of date. The Reverend Reynolds' assessment of his son-in-law's business acumen was remarkably salient, Daniel decided as he climbed back into the waiting hansom.

He directed the driver to the address in Lambeth. Alan Bennington was at home, in much the same position Daniel and Jason had found him the last time. Nell showed Daniel to the chilly parlor and disappeared, presumably to see to her many chores. Daniel briefly wondered if she would remain in Alan Bennington's employ. With her mistress gone, Nell was now living with a man twice her age who was lonely and grieving. Not a safe prospect for any young girl.

"Nancy?" Alan asked, his eyebrows lifting in surprise. "Janet thinks Nancy might have harmed Eliza?"

"Mrs. Reynolds believes Nancy Pruitt held a grudge against your wife," Daniel said, watching Alan Bennington closely.

"Nancy and I were never betrothed, Inspector. We had been courting, that's true, but once I met Eliza, I knew there was no other woman for me. Nancy was hurt, and harsh words were exchanged between us, but she never meant Eliza any real harm. Besides, Nancy is newly married. She's expecting her first child," Alan said. "She came into the shop a fortnight ago and told me the news herself."

"Why would she do that?" Daniel asked.

"I think it was important for her that I know she found happiness with someone else. Perhaps she thought I'd be jealous."

"Were you?"

Alan shrugged, his indifference obvious. "Before that day, I hadn't thought of Nancy in ages. Here." He reached for a small notebook and pencil that lay on an end table, scribbled something, and tore out the page, handing it to Daniel. "This is Nancy's new name and current address. Once you speak to her, you'll see that Nancy had nothing to do with Eliza's death."

"You seem very protective of her," Daniel observed.

"I just don't want you wasting time on suspecting innocent people while Eliza's murderer slips away. Do you even have any leads?" Alan Bennington demanded. "Have you any clues?"

"It's early days," Daniel said, using the banal phrase to justify his lack of progress.

"Whoever killed Eliza didn't just take her life. They humiliated her by putting her on display and making sure that people would talk about the murder for days, even weeks to come," Alan cried, his voice breaking with emotion.

"I'm sorry, Mr. Bennington," Daniel said in a conciliatory manner. "I know how difficult this must be for you."

Alan nodded miserably. His lids drooped with fatigue, and he looked like he hadn't slept or washed in days.

"Perhaps you should get some rest."

"I can't sleep," Alan replied, his red-rimmed eyes misting with tears. "Every time I close my eyes, I see it. The boat gliding out of the mist, Eliza lying there, possibly still alive, alone and beyond all hope," he rasped.

"She wouldn't have been aware of what was happening," Daniel said, inwardly praying that was true.

"Maybe not, Inspector, but I am."

There wasn't much Daniel could say in response to that, so he left Alan Bennington to his grief and headed to Bloomsbury to speak to Nancy Fowler. If the coveted address was anything to go by, then Nancy Pruitt had done well for herself, at least in the practical sense. No wonder she'd felt the need to rub her contentment in Alan's face.

Daniel found Mrs. Fowler at home, all too happy to receive him once he'd explained the purpose of his visit. Like Eliza Bennington, Nancy Fowler was a redhead, but that was where the resemblance ended. To compare the two would be much like comparing a pigeon to a peacock. Eliza Bennington had been stunning. Nancy Fowler was average, in both face and figure. She wore an attractive gown of emerald-green satin trimmed with black velvet, and although the color tended to favor women with red hair, it made Nancy's complexion appear sallow. If she was with child, as she had intimated to Alan Bennington, it was too soon to tell, and Daniel wasn't about to inquire. He would only ask if he felt that Nancy's condition had a bearing on the investigation.

Nancy Fowler invited Daniel to make himself comfortable and immediately rang for refreshments, speaking to the parlormaid who answered the summons in a highhanded, shrill tone. While Mrs. Fowler instructed the maid, Daniel took a moment to examine his surroundings. The room was rather grand, the furnishings and paintings expensive looking. Everything was new and modern, as was the woman herself, who was no older than twenty-one and clearly relished her role as the mistress of a great house. Daniel wondered if Nancy received many visitors, since she seemed eager to entertain him as if he were paying a social call rather than visiting her in his professional capacity.

Once the parlormaid departed, Nancy finally turned her attention to Daniel. Try as she might, she couldn't hide her smugness. "I always said Eliza would get her comeuppance," she said. "She was a terrible person. Positively venal."

"Really? That's not at all the reports I've had of Mrs. Bennington so far," Daniel said, hoping he might unearth a kernel of truth about Eliza Bennington within the jealousy-fueled rant Nancy Fowler was obviously about to engage in.

"She was vain, selfish, and indifferent to the feelings of others. Alan and I were engaged, or as good as. We were planning a life together when Eliza swooped in as if I didn't exist. She set her cap for Alan, and Alan she got. He never stood a chance, and neither did I, frankly. I was too young and inexperienced to go up against someone like her. I grant you, Inspector, she was beautiful. Even I can admit that. But I always knew her beauty would be her downfall."

"Why do you think her beauty was responsible for her death?" Daniel asked.

"Well, look at how she ended up," Nancy exclaimed. "Does a respectable woman wind up floating half naked down the Thames? I think not. Clearly, Eliza had overplayed her hand and lost."

Nancy appeared set to say more, but the maid returned bearing a tea tray. Several minutes were spent pouring out and then sampling the almond biscuits that accompanied the cucumber and fishpaste sandwiches before Daniel was able to redirect the conversation back to the matter at hand.

"What do you think Eliza Bennington was up to?" Daniel asked, hoping Nancy's spite might spur her to reveal something useful.

"I'm sure I don't know," Nancy said primly. "My mind doesn't stretch to such goings-on." She took a delicate sip and set her cup down on the low table.

"How long have you been married, Mrs. Fowler?"

Nancy's expression softened, her eyes shining with happiness. "Just over a year now. I became ill after Alan ended things between us. He didn't even have the decency to tell me outright. Simply stopped calling and refused to reply to my letters. I couldn't eat, couldn't sleep. I felt lost and fearful of what the future held for me. My father tried to reason with me, to show me that Alan was a scoundrel who didn't deserve my tears. He said I should find a man who would provide not only financial security but emotional stability." Nancy shook her head in disbelief as she recalled that uncertain time.

"Papa grew impatient with me and took me to see a doctor." Nancy smiled dreamily. "And that's how I met my husband. He took one look at me and said I didn't suffer from anything that a bit of happiness wouldn't cure. And then he set about bringing joy into my life."

As if on cue, Daniel heard the opening of the front door, a brief exchange with the maidservant, and then the man himself entered the drawing room. Dr. Fowler wasn't nearly as handsome as Alan Bennington but possessed a friendliness of manner that instantly put Daniel at ease. Dr. Fowler introduced himself and took a seat next to his wife, putting his hand over hers in a reassuring manner. The two of them looked a devoted pair.

"Inspector Haze is here about Eliza Bennington," Nancy explained.

"Dreadful business," Dr. Fowler said. "The poor woman. I read about her death in the papers."

"Did you know her?" Daniel asked.

"We met once, shortly before Nancy and I were married. At Kew Gardens, of all places. It made for an awkward few minutes, since Alan and Nancy could hardly pretend not to know each other," he explained with an embarrassed smile.

"And what did you make of her, Dr. Fowler?"

"I found her to be affected."

"In what way?"

"I think she desperately wanted us to believe that she was happy, but there was a void behind the smile, a sadness in the eyes."

"That's quite a lot to deduce about someone you've never met before in only a few minutes," Daniel remarked.

"I am a physician, Inspector Haze, but unlike many of my colleagues, I believe that a patient's mental state has as much to do with their well-being as their physical health. I'm trained to recognize signs of emotional distress."

"Perhaps Mrs. Bennington was simply uncomfortable," Daniel suggested.

"Perhaps," Dr. Fowler replied, but it was obvious he didn't agree.

"And what did you think of Alan Bennington?"

"I thought he was the biggest fool to ever walk the earth," Dr. Fowler said, smiling at his wife. "But his loss was my gain, so I am eternally grateful to him."

Nancy's eyes misted. "I said horrid things about Eliza, Inspector, but I was angry and hurt at the time. I never meant for anything to happen to her, and I really am sorry she met with such a dreadful end. Losing Alan was the best thing to ever happen to me, and I have Eliza to thank for my new life." Her hand subconsciously went to her belly. "We're anticipating a happy event," she said softly, and her husband beamed at her.

"I wish you success in your inquiry, Inspector Haze," Dr. Fowler said. "Seems you have your work cut out for you."

"Thank you," Daniel said with feeling, and pushed to his feet. This investigation was quickly going nowhere.

"If you speak to Alan, please tell him how sorry I am," Nancy said. "I don't think it would be appropriate to call on him just now."

"No," Daniel agreed. "He doesn't seem to be up to receiving visitors."

Dr. Fowler stood too and walked Daniel out to the foyer. "Inspector, I would ask you not to call on us again. Nancy is in a delicate state, and I would hate for her to be upset. She feels awfully guilty, even though her feelings about Eliza Bennington are perfectly natural, given their history."

"Where were you on Wednesday night, Dr. Fowler?" Daniel asked.

Dr. Fowler chuckled, as if the question amused him. "On Wednesday night, my wife and I attended a small party at my partner's house. It was his fortieth birthday. We were invited for six and returned around ten thirty. We retired a few minutes later. My partner's name is Dr. Laurence Stone," he added without any rancor. "In case you need to check our alibi. I can give you his home address."

"If you would be so kind."

Dr. Fowler jotted down the address, and Daniel took his leave. Tomorrow, he'd send a constable to verify Dr. Fowler's alibi, but for today, there were no further leads to pursue, so Daniel hastened home. He was eternally grateful that Superintendent Ransome had to leave early and wouldn't be expecting a report tonight. Ransome did not take kindly to lack of progress, especially when it came to high-profile cases, and resorted to berating and bullying to ensure a result.

Chapter 10

Daniel found Rebecca in the parlor, a tea tray on the low table before her. She looked up and smiled, but there was something guarded in her gaze, something Daniel couldn't quite identify. He assumed Charlotte was still napping, although it was getting a bit late in the day. On any other occasion, he might have pointed that out, but he longed for a few minutes alone with Rebecca, so he kept his counsel.

"Tea?" Rebecca asked solicitously. "There's still some in the pot."

"I think I would prefer something stronger," Daniel said, and walked over to the sideboard to pour himself a Scotch. He'd had quite enough tea for one day. "Did you and Charlotte have a good day?" he asked once he was seated.

"Oh, yes. We went to the park in the morning. You know how she loves to feed the ducks. And then we had luncheon together, drew a picture, and read a story. She's still asleep," Rebecca confirmed as she glanced toward the carriage clock on the mantel. "And how was your day? Are you happy to be working a case again, Inspector?"

Rebecca's tone was playful, but the fact that she had addressed him by his title rather than his name wasn't lost on Daniel. They had been on a Christian name basis for the past two months. What had changed?

"I'm glad to be back, but this case is proving a real challenge," Daniel replied. "I have spoken to nearly everyone who was close to the victim but have yet to identify a single suspect or discover a potential motive for the murder."

"You will get there, Inspector. You always do in the end," Rebecca said. The words were meant to encourage, but Daniel sensed Rebecca's lack of interest. She glanced at the clock again, probably wondering how long she should remain before making an excuse to leave the room.

"I appreciate your confidence in me, Miss Grainger," Daniel replied, reverting to the formality of their earlier acquaintance.

Daniel considered asking Rebecca straight out what was on her mind, but something held him back, perhaps his instinct for self-preservation. He was preoccupied with the case and had a feeling that whatever was troubling her would not be resolved with a few minutes' conversation. And if he were honest with himself, some small part of him was reluctant to discover the source of her sudden aloofness. It rarely boded well when a hitherto warm, lively woman suddenly withdrew behind a screen of politeness and glanced at the clock with unsettling frequency.

Rebecca went to set down her cup and nearly knocked it over when there was a rap at the front door. She froze, clearly alarmed by their unexpected visitor.

"Lord Redmond," Grace announced as she entered the room, the man himself just behind her.

"Miss Grainger. Daniel," Jason said as he walked in and bowed politely to Rebecca.

"Good afternoon, my lord," Rebecca chirped. "How nice to see you again."

"And so soon," Jason added, grinning as his gaze turned toward Daniel in a silent inquiry. Jason obviously thought he'd interrupted a tête-à-tête, but he couldn't be more wrong, Daniel thought sourly. If anything, he'd saved them both from further awkwardness.

"I didn't mean that at all," Rebecca replied, smiling at Jason sweetly. "Now, if you will excuse me, I'll leave you gentlemen to talk while I check on my charge." Rebecca left the room, closing the door softly behind her.

"Tea or Scotch?" Daniel asked dourly.

"Scotch. Don't get up. I'll help myself." Jason poured himself a drink and settled in his favorite wingchair. "Were you able to learn anything of significance after I left you today? Could Nancy Pruitt have had a reason to want Eliza Bennington dead?"

"I have yet to verify their alibi, but I don't believe either Nancy or Dr. Fowler had a compelling motive for the murder."

"If Nancy Fowler had wanted revenge, she would have exacted it years ago," Jason agreed. "Unless something happened recently to reawaken her ill will toward Eliza Bennington."

"Are you suggesting that Eliza may have been meeting Dr. Fowler?"

"If she left the house just after Nell, Eliza would not have seen her husband since that morning," Jason pointed out. "Based on physical evidence, I believe she had engaged in sexual relations shortly before her death. Whether it was with Dr. Fowler I cannot say."

Daniel sighed. "I just don't know, Jason. Everyone we spoke to said Eliza was devoted to her husband. Even Nancy Fowler admitted that she only hated Eliza because of what happened with Alan, and if we're to be honest, Alan is the one to blame for the demise of the relationship with Nancy, not Eliza. She might not have even known that Alan was courting another woman at the time."

Jason set down his glass on an end table and leaned back, crossing his legs at the ankles. "If Eliza Bennington was seeing another man, Alan Bennington would have a solid motive for murder."

"Do you really think it was him? He seemed so broken up when I saw him this afternoon," Daniel said. Alan's desolation had seemed genuine, but Daniel wasn't prepared to rule him out just yet. Alan's despair could be the result of regret, guilt at taking the life of a woman he'd clearly loved, as well as fear for his own future should he find himself charged with Eliza's murder.

"The person who killed Eliza Bennington and had sexual relations with her was likely one and the same. He clearly wanted her to look beautiful in death and was aware of her fondness for mermaids. Why else bother with the display? Had it been a random attack, the killer would have left her where she fell instead of going through the trouble of arranging her body to resemble a work of art."

"So, you think Alan Bennington had discovered the truth, forced himself on his wife, then murdered her and laid her out in a way consistent with a childhood fantasy?"

"The theory does fit the facts," Jason replied.

"Are you suggesting that Eliza was raped?" Daniel asked.

"No, but the lovemaking hadn't been gentle. Which is not to say it was necessarily an act of violence."

"So the killer could have been her lover," Daniel suggested. "A man capable of such frenzy could just as easily kill in a fit of jealousy."

"Yes, that's also a possibility. Perhaps he'd grown tired of sharing Eliza with her husband."

"If only there was a way to identify the man by his secretions," Daniel said. "We'd have our killer."

Jason nodded. "I tend to think that a person's fluids are a sort of signature that would identify them if we had the capability to break them down to a molecular level."

"Is such an undertaking even possible?" Daniel asked.

"I really couldn't say, but just because it's never been done doesn't mean it won't be attempted in the future."

"That would certainly change the face of policing," Daniel said, trying to imagine how such intimate knowledge would alter the value of the evidence. He was just about to suggest as much when there was a loud knock at the front door.

"Are you expecting someone?" Jason asked.

"No."

Grace knocked lightly on the parlor door, then pushed it open. "Sorry to disturb you, sir, but there's a Mr. Gillespie to see you."

Jason and Daniel exchanged looks of surprise. Norm Gillespie was the police photographer, but he had not been available to photograph Eliza Bennington's remains. Calling on Daniel at home was unorthodox, to say the least, but also most intriguing, since he obviously had something urgent to impart.

Norm Gillespie was a short, stocky, dark-haired man with a thicker-than-fashionable moustache and caterpillar-like eyebrows over deep-set dark eyes. He wasn't talkative, nor did he mix with the policemen with whom he worked. He did his job and left, delivering the photographs he'd developed in his darkroom a few hours later. Daniel couldn't account for his presence in his home.

"Mr. Gillespie, do come in and have a seat. Drink?" Daniel asked, feeling it was only polite to offer the man some refreshment.

"Don't mind if I do," Mr. Gillespie said as he sat heavily on the settee Miss Grainger had vacated a few minutes before. It was strange to see him there, a hulking presence that so completely obliterated the memory of Rebecca's feminine beauty.

The photographer accepted a whisky and took a sip, nodding in appreciation. "Good stuff, this," he said.

"Yes, Lord Redmond keeps me well supplied," Daniel joked. Jason usually brought a bottle of Scotch whisky for them to enjoy. "How can I help you?" Daniel asked when the man failed to explain the reason for his visit.

"It's about the murder of Eliza Bennington," Gillespie said. "When I saw the photographs in the newspaper, I recognized her straight away."

"You knew her?" Jason asked, looking at the man with renewed interest.

"Not personally, no."

"So, what's your connection to Eliza Bennington?" Daniel inquired.

Norm Gillespie took an envelope from his breast pocket and handed it to Daniel, his expression inscrutable.

Daniel opened the envelope, extracted two photographs, and sucked in his breath sharply. In the first picture, Eliza reclined on a velvet chaise, her hair loose, her expression serene. She was completely nude, her skin like alabaster, her limbs relaxed. Even in the black-and-white image, she looked full of color, and full of life. In the second image, Eliza sat in a hardback chair. Her hair cascaded over her shoulders, and she leaned back, looking slightly away from the camera. Her right leg was bent at the knee, the heel resting against the seat in a way that offered a tantalizing glimpse of her inner thigh and beyond.

Reminding himself to breathe, Daniel handed the photographs to Jason, whose face remained impassive as he looked at them. Daniel would never admit it, but in his thirty-four years, he had only seen one woman—his wife—in a state of undress, and even then, Sarah hadn't been one to strut around in the nude or remain uncovered in moments of postcoital bliss. The photographs were shockingly intimate and embarrassing.

"Did you take these?" Daniel asked, his voice unexpectedly hoarse.

"No."

"Then how did you come to possess them?"

Jason handed the envelope back to the photographer, who placed it on the low table between them, indicating that Daniel could hold on to the evidence.

"I have four children, Inspector Haze, another one on the way," Gillespie said, the abrupt change of subject taking Daniel by surprise.

"Congratulations," Daniel said, unsure what was expected of him in this instance.

"Thank you. The point is, I can barely make ends meet with the unsteady work from the Yard and the commissions from the photo atelier where I work. About six months ago, I was approached by an acquaintance. He showed me some photos and asked if I would be willing to distribute them. I was to offer the first photograph for free, but in exchange, the recipient would give me his address and agree to pay a subscription fee if he hoped to see more of the same. Once on the list, the customer would receive a monthly mailing of several postcards wrapped in plain brown paper. I would receive a thirty percent commission for each subscription I was able to secure. Naturally, I agreed."

"But why would someone wish to give you their address and agree to pay for a subscription?" Daniel asked. Surely that was a risk, particularly if the man in question was married. And there were easier ways to obtain the sort of images Gillespie offered.

Although he had never worked a case in Holywell Street, Daniel had heard from other policemen that the area was a den of vice. Numerous bookshops dealt in illicit pornography, disguising their wares behind suggestive titles or plain covers. It was a sickness that was spreading through the city and leaving its vile mark. As if it wasn't bad enough that a quarter of London's female population earned their daily bread through prostitution, now there was another, cheaper and longer-lasting way to enjoy explicit eroticism.

Of course, the French had got there first, as they always did with anything that was deviant or unsavory. Pornographic images from France had appeared seemingly out of nowhere and were sold at train stations, book stalls, and taverns. Although technically illegal, the postcards were easy enough to find if one had the desire to spend money on such vulgarity.

Gillespie sucked in his breath, as if striving for patience. No doubt the logistics of the operation made perfect sense to him, but he didn't wish to relay the details to Daniel.

"Some gentlemen don't care to be seen purchasing photographs their mothers or wives would not approve of, nor do they wish to publicly support what is essentially an illegal trade. With a subscription, they receive a discreet package and enjoy the product in the privacy of their study or bedroom. Besides, there's the added element of excitement and expectation, since the gentleman never knows what he will receive. It's like opening a present," Gillespie explained.

"Were the photographs you were tasked with distributing only of Eliza Bennington?" Jason asked.

"No, they were of various women, and I couldn't give them away fast enough."

"Were there other photographs?"

"How do you mean, my lord?"

"These images are not so very different from the classical works of art you might see in a museum. They're tasteful and beautiful. But as we all know, more explicit photographs would fetch a higher price."

Norm Gillespie went beet-red and averted his gaze. "There are those, yes."

"Was Eliza Bennington in any of them?" Daniel asked, having regained the ability to speak after he understood exactly what Jason was referring to.

"No, she was not. The sort of women who pose for those pictures are usually whores who are looking to make a quick profit. It's all in a day's work for them, and they get handsomely paid to do what they're already doing anyway."

"So, Eliza Bennington posed only for what could be loosely described as art?" Jason asked.

"As far as I know."

"Was she always in the photographs alone?"

"Yes. And photographs of Eliza were generally offered through the subscription, so they weren't circulated in the streets."

"I will need the name of the photographer who took these," Daniel said.

"I'm afraid I can't give it to you, Inspector. My livelihood depends on selling these images. I have a family to feed."

"Mr. Gillespie, I appreciate your assistance in this matter, but you do realize I can arrest you for distribution of pornography," Daniel said pleasantly. The photographer blanched.

"I have no interest in ruining your life," Daniel continued, "and I know that arresting one man will make little difference to the amount of contraband on the streets, but I do need to know the name of the man for whom you've been working."

"Do I have your word that Superintendent Ransome will not hear about this?" Gillespie demanded.

"You have my word. No one needs to know where I obtained these photographs."

"For all they know, you're a subscriber," Gillespie joked, but the attempt at humor made Daniel angry.

As a detective with Scotland Yard, he knew he should be immune to the uglier side of human nature and remain unfazed when presented with two relatively tame photographs of a beautiful woman, but he could barely hide his embarrassment and the fact that his gaze kept straying to the envelope. He wanted to see the images again, to study them in private, which made him no better than those disgusting men who pored over these photographs and used them to satisfy their baser needs.

Daniel wasn't about to consult Jason on the subject, but he knew that there were two schools of thought when it came to acts of self-pleasure. There were those who were terrified of nighttime secretions, believing that spilling one's seed unnecessarily weakened the body, and others who thought it promoted good health and a general sense of well-being. Daniel subscribed to the former.

"Dawson. Eric Dawson," Norm Gillespie stated. "He's the man I work for."

"Dawson?" Daniel choked out. "Of Dawson's Portrait Atelier in Regent Street?" Gillespie nodded. "Sarah and I took Charlotte there to have our portrait taken. Mr. Dawson himself photographed us."

"He has a separate studio at the back of the shop. That's where he photographs the women. And then he prints the photographs in his darkroom. As long as he can afford the paper, he can make hundreds of copies of each image," Norm Gillespie explained.

"And he retains seventy percent of the profit," Jason said. "He must be doing very well for himself. Is the shop a front for his activities?"

"Not so much a front as a legitimate business," Gillespie explained. "Eric Dawson is a talented photographer, but he's also a man who understands the nature of his customers. There's a demand, and he supplies it."

"His customers are depraved deviants who ogle other men's wives," Daniel exclaimed, venting his frustration at last.

"Inspector, as far as I know, no woman was either threatened or coerced in any way to pose for the photos. They know what's involved and what the images will be used for. However, this gives them an opportunity to earn a living, the sort of living they could never make by going into service or working in a tavern or mill. And in the case of someone like Eliza Bennington, they could profit very nicely without resorting to being a whore."

"Eliza Bennington was a married woman," Daniel snapped.

"So she was, but clearly something or someone had induced her to seek out Mr. Dawson," Mr. Gillespie said as he set down his empty glass and pushed to his feet. "I'll be off now. I only wished to help you, but I see you're not at all appreciative of the tip."

"Thank you for your assistance, Mr. Gillespie," Jason said. He stood and shook the man's hand, as if he had performed some heroic feat instead of selling lurid photographs of desperate women.

Daniel stood and held out his hand as well, keeping his face blank to hide his disgust. "Thank you, Mr. Gillespie. I do appreciate your help. I'm just a bit shocked, I suppose. I never expected the case to take us in this direction."

"It's the reality of the world we live in, Inspector Haze," the photographer said.

Daniel couldn't help but ask one final question. "Does your wife know you're doing this?"

Gillespie smiled, clearly amused by Daniel's naiveté. "Of course she does. She's seen the photographs. And she's seen the money they bring. Not all of us can afford to have unimpeachable morals."

Once Gillespie had gone, Daniel turned to Jason. "He's shown them to his wife," he exclaimed, scandalized.

Jason smiled at him as if he were a child. "Daniel, those photographs are meant to achieve a desired effect. To titillate. Perhaps there's a reason our Mr. Gillespie has four children and another on the way." Jason laughed softly.

"But it's depraved," Daniel sputtered.

"If a man, or a woman, admires a photograph of a beautiful woman, how is that different from looking at a painting by Rubens or a Roman sculpture of a naked nymph?"

"These are real women."

"Real women posed for those paintings and sculptures," Jason replied calmly.

"So you think there's nothing wrong with a married woman posing nude in some backroom studio and then having her image sold to countless men?"

"If she did it willingly and was paid for it, then no."

"I'm appalled you see nothing wrong with this."

"What I see is that Eliza Bennington had secrets, and they may have led to her death."

Daniel pointed to the envelope. "If her husband found out about these photos, that would give him a motive for murder."

"Indeed, it would," Jason agreed. "But did he know? And what did Eliza do with the money?"

"Perhaps she wished to leave him," Daniel speculated. "But if she did, she could have appealed to her family for help."

"Her father is a vicar," Jason reminded him. "He might not have wholeheartedly approved of his daughter's husband, but I doubt he would have encouraged her to leave him. As a vicar, he would advise her to uphold the sanctity of marriage. As would my own dear father-in-law, who still thinks I'm a reprobate," Jason added with a roguish grin.

"Yes, I suppose you're right," Daniel agreed gruffly. "Tomorrow, I will visit Mr. Dawson's studio, then confront Alan Bennington with the existence of these images. Are you able to accompany me?"

"I wouldn't miss it." Jason tossed back the remainder of his whisky. "But now, I think it's time I went home. I have rather neglected my wife."

"Give my regards to Lady Redmond," Daniel said with a warm smile. "She's a very understanding woman."

Jason's only reply was a smug smile.

Chapter 11

Sunday, February 14

Jason and Daniel agreed to meet at two o'clock, since it was only proper that they accompany the members of their households to the Sunday service and then join them for luncheon. Besides, for all they knew, Mr. Dawson was a God-fearing soul who attended church faithfully and joined his family for Sunday lunch as well. Given Rebecca's recent aloofness, Daniel had no plans to mark Valentine's Day, but he was sure Jason would have a romantic Valentine and a gift for Katherine.

When they arrived in Regent Street at half past two, the atelier was closed, but they found Eric Dawson in his rooms above the shop, the remnants of his meal still on a table set for one. His servant led them past the dining area into a small, cozy parlor, where Eric Dawson sat reading before the fire.

"Inspector Haze, I believe," Eric Dawson exclaimed. He set down his book and got to his feet, smiling as if genuinely happy to receive them. "What a pleasure to see you again. And how is your charming wife? And daughter? Charlotte, was it?"

Either the man had an impeccable memory or Norm Gillespie had warned him of Daniel's impending visit. Daniel recoiled at the mention of Sarah and Charlotte but managed to retain a calm demeanor as he introduced Jason.

"To what do I owe the honor, gentlemen?" Eric Dawson asked. He didn't seem at all put out, behaving as if this were a social call. "Do sit down. I'm afraid I can't offer you any refreshment."

"No refreshment necessary," Daniel replied as the three men found their seats. Once Daniel had Eric Dawson's undivided attention, he placed the photographs of Eliza Bennington on the table.

"Ah, I see you've come across one of my lovelies."

"Your lovelies?"

"I think of my models as my lovelies. And they are lovely, each one in her own way."

"This is exploitation," Daniel stated, his temper flaring despite his best efforts.

"The models are all willing participants and get handsomely compensated for their contribution to my art."

"Art, is it?" Daniel scoffed.

"Art comes in many forms, Inspector. Wouldn't you agree, Lord Redmond?" Dawson asked, turning to look quizzically at Jason, who was observing the exchange with interest.

"It does," Jason said noncommittally.

"There you have it, Inspector. Even Lord Redmond agrees that my nudes are an art form," Eric Dawson announced smugly.

Daniel shot an irritated glance in Jason's direction, then turned back to the photographer. "And what of the others? The ones who pose in the more provocative shots?"

"It's their choice, Inspector Haze. I do not force anyone to do anything. But there's an insatiable hunger in our society, not only for beauty, but for eroticism."

"Is that your professional opinion?" Daniel asked sarcastically.

Eric Dawson fixed Daniel with a sardonic gaze. "I dare you to tell me that you did not find these images arousing, Inspector Haze. Not a twitch?" he teased.

Daniel felt heat rising in his neck and moving upward into his face, his embarrassment not lost on Dawson, who chuckled in obvious delight. Daniel had studied the images once Jason had gone and found them to be not only arousing but sadly depressing, since they served to remind him how long he'd been alone and how desperately he missed having a woman to love, both emotionally and physically. He was starved for affection, and although he missed Sarah, thoughts of her brought him nothing but pain. He longed for a new relationship, one untainted by grief, guilt, and regret.

Tearing his gaze away from the offending images, Daniel looked at Eric Dawson instead. "How did you meet Eliza Bennington?" he asked.

"Through her husband."

That took the wind out of Daniel's sails. His shoulders sagged, and he shook his head in disbelief. "Her husband introduced his wife to you?" he asked, just to be clear.

"I've known Alan Bennington for years. I frequent his shop. In fact, I had asked him to stock my book of photographs. Oh, not the lovelies, Inspector. Photographs of nature. I love capturing the sea in all its moods."

"Did Alan Bennington know about your sideline when he introduced you to his wife?" Jason asked.

"He may have," Dawson replied smoothly. "We had never discussed it openly."

"Does Alan Bennington sell pornography in his shop?" Daniel asked.

"Not as far as I'm aware, but it would benefit him greatly if he did. Maybe he'd finally turn a profit," Eric Dawson added with a cruel laugh.

"How did Eliza Bennington come to pose for you?" Jason asked.

"I asked her to. I called on her when I knew Alan to be at the shop and showed her several photographs. I told her she could make a significant amount of money if she were interested."

"And was she?"

"Not right away. She was understandably shocked and asked me to leave. It took several months for her to come to me."

"Did she tell you what changed her mind?" Daniel asked.

"No, and I didn't ask. Eliza Bennington was a remarkably beautiful woman, and I was happy to have engaged her services."

"How long had she been posing for you?" Jason asked.

"About four months now. She was terrified at first, embarrassed and tense, but as you can see from these images, she came to enjoy herself. She was proud of her body and at ease with her sexuality."

"Are these recent photographs?"

"Yes, these are the last I took of her."

"Are there any other, more explicit photographs?" Jason asked.

"I did not take any. I prefer to create art, but there are others who are not as esthetically minded."

"Do these women actually engage in…" Daniel allowed the sentence to trail off, his meaning obvious.

"Some models are happy to be photographed in *flagrante delicto*. They find it arousing, as well as financially rewarding."

"Good God!" Daniel exclaimed. "What's next? You'll be selling these photographs openly in your atelier, or bind them into a table book?"

"Why not?" Eric Dawson chuckled. "Would you not enjoy looking at risqué photographs of beautiful women? Perhaps of your own wife?" he taunted.

"My wife is dead," Daniel barked.

"I'm sorry to hear that, Inspector Haze. She was a charming woman."

"Please, do not talk about my wife," Daniel hissed.

"I do apologize. I meant no offense."

"I would like to see your studio."

"Of course, but you will not find anything incriminating, Inspector. Only a few pieces of furniture, a camera, and a screen behind which the ladies undress. They might pose nude, but they prefer to maintain their privacy when taking off their bloomers."

The studio yielded no evidence, just as Eric Dawson had predicted. It was just a room. There was a stack of photographs, but they were much like the images of Eliza—nude women draped over a chaise or seated in a way meant to titillate the viewer. As Jason had pointed out, they revealed no more than a classical painting or a marble statue.

"When was the last time you saw Eliza Bennington?" Daniel asked, averting his gaze from the photos.

"The previous Wednesday, a week before she was found dead."

"Did you photograph her?" Jason asked.

"No. We had tea. Eliza wasn't in the mood to be photographed, so we just talked."

"What about?" Daniel asked.

"Alan."

"What did she say?"

"She was upset with him, furious even. Eliza had used the money to pay off some of Alan's debts, but instead of trying to mend his ways, he simply went on as before, taking his wife's earnings as if it were his due."

"Where did he think the money had come from?" Jason asked.

"Alastair Reynolds," Eric Dawson replied. "He assumed Eliza had secured another loan from her brother."

"What did Alan Bennington spend his money on?" Daniel asked.

Eric Dawson shrugged. "Life, I suppose. Food, rent, coal, new publications for his shop. Alan doesn't earn enough to cover his expenses. He simply doesn't have a head for business."

"Unlike you, who found a profitable sideline," Daniel replied acidly.

"Unlike me," Eric Dawson said, without so much as a hint of rancor. "It's simply business, Inspector, just like anything else. Do you judge an executioner or a butcher, who both kill for a living? What I do is remarkably innocent by comparison."

"Mr. Dawson, who are your competitors?" Jason asked.

Eric Dawson laughed. "There are about four hundred photography studios in London, and at least half of them are churning out erotic images. That's where the profit is, not in taking photographs of boring, middled-aged couples and their equally boring children."

Daniel winced at that, feeling the insult was directed squarely at him and his family. The man really was an evil little weasel.

"Surely there are some studios that are better known for this sort of thing than others," Jason interjected, the insult not lost on him.

"There is one particular studio that I had mentioned to Eliza."

"Which studio was that?"

"The Tristan Carmichael Studio."

"Tristan Carmichael?" Daniel nearly choked on the name. "Son of Lance Carmichael?"

"I see you've heard of them."

Jason and Daniel had met Tristan Carmichael while investigating the death of Imogen Chadwick more than a year ago. Tristan had been courting Moll Brody, the niece of the tavern keeper in Birch Hill, and had briefly been considered a suspect in Moll's disappearance. Tristan's father, Lance Carmichael, was a well-known privateer and thug who had his proverbial fingers in various nefarious activities, ranging from smuggling and prostitution to the opium dens that had sprung up in the bigger towns of Essex.

"I thought they kept their activities to Essex," Daniel said.

"They're branching out. Or haven't you heard?" Eric Dawson replied. "There's custom enough for everyone, and Tristan now oversees the London branch of the family business. I hear the Carmichaels have recently opened two new opium dens in Whitechapel."

"And what do you know of the photo studio?" Jason asked.

Eric Dawson smiled wryly. "Their product is the most salacious, and they cater to a particular sort of clientele."

"What sort is that?"

"The sort that crave something off the beaten path, my lord. It's not art, it's debauchery, if you ask me."

"But you said art comes in many different forms," Jason challenged him.

"I did, yes, but there's a line between beauty and ugliness, between self-expression and doing whatever it takes to make the most money."

"Surely every person draws their own line between beauty and ugliness."

"You are absolutely correct, Lord Redmond. That is simply my line, and I choose to remain safely behind it. The money helps, but I want to make this world a freer, more accepting place, not some biblical version of Hell."

"Is that what Tristan Carmichael is doing?" Daniel asked, choosing not to envision what that might entail.

"In my opinion, yes," Eric Dawson said. He no longer seemed as smug as he had a few minutes ago.

"Then why did you give Eliza his name?" Jason asked.

"Eliza urgently needed money."

"What for?" Daniel and Jason asked in unison.

"She wouldn't tell me, but I got the sense that she would do anything, compromise herself in any way, to get what she needed."

"Do you think the money was for her husband?" Jason inquired.

"I really couldn't tell you, but something had changed. Eliza was no longer posing as an act of love. Whatever she did was driven by desperation."

"Where is Carmichael's studio?" Daniel asked.

"He uses a warehouse in Wapping. It's near Oliver's Wharf on the Wapping High Street."

Daniel and Jason exchanged speculative glances. If Eliza's body had been placed in the boat in Wapping, it could very easily have wound up in Westminster, assuming the current had carried it in that direction rather than toward Slough.

"I think we need to pay Tristan Carmichael a visit," Daniel said.

"Without delay," Jason agreed.

"I doubt you'll find him at the warehouse on a Sunday afternoon," Eric Dawson said. "A man in his position has other demands on his time."

"Do you have an address for him?" Daniel asked.

"No, but no doubt you'll be able to obtain it in short order. Now, if you don't mind, it is Sunday—a day of rest."

"Thank you, Mr. Dawson. We'll be in touch," Daniel said.

"That sounds ominous, Inspector," Eric Dawson replied, his lip quirking with amusement.

Chapter 12

It took Jason and Daniel the rest of the day to track down Tristan Carmichael. Although he was a well-known figure in certain parts of London, no one was too eager to either give out his home address or point them in the direction of his businesses. A smart decision, no doubt, and highly beneficial to the health of those they had asked, but frustrating for anyone trying to locate the man.

Daniel finally managed to intimidate a low-level thug into revealing that Tristan had purchased a house in Upper Brook Street and had moved in only last month. It was a far cry from living above an opium den in Brentwood, but given that Tristan was newly married and could probably afford any house he wanted, it made sense that he had chosen a fashionable neighborhood where he could play at being a gentleman.

Forty Upper Brook Street was a neo-classical terraced house that was nearly identical to its neighbors to the right and left. It was attractively stuccoed, high-ceilinged, and boasted an abundance of tall, very clean windows that currently reflected the delicate lavender hue of the twilit sky. Two windows on the ground floor glowed with gaslight, signifying that the master was most likely at home. A smartly dressed butler answered the door and glared at Jason and Daniel as if they were hungry street urchins, or worse yet, do-gooders collecting money for charity.

"Yes?" he demanded.

"Inspector Haze and Lord Redmond to see Tristan Carmichael," Daniel said, holding up his warrant card.

"Mr. Carmichael is not at home to visitors this evening," the butler replied haughtily.

"This is not a social call," Daniel replied. "And Mr. Carmichael and I are acquainted," he added in the hope that the man would admit them.

"Then you should know, Inspector, that Mr. Carmichael does not see anyone on Sundays."

"Oh, just let them in, Simcoe," a voice called from somewhere behind the butler.

"As you wish, sir."

Simcoe stepped aside, and they came face to face with the man himself. Years of criminal activity and the taxing demands of being his father's second-in-command had done nothing to coarsen Tristan Carmichael's looks. As on their first meeting, Daniel reflected that Tristan Carmichael resembled a Pre-Raphaelite angel. He wore his golden curls longer than was fashionable, his blue eyes were wide and guileless, and his physique attested to hours spent at an exclusive gymnasium. His clothes were of the highest quality and tailored so finely, Beau Brummel himself would have given his approval had he still been alive.

"Inspector Haze and Lord Redmond. What an unexpected pleasure." The last was said with the sarcasm it deserved. "Do come in and make yourselves comfortable."

Having surrendered their coats, hats, and in Jason's case, walking stick, to Simcoe, they adjourned to the beautifully appointed drawing room and settled on aquamarine damask sofas flanked by pretty occasional tables that displayed vases filled with fresh flowers. Their feet sank into the thick Turkish rug patterned in celadon green and pink, and a warm fire filled the room with its comforting glow, the mantel constructed of pale-green and pink marble quarried only in certain parts of Italy and adorned with gold leaf. Having divested himself of their things, Simcoe returned to pour the drinks. Once everyone had a glass and the butler had departed with a soft click of the door, Tristan turned to his guests.

"To what do I owe the pleasure, gentlemen?"

"You may have seen in the papers—" Daniel began, but Tristan held up his hand.

"I make it a habit never to read the papers. Nothing but bad news," he said, shaking his head. "I see enough tragedy in my daily life. I don't require any more."

Daniel was burning to point out that the tragedy Tristan Carmichael saw was no doubt of his own making but chose to keep silent. He needed the man's help to solve this case, so antagonizing him wouldn't be the most prudent approach.

"Eliza Bennington was found dead on Thursday morning, floating in a dinghy on the Thames," he said instead.

Tristan looked from Daniel to Jason and back again. "And?"

"And we think you might have been acquainted with the lady," Jason said.

"That doesn't mean I had anything to do with her death."

"No one is saying you did," Daniel replied patiently. "But you had met?"

"Yes. Eliza was charming."

"Is Mrs. Carmichael at home?" Jason asked, clearly surprising Tristan Carmichael with the inquiry.

Daniel realized then that the house was very quiet, no sign of anyone besides the butler, not even a parlormaid.

"My wife is at our home in Brentwood," Tristan replied. "She doesn't much care for London."

"And your father?" Jason asked. "I trust he's in good health?"

"Yes. Thank you for asking, my lord. My father is in Essex as well, keeping my wife company. They always spend Sundays together, it being the Lord's Day and my father believing himself the lord of all he surveys. And given that he handpicked my bride, he has a great deal more affection for her than do I," Tristan added bitterly. "Treats her like one of his beloved daughters."

"Mr. Carmichael, how well did you know Eliza Bennington?" Daniel asked.

"I didn't know her in the biblical sense, if that's what you're asking, Inspector."

"But your acquaintance wasn't a social one, was it?"

"No. Eliza Bennington wished to work for me."

"In what capacity?"

"Given that you're here, I can only assume that you've done your legwork, Inspector, and already know that Eliza had been posing for risqué photographs for the past few months. They were rather beautiful," Tristan said wistfully. "But the arrangement no longer suited her."

"Why not?" Jason asked.

"I don't know, but I got the impression that she needed to make more money."

"For what?"

Tristan shrugged. "For the usual things, I imagine. She did mention that her husband was something of a wastrel. Seems she was supporting him."

"So, you think the money was for her husband?" Daniel pressed.

"I never asked. None of my affair. If a woman comes to me and says she wants to work, I assess her attributes and decide whether I want to purchase what she's selling."

"And did you?" Jason asked.

"I did. Alas, Eliza was murdered before I had a chance to fully utilize her talents. I only saw her professionally once."

"What, precisely, did Eliza do for you?"

"Really, my lord," Tristan said, rolling his eyes theatrically. "I think you know the answer to that already. Eliza posed for photographs of a certain nature. Willingly, I might add."

"What sort of nature?" Daniel asked. He needed to hear it from Carmichael himself to know how far Eliza had fallen.

Tristan sighed and took a sip of his brandy. "I'll be frank with you, Inspector. Eliza had asked for rather a lot of money. Twenty quid per session. That's a fortune," Tristan pointed out.

Daniel balked at the sum. That was more than many families earned in a year. He paid Grace six pounds per annum, and her wages included room and board.

"And what precisely was she willing to do for such an exorbitant sum?" Jason asked.

"Anything," Tristan replied with a lewd smile.

"You mean she was no longer just posing."

"Oh, no. I wanted to test her mettle before committing to such an arrangement, so I asked her to pleasure a gentleman in a way that required no hands," Tristan explained. He was enjoying himself. That was evident.

"And did she?" Jason asked.

"She wasn't skilled, but when one looks at a photograph, they don't see the technique, only a moment in time. And she was able to hold the position for the time it took the photographer to take the picture. In fact, he took several. Would you like to see them?" Tristan asked.

"No, thank you," Daniel was quick to reply. He wasn't prepared to see what the photos contained.

"And did she come to your studio last Wednesday?" Jason asked.

"Yes, she did."

"What took place at the session?"

"I'm sure that's none of your affair, my lord," Tristan replied, his smile infuriatingly smug.

"When I performed the postmortem, I discovered evidence of recent sexual congress. I need to know whether the act was consensual or whether the victim had been assaulted," Jason replied calmly.

Tristan nodded. "Eliza was photographed with two gentlemen. It was consensual, and she was paid twenty quid per our agreement."

"Did either of them penetrate her?" Jason asked, making Daniel cringe inwardly.

He'd worked on several cases involving crimes against prostitutes, but the fact that Eliza Bennington was the daughter of a vicar and the wife of a respectable businessman made it nearly impossible for Daniel to reconcile her activities to those of common streetwalkers. Eliza had not needed to do what she did to survive, so there had to be another reason, one that got her killed.

"They both did," Tristan replied. "That was the arrangement, and Eliza had agreed to it ahead of time. She could have refused when I proposed it, just as she could have changed her mind at any time thereafter. I wouldn't have held it against her. But she didn't change her mind. She was willing."

"And the money?" Jason asked. "What did she do with it?"

"She stowed it away in her reticule. And before you ask, she was very much alive the last time I saw her."

"When was that?"

"Wednesday, early evening."

"So, Eliza Bennington came to your studio on the Wednesday she died, was used by two men, then left unharmed?" Jason asked, his tone betraying his incredulity.

"That is correct, my lord. I saw her off myself. In fact, I even offered to put her in a cab, but she said she wished to walk."

"What time did she leave?" Daniel asked.

"Just past five. It was already dark outside, and I was concerned about her walking around with all that money in her purse."

"How very chivalrous of you, Mr. Carmichael," Jason said with disgust. "Or you could have killed her and taken the money back, since you already had what you wanted."

"I stood to make a lot of money off Eliza Bennington," Tristan replied, his gaze challenging Jason's. "It would be counterproductive to kill her. How did she die, by the way?"

"She was bashed on the head, undressed, and set adrift in a dinghy. There's a strong possibility she was still alive and died slowly as she froze to death."

"Hmm," Tristan said. "Odd way to kill someone."

"How would you do it?" Jason asked, tilting his head as if he were really curious.

"I don't kill people, my lord, but if I took it into my head to murder someone, I'd most likely slit their throat. Quick and efficient, if a bit messy. But if done from the back, the killer can avoid the spray of arterial blood."

"I wouldn't expect you to be familiar with the term," Jason said, clearly surprised by Carmichael's statement.

"I enjoy reading medical journals, my lord," Tristan replied. "Most illuminating."

"Indeed," Jason snarled.

"Did Eliza Bennington own a blue shawl?" Daniel asked, inserting himself into the impasse between the two men. The tension between them practically crackled, and in Tristan Carmichael's own terminology, it was counterproductive to the investigation.

Tristan shrugged. "I have no idea."

"Was Eliza upset or frightened on that last day?"

"She didn't seem to be. She was visibly pleased when I paid her. She counted the notes twice before putting them away. Did you find her reticule?" Tristan asked, cocking his head in exactly the same way Jason had done, possibly mocking him.

"No. The only thing we found was the shawl. Her legs were wrapped in it to make her look like a mermaid."

"How very curious," Tristan exclaimed. He shook his head and sighed deeply. "You might not believe me, but I am sorry she's dead. She was a beautiful woman who deserved better than what she got. If you ask me, her husband is guilty of criminal negligence. When you possess a woman like Eliza Bennington, you do whatever it takes to keep her happy."

"You don't think her husband made her happy?" Jason asked, his eyes narrowing in speculation.

"Not in any way that matters."

"Meaning?" Daniel asked.

"Eliza was starved for attention and affection. She needed a man she could rely on to look after her. Alan Bennington was worthless, as both a husband and a provider."

"She told you all this, or is this your own assessment of Eliza Bennington's marriage?" Jason asked.

Tristan grinned, the smile infuriatingly condescending. "If a man wants to succeed in his line of work, then he must understand the nature of his clients in order to appeal to their deepest desires. I have learned to assess every person I come in contact with because my dealings with them could either lead to a profitable partnership or to an unfortunate break. Eliza wasn't so very difficult to read, nor did she try to hide her disappointment and frustration." Tristan lifted an eyebrow as he looked from one man to the other. "And I don't think I'm wrong in saying that Eliza enjoyed the work she did. It had awakened certain needs she hadn't realized she had."

"You mean a need to be used by two men?" Daniel demanded. He could barely contain his disdain.

"She wouldn't be the first or the last woman to enjoy a vigorous rogering."

"Did you have relations with Eliza Bennington?"

"I'm a married man, Inspector. I'm faithful to my lovely wife."

"Are you?" Daniel was unable to hide his sarcasm.

"My father taught me from an early age not to mix business with pleasure. I think that's sound advice."

"Who was the last person to see Eliza Bennington on Wednesday night?" Jason asked.

"I was. The photographer and the other participants left first."

"Why did it take Eliza so long to leave?" Daniel inquired.

"Ladies do take rather a long time to get dressed, Inspector," Tristan Carmichael pointed out.

"Did she dress herself?" Jason asked.

"Mary helped her."

"And who's Mary?"

"She's one of my girls," Tristan replied, his meaning obvious. "She helps out with things us gentlemen can't."

"We'd like to speak to Mary," Daniel said.

"You'll find her at the Gilded Lily Brothel in Covent Garden tomorrow. Mary Smith," Tristan added, enunciating the name.

"Is that even her real name?"

"Does it matter? Look, are we done here? I'm expecting a guest for dinner."

Daniel pushed to his feet. "If you are in any way responsible for Eliza Bennington's death..." He didn't bother to finish the sentence or keep the threat out of his tone.

"Murder is bad for business, Inspector Haze. As are visits from the police. Goodnight to you both." Tristan walked to the drawing room door and held it open for them, his meaning clear.

Simcoe was already in the foyer, their coats slung over his arm and their hats and Jason's stick in his hands. He handed them over silently and unlocked the front door, closing it with a bang behind them.

Outside, the two men stood in the gathering darkness, the fog rolling off the Thames cloaking them in a shroud of dirty white gauze.

"I'm done for today," Daniel said. He was bone-weary and disheartened. Some righteous part of him was convinced that Eliza Bennington got her just deserts, but as a policeman, he had no right to think along those lines. Whatever Eliza had done and whatever dangerous situation she had put herself in, she hadn't deserved what happened to her.

Jason nodded. "I will be at the hospital until noon tomorrow, but then I am at your disposal."

"Good. I'd like to speak to Alan Bennington again, then pay a visit to the Gilded Lily. I would appreciate it if you would come with me to the brothel."

"I'd be happy to. I'll collect you from Scotland Yard at half past twelve?"

"Yes."

"Can I offer you a ride home?" Jason asked.

"Thank you. I'll walk."

"Till tomorrow, then," Jason said, and climbed into the waiting brougham.

Chapter 13

When Daniel got home, Grace was in the nursery with Charlotte. Charlotte's grandmother, Harriet Elderman, had sent her a pretty dollhouse for Christmas, and the child's attention was focused on rearranging the tiny furniture to her satisfaction.

"Papa," she said happily. "Play?"

"Where's Miss Grainger?" Daniel asked Grace.

Rebecca's half day was on Saturday, when Daniel was most likely to be at home to spend time with Charlotte. To take unscheduled leave two days in a row was highly unusual, not to mention inconsiderate when Grace had her own work to do and at this time of day and had to see to their dinner.

"She went for a walk," Grace said, averting her gaze and fixing it on the little cradle in Charlotte's hand.

"It's dark, and the fog is rolling in."

Grace shrugged. It wasn't her job to school Rebecca in safety. She took her half day on Tuesday mornings, once she had made breakfast for the family and prepared a cold luncheon, which she left in the larder. Grace went to visit her family in Stepney and always got back well before darkness fell, even though it cut into her visit in the winter months when it began to grow dark by four.

"If you'll mind Charlotte, Inspector, I'll see to dinner," she said, already halfway out the door.

"Of course," Daniel replied, happy to spend an uncomplicated hour with his daughter.

Rebecca returned in time to put Charlotte to sleep and joined Daniel in the dining room. It was their habit to sup once Charlotte was in bed so they could enjoy dinner uninterrupted, but tension thickened the air as they took their seats, and Daniel found himself avoiding Rebecca's gaze as he unfolded his napkin and straightened the cutlery.

"Did you have a nice walk?" Daniel asked once there was nothing left for him to do save make polite conversation.

"Yes. Very pleasant. Thank you."

That was a blatant lie, since no sane person would go walking in the soupy fog that had descended on the city and muffled not only the sound of carriages but also footsteps. It was a dangerous business to be out on such a night, especially for a woman without a chaperone.

"Did you walk by yourself?" Daniel asked, unable to help himself.

Rebecca looked up from her soup, her expression guarded. "No. I met a friend."

"Good. Safety in numbers," Daniel mumbled.

"Indeed, there is," Rebecca agreed. She looked down into her plate, avoiding his probing gaze.

"Rebecca, is everything all right?" Daniel asked.

He couldn't sit there and pretend that the awkwardness between them didn't feel like a tangible thing, filling the room and wrapping itself around them like a funeral shroud. They were no more than three feet apart, but they may as well have been on opposite ends of the city for all the closeness he felt to a woman he had confessed to loving.

Rebecca reached out and covered his hand with her own. Her skin was cool and dry, and the touch, although intimate, did little to reassure him.

"Of course. I'm sorry to have worried you, Inspector."

"It's just with this recent murder…"

"I completely understand. It was thoughtless of me."

Daniel suddenly felt old, as if he were Rebecca's father and not a man she might consider marrying. The connection he'd felt with her before the stabbing had vanished, leaving behind two people who were forced to endure each other's company. He would have liked nothing more than to recapture the warm, flirtatious relationship they'd briefly shared, but the relations between them seemed irrevocably changed, and he wasn't sure why.

"Shall we have a nightcap after dinner?" he asked, hoping they might talk more easily when seated before the fire and without Grace coming in every few minutes to bring in the next course or take away the used plates.

Rebecca smiled apologetically. "If you don't mind, I think I'd like to retire early. I'm rather tired."

"Of course," Daniel said. He could hear the stiffness in his tone, and the underlying disappointment. Rebecca had carefully avoided him all week and clearly intended to continue to do so.

The prospect of having a nightcap on his own didn't appeal, so Daniel retreated to his own bedroom to brood in peace. Something had changed, but he had no right to press Rebecca for answers. She was in an awkward situation as it was, her relationship with Daniel not quite professional yet not quite intimate.

Daniel stared at the glowing coals in the hearth, startled by a moment of clarity. Of course. That was it. Rebecca was worried about the future, and as a woman, she felt she had to wait for him to propel their relationship forward. She was expecting a proposal, and he, like a dolt, had acted in a manner so obtuse as to make her doubt his intentions toward her.

As soon as this case was over, he would purchase a ring and propose. Getting engaged would defuse the awkwardness between them and put them on equal footing within the household, as well as where Charlotte was concerned. It would be disrespectful to Sarah's memory to wed before the year of mourning was up, but as long as Rebecca knew that he was fully committed to her, she could allow herself to move forward with the planning, not only of their wedding but of their future life together. Having had this epiphany, Daniel adjusted the fire screen, undressed, turned out the lamp, and climbed into bed, sliding beneath the covers and hoping for a good night's sleep.

Chapter 14

Jason felt an immense sense of relief when the dinner guests finally departed in a flurry of promises to see each other again soon. Katie had become fast friends with Adelaide Powell, of whom Jason wholeheartedly approved, but he didn't much care for Adelaide's husband, Andrew, now that he knew him better. He was the sort of man who shared little of himself but was always asking pointed questions and spouting opinions on subjects he knew little about. Jason had spent the past several hours engaged in a game of verbal tennis, hitting back at Andrew's intrusive inquiries with vague responses, especially once the conversation had turned to the murder of Eliza Bennington. Jason didn't think it appropriate to discuss the details of the case with the Powells, nor did he wish to hear Andrew's summation, which would be based on nothing but hearsay and unfounded speculation.

"I'm sorry you didn't have a good time," Katherine said as she slid onto Jason's lap and wrapped her arms around his neck.

He was seated before the fire in the library, where the two men had retired for brandy and cigars after dinner. Jason did not smoke and couldn't abide the smell of the foul things, but Andrew had puffed away undaunted, blowing the smoke in Jason's face.

"I'm glad you found a friend in Adelaide," he said, running a hand along Katherine's back. "She's a charming woman."

Katherine smiled. "Andrew is rather boorish, isn't he?"

"At times."

"You seem reluctant to speak about the case," Katherine pointed out as she settled more comfortably, leaning into him, and resting her head on his shoulder.

"I simply wish to spare you the sordid details."

"I'm not a child, Jason," Katherine admonished softly.

"No, you're not, and I value your input. Always," he added. "But this case is…" He paused, searching for the right word. "Ugly," he said at last.

"Uglier than the other murders you have worked on?" Katherine asked, raising her head to look him in the face.

"Yes."

He hadn't realized until he said it that he really did find this case disturbing. He could understand jealousy, greed, even fear of discovery as a motive for murder, but whoever had killed Eliza Bennington had been driven by something he couldn't quite comprehend, just as he couldn't conceive of why a supposedly happily married woman, the daughter of a vicar, would debase herself for money she didn't obviously need. The Benningtons were hardly starving, and Eliza had a family she could turn to for help. Surely her father and brother would have stepped in if the situation became dire.

Jason pulled out the ornate combs that held Katherine's hair in place and ran his fingers through the dark tresses, wishing the two of them could stay like this forever, safe in their love. It was at that moment that he came to realize why the death of Eliza Bennington bothered him so much. Eliza's origins reminded him uncomfortably of his own wife. Katherine was the daughter of a fire-and-brimstone vicar and had married for love despite her father's disdain for her choice of husband. Katherine seemed content, but was it possible that something might change to such a degree that she would be driven to betray everything she knew? Would she sacrifice herself to help Jason if she thought the situation called for it? Because to some degree Jason was certain that Eliza Bennington had done what she had out of love for her husband. Or had she? Try as he might, he just couldn't come up with a theory that encompassed all the facts.

"Go on up to bed, darling," Jason said, gently easing Katherine off his lap. "I'll join you in a minute."

Katherine got to her feet, picked up the combs off the side table, and fixed Jason with a quizzical look over the rim of her spectacles. She looked set to argue, but then turned on her heel and walked toward the door, leaving Jason to his own uncomfortable thoughts.

Chapter 15

Monday, February 15

When Daniel arrived at Scotland Yard in the morning, he headed directly for Superintendent Ransome's office. Ransome was often abrasive and demanding, but he was also a damn good policeman and kept abreast of all the open cases. Ransome commanded respect among the men, and Daniel had to admit, if only to himself, that he'd learned a lot from the superintendent and owed him a great deal. In his more hopeful moments, Daniel imagined that Ransome was grooming him to take over once Ransome moved up, getting ever closer to replacing Commissioner Hawkins when the older man retired.

"Good morning, sir," Daniel said as he entered the superintendent's office.

"Morning, Haze. The mermaid case. What have you got?" John Ransome demanded, not one to waste time on superfluous chitchat.

Daniel filled him in on everything he'd learned so far and watched Ransome's dark eyebrows lift in astonishment.

"How did you come by these photos, Haze?" he asked, his gaze sliding to the photographs of Eliza Bennington now resting on his desk.

"I'm sorry, sir, but I promised not to reveal my source."

John Ransome nodded. He understood the value of a secret source and didn't appear set to press Daniel for details. "How do you mean to proceed?"

Daniel was just about to reply when Constable Collins put his head around the partially open door. "Pardon the interruption, Superintendent, but there's someone here to see Inspector Haze."

"They can wait," Ransome replied.

"It's Mr. Reynolds, sir, Eliza Bennington's brother, and he seems rather anxious."

Ransome sighed. "Off with you, Haze," he said, jutting his chin toward the door. "We'll speak more later. Let's see what Mr. Reynolds is so anxious to share with us."

"Sir," Daniel said, and followed Constable Collins to the reception area.

Alastair Reynolds was tall and powerfully built. He wore a caped coat of dark brown wool, and the beaver top hat in his hands looked shiny and smooth. Though he was standing still, his demeanor was one of unease and impatience, and his dark blue eyes darted toward Daniel as soon as he stepped into the foyer.

"Are you Inspector Haze?" he asked.

"I am. Good to meet you, Mr. Reynolds."

"Likewise. Is there somewhere we can talk?" he asked, casting a sideways glance at Sergeant Meadows behind the polished counter and Constable Collins standing beside Daniel.

"Of course. This way, please, sir."

Daniel escorted Alastair Reynolds to an interview room and invited him to sit. The significance of the room and its utilitarian furniture wasn't lost on the man, whose eyes narrowed in suspicion.

"Am I to be questioned in connection with my sister's death?"

"This is an informal chat, Mr. Reynolds. You did come here voluntarily," Daniel reminded him, hoping to put the man at ease, but Alastair Reynolds' apprehension only seemed to escalate. He was like a bubbling cauldron of emotion, his hands still gripping the hat and his feet firmly planted on the floor, as if he needed to anchor himself.

110

Daniel pulled out a chair for himself and settled across from Alastair Reynolds, who finally set his hat on the table and unbuttoned his coat with unnatural, jerky movements.

"I'm sorry for your loss, Mr. Reynolds," Daniel said when the other man failed to speak.

"Thank you. We're all shattered." Alastair Reynolds looked down at his hands, which were clasped tightly on the scarred surface of the wooden table, then lifted his head to meet Daniel's gaze. "Inspector, I came here to ask you to close the case," he said at last.

"Oh?" Daniel hadn't expected that but didn't want to interrogate the man. Instead, he waited for Mr. Reynolds to explain himself.

The man's eyes were filled with pain, his skin mottled with either anger or the absurdity of finding himself in an interview room at Scotland Yard. Looking more closely, Daniel realized there was a marked resemblance between brother and sister. Alastair's hair was a shade darker, as were his irises, but the shape of the eyes, the high cheekbones, and the finely shaped mouth were all there. He was a remarkably handsome man, one who probably exuded an air of authority and solidity when not working under great emotional strain.

Reynolds inhaled sharply and spoke at last, his words coming quickly, as if he were afraid to change his mind. "I know, Inspector."

"Know what, Mr. Reynolds?"

"I know what my sister got up to. I wish I didn't, and I came to learn of her shame in a most unexpected way, but I beg you to close the case. Our family has suffered enough. If word of Eliza's activities got out, my father would lose his position, and my own family would be compromised. In my line of work, I depend on my good name and my reputation as a man of integrity. All that will be destroyed if it becomes public knowledge that my sister…" His voice trailed off and he bowed his head, unable to meet Daniel's gaze.

"I'm truly sorry for what you're going through, Mr. Reynolds, but I'm afraid I can't simply close an investigation because the family doesn't want the truth to come out. Your sister was brutally murdered, possibly by someone she knew. It is my duty to bring that person to justice."

Reynolds nodded, as if he had expected that very answer. "Then I implore you to keep the sordid details from the press."

"I will do my best to protect your privacy," Daniel promised. "How long have you known about Eliza's eh…activities?" he asked, unsure how to phrase the question politely.

"Since Friday. I was in Manchester on business when one of my colleagues showed me a newspaper. He had only just arrived that morning and had the Thursday edition of the *London Illustrated News* on him."

"Did he realize the victim was your sister?"

"No. He simply thought I would share in his glee. He was so amused, he could barely contain his mirth."

"And what was it that had amused him so?"

Alastair Reynolds sighed explosively. "He said the victim was a filthy whore who had it coming to her. I was shocked and asked why he would say such a thing about a woman he knew nothing about, and he said that he knew more about her than her fool of a husband. It was then that he showed me the photographs. He had them in his case, concealed in a plain brown envelope."

"Did you apprise him of the relationship between you and the victim?" Daniel asked, but the shock on Alastair Reynolds' face was answer enough.

"Of course not. How could I? I simply said that it was up to God to judge her, not him."

"And what did he say to that?"

"He made a remark about me being a vicar's son through and through and asked if I had ever even seen anything like what he had shown me."

"And had you?"

"Inspector, I spend my time among men, some of them rather rough specimens, I might add. Yes, I have seen photographs of that nature before. I just never expected to see my sister in any of them."

"Have you spoken to Alan Bennington?" Daniel asked.

Alastair Reynolds shook his head. "I don't want to see him."

"Why?"

"Because I can't be held responsible for my actions."

"Do you feel Mr. Bennington is to blame?" Daniel asked.

"Of course he is," Alastair exploded. "Had he kept a tighter rein on Eliza, she would never have stooped so low."

"Why do you think your sister decided to pose for the photographs?" Daniel couldn't help wondering if Alastair had seen any of the more recent photos, the ones commissioned by Tristan Carmichael.

"Eliza was always rebellious. She went against my father's wishes by marrying Bennington."

"What was your father's objection to Alan Bennington?"

He had already heard from the reverend, but there was a good chance that Alastair would reveal some deep-seated prejudice or past incident that would explain the reverend's deep dislike for his son-in-law.

Alastair drew in a deep breath, clearly striving for patience. "We're not titled, Inspector, but my mother came from a long line of landed gentry, and Eliza was set to receive a respectable portion when she married. Being uncommonly beautiful, Eliza had the potential to marry up, which would, in turn, have elevated the entire family. There were two noble gentlemen who had expressed an interest in her, but she rejected them flat out. They were old and stodgy, she said. Alan Bennington is handsome, I suppose, but he had nothing to offer a wife save genteel poverty. And we still have no idea who his people are. It's as if he'd sprung from the earth, fully formed. There are no parents, aunts or uncles, or even distant cousins. There is no one to recommend him."

"But Eliza fell in love with him?" Daniel prodded.

"Yes. She was blinded by him. She thought him charming and intelligent and kind. The fact that he seemed to have no interest in bettering his situation only spurred her on. It seemed saintly to her that he was above such trivial matters."

"Did your father forbid the marriage?"

"No, but he did try to dissuade her," Alastair said. "But Eliza wouldn't budge. She would marry Alan Bennington or no one at all, so eventually Father relented. He didn't want to lose her, you see. Eliza had always been his darling girl, and he indulged her more than he should have."

"Which makes her actions all the more puzzling, don't you think? Why would she risk destroying everything she had?"

Alastair Reynolds hung his head in defeat. "Look, I don't know why she did what she did. Perhaps she wanted to spite Alan, or maybe it was because they desperately needed money, since Alan had squandered Eliza's inheritance. For all I know, he might have forced her to do that in order to pay his debts. I never imagined—" He went silent, clearly devastated by what his sister had come to.

"Does your father know?"

"No!" Alastair cried. "Neither my father nor my wife know anything beyond the fact that Eliza was found dead in mysterious circumstances. And I would like to keep it that way. I want to protect them from the shame and the guilt."

"Why would they feel guilty?" Daniel asked.

"Don't people always feel guilty when something awful happens to someone they love? My father was too indulgent with Eliza when she was growing up. He loved her so dearly, he couldn't bear to discipline her when discipline was sorely needed. And Janet, well, she was the one to encourage the relationship with Alan Bennington. But how could she have known what an ineffectual husband he would be?"

There was that word again. Ineffectual. Used by both the Reverend Reynolds and his son. They had judged Alan Bennington and found him lacking in all the ways that measured a man's worth.

"Please, Inspector Haze. Is it not possible to simply close the case to avoid further disclosures?"

"Mr. Reynolds, do you not think your sister deserves justice?" Daniel asked.

"My sister is beyond caring, but we have to go on and find a way to get past this tragedy."

"I will do my utmost to keep the lurid details from the press," Daniel said. "I'm afraid that's all I can promise at the moment."

"Thank you. You seem an honorable man. I do hope you will be discreet." Alastair Reynolds pushed to his feet and reached for his hat. "I will send the undertakers to collect the body."

"Will Mr. Bennington not wish to bury his wife?"

"Mr. Bennington," Alastair said with ill-disguised venom, "can't afford to pay for a proper funeral. I will see to all the arrangements."

"As you wish," Daniel replied, rising as well. It mattered little to him who paid for the funeral once the body was released. He had a murderer to find.

Chapter 16

Daniel glanced at the clock. He had enough time to walk to the Strand and speak to Alan Bennington, but he would prefer to wait for Jason. He hated to admit it, but he relied on Jason's opinion, and his impetuous manner. Jason was not employed by the Metropolitan Police Service. He could say and do what he pleased, whereas Daniel was bound by a certain code of behavior and was answerable to Ransome, who would gladly throw Daniel under the wheels of an oncoming omnibus to protect his own reputation and ambition if the situation called for it.

In comparison to Daniel's previous case, which had involved an earl with connections to the Palace, the murder of Eliza Bennington was not nearly as career-making, but given the unexpected nature of Eliza's indiscretions, he still had to tread lightly, especially in view of Alastair Reynolds's request. He could hardly blame the man for wishing to keep Eliza's activities under wraps. What respectable man wouldn't?

And then there was the question of the husband. How much did Alan Bennington know? How much had he guessed? If he was aware of what his wife was up to, he would certainly have a motive for murder, but the manner of the disposal of Eliza's body was most puzzling. Why would anyone wish to draw attention to Eliza's murder in such an indecent manner if they were hoping to keep the truth from getting out?

Putting on his coat, hat, and the woolen muffler that had been a gift from Rebecca, Daniel left the building and went for a walk along the embankment. It was cold and gray, the mist rising off the water and a pungent smell permeating the surrounding area. The Thames was a valuable asset to the inhabitants of London and had been since Roman times, but they treated it like a sewer, dumping all manner of refuse into its murky depths, including an astounding number of corpses. Not a week went by that some poor sod wasn't pulled from the water, having either been murdered and tossed into the river to wash away the evidence or committed suicide by jumping off one of the bridges that spanned the waterway. Bloated corpses of dead dogs, cats, and rats routinely washed up on the banks that were littered with rotting fish and various debris expelled by the Thames. Daniel supposed it was absurd to expect Londoners to respect their natural resources when they had so little regard for human life.

He hadn't realized where he was heading until his steps took him to the area where Eliza's body had been discovered by Dick Hawley. Daniel surveyed the muddy stretch of bank before fixing his gaze on the impenetrable expanse of water that flowed with surprising speed past the shore. Had the fog not lifted when it did, the ferryman might never have spotted the dinghy and it would have sailed past the populated areas and drifted out to sea, taking Eliza's remains with it. But if the killer had been hoping for just such an outcome, what was the point of the dramatic display? Surely Eliza was meant to be found.

Daniel might have stayed longer, but the cold and damp of the river tended to get into one's bones, wrapping the passerby in a frigid embrace. Daniel turned and walked briskly back to Scotland Yard. Jason would arrive within the hour, which gave Daniel just enough time to enjoy a mug of hot tea and a biscuit, if Sergeant Meadows had saved one for him. Mrs. Meadows was known at the Yard as the Marzipan Fairy. She sent in a tin of freshly baked biscuits, homemade marzipan, or a cake at least once a week, and Sergeant Meadows guarded his wife's offerings jealously, allowing the men only one piece so that there was enough to go round.

Chapter 17

Daniel and Jason found Alan Bennington in his bookshop, book in hand and a mug of milky tea on the counter beside him. He sat huddled on a three-legged stool, his coat still buttoned, a green muffler wrapped around his neck, and fingerless woolen gloves on his pale hands. The interior of the shop was nearly as cold as the outside, and there was a noticeable air of neglect, evident in the dusty surfaces, moldy-smelling volumes, whose spines were dull with age, and the lack of an appealing display in either the windows or at the entrance of the shop. If Alan Bennington carried the latest bestsellers, they weren't prominently placed, forcing the customer to either ask for assistance or simply take themselves off to a more welcoming establishment.

Alan Bennington placed his open book face-down on the counter and gave them a belligerent stare. "Have you found him, then?" he demanded.

"Not yet, but we would like to ask you a few more questions, if we may," Daniel replied.

"More questions? All you people do is ask questions," Alan sniped bitterly, but it was obvious he was distressed and needed a target for his anger.

Jason unceremoniously leaned against the counter and placed his top hat next to the open book. "Mr. Bennington, do you sell pornography in your shop?" he asked without preamble.

Alan Bennington's eyes nearly popped out of his head. "I beg your pardon?" he sputtered.

"You heard me. Do you sell pornographic images to individuals who are willing to pay for them?"

"I do not," Alan stated, his cheeks growing pink with indignation.

"Maybe you should," Jason continued conversationally. "Seems you could use the income such an undertaking would generate."

"That's illegal," Alan Bennington replied, his gaze narrowing as he was obviously trying to figure out if this was some sort of trap.

"But you are familiar with the sort of merchandise I'm referring to?" Jason asked.

"I am."

"Have you ever purchased illicit photographs for your personal use?"

"No."

"A significant number of London booksellers are involved in illegal trade," Jason said. "I find it difficult to believe that no one has ever approached you with a proposition to sell their product in exchange for a percentage of the profit."

"What is this about? And what does the distribution of pornography have to do with the death of my wife?"

Alan Bennington's confusion seemed genuine, and Daniel was tempted to believe that he truly was ignorant of the connection, but as Jason had pointed out, it was nearly impossible that no one had approached Alan, especially when Eric Dawson had come into the shop regularly and had recruited Bennington's wife.

"Mr. Bennington, your wife had been posing for Eric Dawson for months, and photographs of her were mailed to members of a subscription service. Were you really not aware of her lucrative sideline?" Jason asked.

Alan Bennington went white to the roots of his hair, his mouth opening and closing, as if he couldn't breathe, and his eyes darting around like those of a frightened animal. The acrid smell of the man's sweat, indicative of his fear and distress, hung heavy in the air.

"No," he whispered at last. "A hundred times, no."

Alan grabbed his mug and downed the contents, then wiped his mouth with the back of his hand and promptly vomited into a rubbish bin he'd had just enough time to grab from behind the counter.

"Are you quite all right?" Jason asked once the man had recovered himself somewhat.

The stink of vomit was unbearable, so Daniel opened the door, letting in a blast of cold air.

"I'm sorry," Alan Bennington muttered.

Daniel watched the man carefully. He couldn't tell if it was the news of Eliza's activities that had made him ill or the knowledge that what she'd done was no longer a secret from the police, and therefore the public.

"Mr. Bennington, did you know?" Jason asked again, his tone merciless.

Alan Bennington shook his head. "No," he rasped. "I didn't. But I suspected she was up to something. She suddenly had money."

"Where did she tell you the money had come from?" Daniel asked.

"Eliza said she was able to secure another loan from her brother. He'd given me a loan a few months back, but I have yet to pay it off."

"And you believed her?" Jason inquired.

"I had no reason not to."

"Mr. Bennington, what happened to the money?" Daniel asked.

Alan looked like he was going to be sick again. "I don't have it."

"Where has it gone?"

"I spent it."

"On what?" Jason asked, pinning the man with a relentless stare.

"On my mistress."

"How long have you kept a mistress?" Daniel asked, doing his best to hide his surprise at Alan Bennington's confession.

"About six months now."

"Did your wife know?"

Bennington shook his head. "She couldn't have."

"And was this a serious relationship or just a passing fancy?" Jason asked.

"I don't know," Alan Bennington muttered. He still looked ill, his attention not quite focused on the questions.

"Who is this woman?" Daniel asked as he flipped his notebook to a clean page and took out a pencil.

"Her name is Lorna Simpson."

"Address," Daniel spat out. Alan Bennington recited an address in Blackfriars.

"That's not too far from here," Daniel remarked. "How often did you see her?"

"About twice a week. I'd close the shop for luncheon and go over to Lorna's."

"And is Lorna Simpson married?" Jason asked.

"No. She's a widow."

"What drew you to her?" Jason asked. He seemed genuinely curious, and little wonder. With a woman as lovely as Eliza for a wife, what would drive a man to seek an ongoing arrangement with another?

"She made me feel like a man," Alan Bennington said after a long pause.

"Can you kindly elaborate?" Jason invited, his tone softer now.

Alan Bennington nodded. "When I first met Eliza, I thought she was the most beautiful woman I had ever seen, both inside and out. She was ethereal, inspiring. That she was interested in me seemed a miracle. I never imagined she would welcome my suit, but she did, despite her father's disapproval. And for a short while, we were happy."

Alan looked away, his gaze fixing on the window, his arms going around his middle, either for warmth or to hold in his vulnerability. "Eliza's father and brother had spoiled her. She always had the best of everything: gowns, shoes, trinkets, and most of all, unconditional love. They doted on her."

"And you?" Jason asked.

"I did too, but after a while, I began to experience feelings of inadequacy. I couldn't hope to keep her in the style she was accustomed to. I thought she understood that when we married, but she was constantly making comments that were innocent in themselves but loaded with meaning."

"What sort of comments?"

"Such as, 'Oh, Janet has just ordered an entire new spring wardrobe,' or 'Alastair is making plans for a trip to Italy this summer.'" Alan sighed. "She was reminding me that I couldn't afford to give her those things."

"And Mrs. Simpson?" Daniel asked.

"Lorna is a simple soul who understands that joy is not about material possessions. Joy is about having a companion who makes one happy. Lorna and I never run out of conversation, whereas with Eliza, it was all angry silences and accusing looks. I thought she might feel more fulfilled once she had a child to love, but Eliza never conceived."

"Did you blame her for that?" Jason asked.

"No, of course not, but she became increasingly despondent, especially once Janet and Alastair Reynolds had shared their happy news."

"Did you seek medical advice?"

"Eliza spoke to our family physician, and he told her that she simply needed to allow nature to take its course. He was of the opinion that anxiety could sometimes prevent a desirable outcome."

"Does Mrs. Simpson have children?" Daniel asked. Alan shook his head.

There was something furtive in Alan Bennington's demeanor, a nervousness that went beyond the obvious distress of being questioned by the police and learning unexpected things about a spouse who had been murdered.

"Mr. Bennington, we are going to speak to Mrs. Simpson, so you may as well tell us the whole truth," Daniel said.

"Lorna is with child," Alan Bennington choked out.

"Is it yours?" Jason asked.

Alan Bennington nodded miserably. "I suppose you now think that I killed Eliza so that I could marry the mother of my child."

"Did you?" Daniel barked.

"No."

"So, what were you planning to do?" Jason asked.

"I hadn't really thought about it. I had only just found out about the baby a fortnight ago," Alan said.

"How far along is Mrs. Simpson?"

"About three months." Alan threw Jason a defiant look. "I would gladly have married Lorna had I been free to do so, but it was always my intention to look after my child. You might think this gives me a motive, but I did not kill Eliza."

"Then you should have no objection to my men searching the premises," Daniel replied.

Alan Bennington looked shocked. "I suppose refusing will make me appear guilty, so go on, Inspector. Search the shop. In fact, I will make it even easier for you. I will give you the keys and leave the premises. You can return the keys to me once your flunkies have turned the place over."

Sliding off his stool, Alan Bennington donned his hat and handed the keys to the shop to Daniel.

"Shall we?" Daniel said as he pointed toward the door.

The three of them stepped outside, and Daniel locked the door, dropping the keys into his coat pocket. Without another word, Alan Bennington walked away, his stride determined, his back ramrod straight, and his head held high. It was only once Alan turned the corner that Daniel realized Jason was speaking to him.

"I think we should interview Mrs. Simpson before Alan Bennington has a chance to forewarn her of our visit," Jason was saying.

"If he hasn't already. Let's drop the keys off at the Yard first." Daniel sighed with frustration. "I think it's safe to assume that we'll find nothing on the premises to implicate Mr. Bennington in the murder of his wife," he observed bitterly.

"I think you're right. There was either nothing there to start with, or Bennington has disposed of anything that might incriminate him on the off-chance that the shop might be searched."

"I must admit, I'm rather puzzled by this family," Daniel said once they had delivered the keys to Sergeant Meadows and set off for Blackfriars.

"In what way?"

"First, we have the Reverend Reynolds, who was supposedly married to a woman of means. Landed gentry, according to Alastair Reynolds. If that was the case, what became of the estate? And then we have Alastair Reynolds, who, although understandably concerned with his reputation, is married to a former chorus girl. Alan Bennington is expecting a child with his mistress, which in itself is sufficient motive to want his wife out of the way, yet he admitted to his indiscretions willingly. Had he not told us, we might never have learned of Mrs. Simpson."

Jason considered Daniel's misgivings before replying. "The reverend's wife might have had a brother who inherited the estate, or a father that's still living. A part of her marriage settlement must have been earmarked for Eliza, which would account for the sizeable dowry Alastair Reynolds mentioned, but at this stage, I don't see that it's relevant to the investigation. Even if Alastair Reynolds had a reason to kill his sister, he wouldn't benefit from her death financially, nor would he wish to attract the sort of attention her death has generated."

Jason appeared amused as he addressed the next point. "And he certainly wouldn't be the first man to fall in love with an actress. However, there's the possibility that Miss Bloom was mistaken, and Janet Reynolds is not the person she knew as Janet Brody. She does seem rather a spiteful woman, so it is possible that she was only looking to stir up trouble." Jason took a deep breath and continued. "Alan Bennington didn't have to tell us about his mistress, but I expect the move was a calculated risk on his part. To keep a mistress is not a crime, but if said mistress can provide him with an alibi, we have no grounds to arrest him for the murder of his wife."

"If that's the case, then he's a lot cleverer than anyone gives him credit for," Daniel replied. "Or perhaps he is simply telling the truth."

"Thus far, Alan Bennington is the only person who had reason to murder Eliza."

"As far as we know," Daniel pointed out.

"As far as we know," Jason agreed.

Chapter 18

Lorna Simpson lived in a nondescript two-story redbrick house on John Carpenter Street. The windows and front door could have used a lick of paint, and there were several tiles missing from the roof, but someone had recently swept the steps, there were colorful curtains at the windows, and the chimneypots belched smoke into the air. The residents not only made an effort to keep the place clean but could afford to have a fire burning in the middle of the day, when the temperature was at its highest.

The door was opened by a heavily pregnant young woman who had a fair-haired toddler perched on her hip. She looked at the men with surprise, studying them for a moment before inquiring as to the purpose of their visit.

"We're here to see Mrs. Simpson," Daniel said, not bothering to offer a more detailed explanation or show his warrant card. The woman shrugged with indifference, then called out to Lorna Simpson before simply walking away toward the rear of the building, where a door, presumably to her lodgings, stood ajar.

A dark-haired woman opened the other door and peered out. She was older than Eliza Bennington and wore round wire-rimmed spectacles and a prim gown of russet wool. Her large black eyes widened behind the lenses of her specs as she took in the two well-dressed gentlemen who'd come to call on her.

Daniel held up his warrant card. "Inspector Haze of Scotland Yard, and this is my associate, Dr. Redmond. May we come in, Mrs. Simpson? We'd like to ask you a few questions."

"What's this about, Inspector?" she asked, looking from one man to the other.

"It's about the murder of Eliza Bennington," Daniel said, watching the woman closely for a reaction.

Lorna Simpson went deathly pale, her mouth opening in shock as her hand flew to her bosom.

It stood to reason that she was aware of the death of her lover's wife, since the murder had been the talk of the town for the past few days, so Daniel put her reaction down to finding a Scotland Yard inspector at her door. Either she was feigning shock to demonstrate her innocence, or she hadn't expected her relationship with Alan Bennington to come to light as part of the investigation and was genuinely surprised to discover that Alan had involved her in their inquiries.

Lorna Simpson stepped aside to let them in, then led them into a parlor that faced the street. She quickly collected several cuts of cloth off the surprisingly fashionable settee, so they'd have a place to sit. A narrow table was positioned against the wall, an assortment of tailor's scissors, thimbles, skeins of thread, and patterns littering the surface, but the truly amazing thing was the contraption that stood before the only window in the room, a sleek, black apparatus decorated with a fanciful golden scroll. Perched on a stand, it boasted several wheels, a crank, and an oddly shaped part on the left side that was positioned over a piece of delicate fabric. Daniel had never seen the like but could only assume it was one of those newfangled sewing machines he'd heard about from Grace, whose desire for one bordered on an obsession.

Lorna Simpson pulled up a chair and positioned it to face them before sitting down. She looked from Daniel to Jason as she waited for them to begin the interview. Now that Daniel was presented with an opportunity to study her, he thought her attractive, in an understated, earthy sort of way. She could never compete with someone as ethereally beautiful as Eliza Bennington, but there was a dignity about her that Daniel found both appealing and reassuring in equal parts.

"Mrs. Simpson, it has come to our attention that you are conducting an extramarital liaison with Alan Bennington." Daniel was fully aware that he sounded like some priggish minister, but he needed to get the woman talking, if only to defend herself from accusation.

"Yes," she replied simply. "I am."

"Where did you meet Mr. Bennington?" Jason asked politely.

"We met when I stopped into the shop to purchase a copy of *Mrs. Beeton's Book of Household Management.*"

"And when was this?"

"June of last year."

"Was that when the relationship began?" Daniel asked.

"No. We started seeing each other a few weeks later."

"And now you're carrying Mr. Bennington's child," Daniel announced bluntly.

"I am."

If Daniel had been expecting a simpering, apologetic woman, he wasn't going to find one here. Lorna Simpson seemed to feel no shame, either over the affair or the pregnancy.

"You do realize that your admission goes to show that Mr. Bennington had a motive for murder," Daniel said.

Lorna Simpson's lip curled at the suggestion, and she made a dismissive gesture with her hand. "I know you're only doing your job, Inspector, but you will not find any evidence against Alan. He's the kindest, gentlest man I've ever met, and he would have never murdered his wife. He was disappointed in her, resented her for the way she made him feel, and wished he could turn back time and undo his marriage to her, but he never once wished her ill."

"And what makes Alan Bennington such a paragon of virtue?" Daniel asked, his ill will toward the man all too obvious.

Lorna Simpson gave him a pitying look. "I suppose like most people, you judge Alan by his material possessions, or lack thereof. He resides in Lambeth, and his shop is not a profitable concern, but did you know that he visits the Fetter Lane orphanage every week?" Mrs. Simpson demanded. "That's right," she said triumphantly when Daniel's surprise must have shown plainly on his face. "Alan reads to the orphans and teaches them their letters. He also donates books from the shop every Christmas so the children have a small library of their own where they can borrow books. Alan says that reading is the greatest of comforts and wants to offer the poor orphans a glimpse into another world."

Lorna Simpson glared at Daniel like an avenging angel. "And he allows individuals who can't afford to purchase the books outright to borrow from the shop with the promise that they will return them when they've finished reading them. He helps people, Inspector, without expecting anything in return. How many businessmen in this city can make such a claim?"

"That's very commendable, indeed," Jason said. "But a desire to help and an instinct to kill are not mutually exclusive, Mrs. Simpson."

"I wouldn't expect you to understand, *my lord*," Mrs. Simpson said acidly. "I know who you are. I read the papers. You've lived a life of privilege and ease, so how can you possibly comprehend what a bit of kindness means to an orphaned child?"

Daniel opened his mouth to defend Jason, but Jason gave him a warning look. It was none of Lorna Simpson's affair what Jason had been through or the orphans he'd helped, and was still helping, nor that he treated the patients he operated on pro bono regardless of their social status or ability to pay. This was a murder inquiry, not a competition.

"How do you earn your living, Mrs. Simpson?" Daniel asked instead.

Mrs. Simpson made a face that implied the answer was perfectly obvious. "I take in sewing, Inspector Haze. I work for Imelda Linton, who's a well-known modiste."

"You do not work in her atelier?" Jason asked.

"I prefer to work at home and make my own hours. As long as I deliver the items on the agreed-upon day, Mrs. Linton is happy with the arrangement."

"Will you continue to work for Mrs. Linton once the child is born?" Daniel asked.

"Of course. I will need to support us, won't I?"

"And if your employer discovers that you've given birth to an illegitimate child?"

"I don't see how that's any of her affair," Mrs. Simpson replied haughtily. "Unless you tell her, she need never know."

"When was the last time you saw Alan Bennington?" Daniel asked.

"I saw him on Wednesday."

"What time did he leave you?"

"Around two. He had to return to the shop."

"How was his demeanor at that time?" Jason asked.

"He was happy. He was excited about the prospect of becoming a father."

"Did he mention his wife?"

"No. We had agreed early on that we wouldn't speak about Eliza during our time together."

"Do you have any family, Mrs. Simpson?" Jason asked.

Lorna Simpson seemed surprised by the questions but answered readily enough. "My sister, Laurel, lives in Newcastle with her family, but I haven't seen her since I left for good fifteen years ago. My father was still alive then, but he has since passed. Laurel and I write to each other regularly," she added.

"Does your sister know about Alan Bennington?"

"She does. She thinks I'm a damn fool for allowing myself to become involved with a married man and believes I will cry bitter tears once he leaves me."

"What does your sister's husband do?" Daniel chimed in.

"He's a shopkeeper. Why does that matter?"

"Because if your sister thinks you're a damn fool, perhaps she might take it upon herself to free your lover of his inconvenient wife so that he could marry you."

Lorna Simpson's peal of laughter filled the small room. "What an imagination you have, Inspector. You think that my sister, who's expecting her seventh child, came to London and murdered a woman in cold blood, then undressed her, laid her in a dinghy she had conveniently found nearby, and set her afloat?"

"Perhaps she put her husband up to it," Daniel suggested.

"My brother-in-law adores his wife and children and would never risk the noose for the likes of me. If you think I'm lying to you, then by all means, cable the local constabulary, if there is one, and have them verify his whereabouts. That's Laurel and Isaac Moore, Inspector. Of Newcastle," she added saucily. Daniel thought she might be mocking him.

"I will do just that," Daniel promised. "And where were you Wednesday night?"

"Right here, working on a trousseau for Miss Victoria Mulvaney. Lizzie next door brought me a slice of fish pie for my supper around seven, since I hadn't had time to make anything."

"Eliza Bennington may have been killed before seven," Jason said.

"I never went out on Wednesday. The only time I stopped working was when Alan came to see me around one. He stayed for an hour and left."

"You could easily have left the house, made your way to Wapping, killed Eliza Bennington, and returned by seven," Daniel mused. "No one would be the wiser."

"Yes, I suppose I could have, but I would have to have known that Eliza Bennington would be in Wapping, wouldn't I?" Lorna Simpson pointed out. "As far as I was aware, Eliza was at home, awaiting the arrival of her husband."

Daniel nodded in acknowledgement of the validity of that statement. Unless Lorna had followed Eliza and then waited for her to emerge from Tristan Carmichael's warehouse, she would have had no way of knowing where to find Eliza on Wednesday evening. Which wasn't to say that it wasn't possible. They only had Lorna's word for her whereabouts that day.

"Do you have any blue silk?" Jason asked.

"Yes. I'm working on a ball gown for one of Mrs. Linton's clients." Lorna's face was devoid of subterfuge, and she seemed genuinely puzzled by Jason's question.

"Eliza was wrapped in a peacock-blue shawl," Daniel explained.

"I see." Lorna smiled wryly. "Inspector, I work hard to make ends meet, and I have a child on the way, one I might be raising on my own. Do you think I would throw away a silk shawl on a corpse? To what end?"

"The killer wished to make Eliza Bennington look like a mermaid."

Lorna's lip curled again. She seemed to have a habit of doing that when she found something amusing. "A rather peculiar notion, if you ask me," she said, shaking her head.

"Perhaps," Jason replied, "but with Eliza out of the way, Alan Bennington is now free to marry you, and well-to-do or not, he's been a great help to you these past months."

"How do you mean?" Lorna asked, clearly taken aback by Jason's observation.

"If I'm not mistaken, that's a Singer Grasshopper model sewing machine. My mother had one just like it," he added. "A gift from Mr. Bennington?"

"Yes," Lorna replied hesitantly.

"As well as the settee and the sideboard?" Jason asked, his tone conversational. Daniel hadn't noticed the sideboard, but now that he looked at it, it did appear almost new.

"What of it, my lord?" Lorna asked.

"I could be wrong, of course, but it is my understanding that this model of sewing machine is manufactured in the United States, which would mean that Mr. Bennington had ordered it for you and had it shipped across the Atlantic, not an inexpensive undertaking. He also bought you new furniture, and I expect there are other items he paid for during the course of your relationship. He was using the funds he'd borrowed from his wife's brother to support you."

"I never asked Alan for anything," Lorna spat out. "He wished to help me, and I never asked him where the money came from."

"Nevertheless, your lover was keeping you in finer style than you could ever afford on your own, no matter how much sewing you took in, and if his wife or her family were to find out, the bounty would be sure to stop. Eliza's death ensures that Alan Bennington continues to support you and your child."

Lorna's eyes blazed with indignation. "I challenge you to find a witness who either saw me leaving the house on Wednesday or returning, or who can place me anywhere near Wapping. Until you do, I think our business is at an end, gentlemen. I have work to do, and you have a murder to solve. Good day to you both."

Lorna stood and walked over to the door, which she held open for them with an air of vindictive pride.

"That's one spirited woman," Jason said once they were back in the street.

"And unapologetic," Daniel added. "As if having a liaison with a married man and getting pregnant by him is the most acceptable thing in the world."

"She doesn't seem troubled by it."

"Perhaps because she's sure Alan Bennington will marry her now that he's free," Daniel mused.

"Not if he hangs."

"She seems convinced that we won't find any evidence against either of them."

"Either she truly believes that or it's just bravado talking," Jason said.

"Let's question the neighbor before Mrs. Simpson has a chance to ask her to lie for her."

Daniel knocked on the other door and presented his warrant card when it was opened by the same woman they'd seen earlier.

She didn't budge, blocking the door with her massive belly. "What ye want, then?" she demanded.

"Your name, for a start," Daniel replied, annoyed by the woman's hostility.

"Elizabeth Coulter," the woman replied, her gaze never leaving Daniel's face. "What of it?"

"Did you see Mrs. Simpson on Wednesday?" Daniel asked.

"'Course I did."

"What time?"

The woman shrugged. "First time, round ten, I s'pose, when I were hangin' out me washing, and then round half seven. I brought 'er back a fish pie for 'er supper."

"Do you normally bring her food?" Daniel asked.

Mrs. Coulter looked taken aback. "Yeh. Sometimes. She watches me boy from time to time, so I repay 'er when I'm able. Me husband 'ad a 'ankering for a fish pie, so I got one for Lorna as well. Small price to pay for 'er kindness. That a crime, Inspector?"

"It's not," Daniel replied. "Did you see Mrs. Simpson go out on Wednesday?"

"I 'ave no time to spy on me neighbors. If she went out, I didn't see 'er. Are we done 'ere? I 'ave stew on the simmer and don't want it to burn."

"One last question, Mrs. Coulter. Did you see anyone coming to see Mrs. Simpson on Wednesday?" Jason asked.

"Saw 'er fancy man come round one."

"What about later, in the evening?"

"If anyone 'ad come to see Lorna, I'd not 'ave 'eard it. Me Mark snores like a locomotive. That's all I 'ear all the night long."

"Thank you, Mrs. Coulter," Jason said politely. "You've been a great help."

"'Ave I?" Mrs. Coulter asked with obvious amusement. "Never thought I'd be 'elping the police," she said, shaking her head. "Will wonders never cease?"

She unceremoniously shut the door in their faces, and they heard her calling to her son to get away from the window.

"Let's stop by the Yard and see if the men found anything at the shop, then head over to the Gilded Lily to speak to Mary Smith."

"Perhaps we should question Mrs. Linton, as well," Jason suggested.

Daniel considered it. "Do you think she might know something?"

"At the very least, we can verify whether Lorna Simpson actually works for her and if she was as busy as she claims to be."

Daniel glanced at the clock on a nearby church tower. He supposed they could stop off at Mrs. Linton's shop on the way to the brothel. It wasn't as though Mary Smith was going anywhere.

Chapter 19

"Anything at Bennington's bookshop?" Daniel asked Sergeant Meadows once they were back at the Yard.

"See for yourself," the sergeant answered, and directed Daniel and Jason to a room furnished with wall-to-wall wooden cabinets where they kept the case files as well as incriminating evidence. The box containing the items removed by the constables from Alan Bennington's shop was pitifully small. It contained several packets of arsenic, headache powder, and a plain brown envelope. Daniel eagerly opened the envelope, hoping to find lewd photos of the man's wife, but it contained several bank notes in the sum of twenty pounds.

Daniel supposed he had expected as much, but he was still disappointed, since the items weren't all that incriminating. The arsenic would be to kill the rats in the shop. The headache powder was self-evident. And the money, although the exact amount of the fee Eliza had received from Tristan Carmichael, was hardly damning evidence. Daniel returned the box to Sergeant Meadows, who locked it in a drawer, and left the room.

It was just past three, so as good a time as any to pay a call on Mrs. Linton, whose atelier was located in Bond Street. The shopfront consisted of two large plated windows that displayed stylish and, from the looks of them, expensive gowns. An awning of pale green and white matched the apple-green door between the window displays, and *Mrs. Linton's House of Style* was etched into the discreet copper plate beside the door.

Jason and Daniel entered the establishment, which wasn't very large and was furnished with pink-and-cream striped chairs, a thick carpet in shades of cream and pink, and several gilded mirrors. A blonde-wood counter ran the length of one wall and displayed thick, velvet-bound books, presumably full of patterns and sketches of the latest styles.

A fashionably attired young woman stood behind the counter and smiled warmly, her brown eyes lighting up as if she'd been waiting for them all afternoon. "Good afternoon, gentlemen," she said. "How can I help you today? Are you looking to order a gift for that special lady?"

Daniel showed her his warrant card. "I'm Inspector Haze of Scotland Yard, and this is my associate, Lord Redmond. Are you Mrs. Linton?"

The young woman seemed taken aback by both the identity of the callers and the question. "No, I'm not, Inspector," she said. "Mrs. Linton would never stoop to greeting customers herself. She's in the back. I'll get her, shall I?"

Not bothering to wait for a reply, she hurried through a discreetly placed side door and returned a few moments later, followed by a handsome woman of middle years. Mrs. Linton's chestnut curls were elaborately coiffed, her pale green eyes were accentuated by lashes too dark to be natural in a woman of her coloring, and her waist was so narrow, it was a wonder she could draw breath and not faint from lack of oxygen. She wore a gown of burgundy silk, decorated with cut black velvet that formed whimsical patterns on the bodice, the back, and the hem. A velvet ribbon encircled her slender white throat and showcased a diamond-encrusted ruby that sparkled in the light from the windows and perfectly matched the dangling earrings that swayed gently as the woman moved.

"I am Imelda Linton. How may I be of service, Inspector? My lord," she added, giving Jason a slight bow of the head.

"We are investigating the murder of Eliza Bennington," Daniel explained.

"The mermaid?" Mrs. Linton asked, clearly surprised to find herself connected to the inquiry. "Then perhaps we'd better speak in my office."

Mrs. Linton led them through the door she'd come through into a comfortably furnished room dominated by an inlaid rosewood desk with a matching chair and a tall cabinet. There were two guest chairs, an ornate brazier, the contents of which glowed behind the grill and gave off a surprising amount of heat, and several potted plants. The pink-and-white patterned wallpaper gave the room a distinctly feminine feel.

"Do sit down, gentlemen," Mrs. Linton invited, and settled behind her desk, folding her hands as if she were about to pray. "I fail to see how I might be connected to the unfortunate woman, but I'm happy to answer your questions."

"Mrs. Linton, do you employ Mrs. Lorna Simpson?" Jason asked.

"Yes. Why?"

"She works at home?" Daniel asked.

"She does. Most of my girls work at home, Inspector."

"Why?"

Imelda Linton looked at him as if he were daft. "Because it reduces costs and enables me to pay my seamstresses a more competitive wage. I keep a small workshop in the back room for time-sensitive alterations and fittings, but I don't need to maintain separate premises for the rest of the seamstresses, which is a costly business, even if I rent a space in the East End or even across the river."

"How many seamstresses do you employ?" Jason asked.

"Nearly forty," Mrs. Linton replied.

"Forty?" Daniel echoed.

Mrs. Linton smiled indulgently. "You clearly have no idea how much work goes into creating a garment, Inspector. And we make many. Still, even with forty girls, the wait time for a Linton original is nearly two months."

"When was the last time you saw Lorna Simpson?"

"On Monday, but what does Mrs. Simpson have to do with the murder of Eliza Bennington?"

"We believe they were acquainted," Daniel replied, not wishing to give Mrs. Linton any ammunition against a potentially innocent woman.

"I see. Well, as a rule, Mrs. Simpson comes in on Monday morning to collect the fabrics, patterns, and measurements I have prepared for her. She then returns the finished items to me on Thursday morning, since I schedule most of the fittings for Thursday afternoon and Friday," she explained. "I furnish her with the next set of orders on Thursday, and she brings them back on Monday morning, so I see her only twice a week."

"And did Mrs. Simpson deliver the orders this past Thursday, as expected?" Jason asked.

"She did. Mrs. Simpson is always prompt, and her work is exemplary. I've never seen such even stiches."

Mrs. Linton clearly wasn't aware that Lorna Simpson relied on a sewing machine to produce the stitches that had so impressed her employer, but Daniel saw no reason to divulge her secret. Using machinery wasn't against the law, nor was Mrs. Simpson obligated to report it.

"Do you expect the seamstresses to work seven days a week?" Jason asked. His tone was distinctly unfriendly, and his censure wasn't lost on the proprietress.

Mrs. Linton smiled at him. "No, my lord. The workers decide how many days they wish to work. I pay them per item, not per hour or even per week."

"Is that common?" Daniel asked.

"Most of the seamstresses have small children to care for, Inspector. They create their own schedule, often sewing at night once they can work uninterrupted. As long as they finish the orders on time, it makes little difference to me when they find the time to

142

fulfill their obligations, but I will not pay them for hours they do not work. Lorna doesn't have small children now, but when her son was younger, the arrangement suited her very well."

"Mrs. Simpson had a son?" Jason asked, his surprise evident.

"Mrs. Simpson *has* a son," Mrs. Linton replied. "In fact, he often accompanied his mother when she came to deliver and collect the orders, to help her carry the parcels. But I haven't seen him in months."

"Do you know his name?"

Mrs. Linton made a vague gesture with her beringed hand. "Sorry, I can't recall."

"And how old would you say he was the last time you saw him?" Daniel asked.

"Thirteen, maybe. Is that relevant?"

"At this stage, we're not yet sure what is relevant. We're speaking to everyone who knew Mrs. Bennington."

"Well, I never met her, so I really don't see how I can be of further help."

"Which is why we won't detain you any longer," Daniel said, and pushed to his feet. "Thank you for your time, Mrs. Linton."

But Imelda Linton wasn't interested in Daniel. She turned to Jason, smiling beguilingly. "My lord," she purred. "And is there a Lady Redmond?"

"There is," Jason replied, smiling back.

"Perhaps you will consider Linton's House of Style the next time your dear wife requires a ball gown or even a riding habit or a walking dress," she said. "Our prices are competitive, and the results speak for themselves. We cater to a most exclusive clientele, and our every design is an original."

Jason acknowledged Mrs. Linton's sales pitch with a slight incline of the head. "I will certainly mention your establishment to my wife, but I'm certain she's familiar with it already."

The implication was that Katherine had heard of Linton's House of Style but chose to withhold her patronage, but Mrs. Linton's face lit up with pleasure. "I would be very grateful, my lord."

"Good day, Mrs. Linton." Jason bowed from the neck and followed Daniel to the door.

"Lorna Simpson has a son," Daniel said as soon as they were in the street.

"Either Mrs. Linton has confused Mrs. Simpson with another seamstress or both Lorna Simpson and Alan Bennington deliberately failed to mention him."

"But to what end?"

"Perhaps they fear he had something to do with Eliza's murder."

Daniel considered this. "He may have been angry with Alan Bennington for taking advantage of his mother and perhaps hoped to frame him for the murder, or he may have thought that disposing of Alan's wife would free Alan to marry Lorna before their child is born."

"There's nothing to suggest the younger Simpson was involved in any way, but I think we should speak to Mrs. Simpson again and account for the boy's whereabouts, if only for the purpose of elimination."

"I agree, but first, we should speak to Mary Smith."

Chapter 20

By the time they arrived in Covent Garden, dusky shadows had begun to wrap the city in a lavender haze, and the remaining vendors at Covent Market hurried to pack away their unsold wares and load the wagons for the journey home. The stench of rotting vegetables hung in the air, and piles of broken crates and half-unraveled baskets littered the plaza. Several thin, ragged children had converged on the square, waiting for the farmers to depart so they could pick through the refuse for anything that might still be edible and either devour it on the spot or bring it home to share with their families. The broken crates wouldn't go to waste either, since they could be burned in lieu of coal and guarantee several poor families a warmer night than they would have otherwise.

Daniel and Jason cut across the market and continued on foot to Maiden Lane, an ironic location for a brothel, but this was London, and prostitutes could be found just about anywhere there were potential clients. The girls ranged from glittering, silk-clad beauties who dwelled in opulent establishments that catered to the highest echelons of London society to toothless hags that serviced their clients in doorways and filthy alleyways for lack of a place to conduct their business. Daniel expected the Gilded Lily housed the former.

The brothel door displayed no number, but the establishment was easily identifiable by a brass fleur-de-lis knocker, a somewhat unpatriotic symbol given England's history of conflict with France, but a clear indication of what lay behind the shiny blue door. Daniel banged the heavy knocker, eliciting an almost immediate response from a burly fellow with neatly oiled dark hair and a handlebar moustache. His scowl was instantly replaced by a look of forced amicability when Daniel presented his warrant card and introduced himself and Jason before stating their business.

"Come in, Inspector. My lord. Mr. Carmichael did say as you'd be stopping by. Mary will receive you in the Rose Parlor." Evidently, the flower theme continued beyond the front door.

The men were escorted to a cozy receiving room just off a corridor that culminated in a large, beautifully furnished drawing room in shades of purple and gold. Even in the light of day, the furnishings and carpet looked new and expensive, and the heavy velvet curtains were neither faded nor threadbare. The Carmichaels spared no expense when it came to attracting a certain class of gentleman.

The furniture in the Rose Parlor was all dusky pink satin and spindly legs, and the mauve and cream carpet was so thick, their feet practically sank into the fibers. A pretty painting of a single rose hung above the mantel, and on closer inspection of its delicate pink folds, Daniel found himself averting his eyes in embarrassment as it brought certain thoughts to mind that were best avoided in his current situation.

"Would you care for some refreshment, gentlemen?" the man asked. "A glass of champagne perhaps, or a snifter of brandy?"

"No, thank you," Jason replied politely for them both.

"Then I'll send Mary in," the man said, and departed, closing the door softly behind him.

"Tristan Carmichael is a shrewd businessman," Jason said as he took in the room and chuckled once his gaze settled on the painting.

"That he is. Just like his father. Those two don't do things by halves."

"I'm sure there's a seedier establishment somewhere in this city that caters to the less affluent client," Jason remarked. "I can't imagine that Tristan Carmichael would limit himself to the wealthy."

"It really is astonishing how many women would rather sell their bodies than try to find honest work," Daniel remarked, deeply irritated by the response this case had elicited in him.

"If honest work paid as much as prostitution, I'm sure they'd be lining up to apply for any available position," Jason replied sadly. "How much do you think Lorna Simpson earns in a week?"

"I couldn't begin to guess."

"I doubt it's very much, and she spends hours hunched over her sewing in that dimly lit room, straining her already impaired eyes until her vision fails completely. She can probably earn the same or more by servicing just one client in an establishment like this."

"Are you suggesting that a woman's life choices should be dictated only by financial gain?" Daniel asked, shocked. Sometimes Jason's views were disturbingly radical, even for an American.

"I'm suggesting that working women should be paid enough to support themselves and their children and afford them sufficient food, coal, and whatever other necessities they require besides a roof over their heads."

"That would entail extensive social reform that no one in power is particularly interested in," Daniel replied.

Jason never got a chance to respond because a girl of about thirteen entered the room. She had dark curls that bounced gaily around her round face, and huge dark eyes fringed by thick lashes. She wore a simple gown of dark blue wool and an apron tied around her waist.

"Good afternoon, gentlemen," she said primly.

"You're Mary Smith?" Daniel asked. She wasn't at all what he'd expected, but perhaps she was dressed this way on purpose.

"I am, sir."

"Sit down, Miss Smith," Jason invited, smiling at her as if she were a charming child rather than one of Tristan Carmichael's doxies.

Mary sat down on the dusky rose settee across from the two men and looked from one to the other expectantly. She didn't appear anxious in the least, which Daniel found surprising. Most people fidgeted and fretted when confronted by the police.

"How old are you, Mary?" Jason asked.

"Nearly fourteen, sir."

"And how long have you worked here?"

"Two years now, sir."

Mary's speech was more cultured than that of the average harlot, at least the ones Daniel had come across in his line of work, and he wondered how she'd wound up in a place like this. She clearly wasn't one of an army of country girls who flocked to London in the hope of a better life and promptly found themselves servicing countless men, either in the comfort and style of an exclusive brothel or in alleys of the city's many slums.

"And what are your duties?" Jason asked, having clearly thought the same thing.

"I help the girls," Mary said simply.

"With?"

"Whatever they need. I help them dress. I look after their unmentionables. I make sure they have the necessary supplies in their rooms," she added, averting her gaze.

That could mean anything from menstrual rags to rubber bulbs filled with vinegar water used for douching between clients.

"You are not…" Daniel wasn't sure how to ask the question politely.

148

"I don't take clients, Inspector," Mary replied. "My father was an associate of Mr. Carmichael's father before he died. Mr. Tristan took me on to make sure I had a roof over my head and food in my belly. He wouldn't permit me to service punters even if I had expressed a wish to do so. He's very protective of me."

"He's very chivalrous, our Mr. Carmichael," Daniel said sarcastically, but the jibe was lost on Mary.

"He's a kind man, to be sure," she replied.

"Mary, were you at Mr. Carmichael's Wapping warehouse last Wednesday?"

"I was."

"What time did you arrive?" Jason asked.

"Mr. Carmichael collected me around three and took me to Wapping. He told me I was to assist a new model, then go for a walk and return in an hour."

"What happened when you came back?"

"The photographer was packing away his things, and the other two gentlemen were smoking while they waited to be paid."

"And the model? Was this the woman you helped?" Daniel showed Mary the photograph from the newspaper.

"That's her. Eliza, she was called. She was behind the screen when I returned, already wearing her camisole and bloomers. I helped her with her corset and then buttoned her dress and pinned her hair."

"How did she seem to you?" Jason asked.

Mary shrugged as if unsure what he was really asking of her. "She just stood there, staring at the screen while I dressed her."

"Was she ill, do you think?"

"No, just a little dazed."

"Did she say anything?"

"She thanked me for helping her."

"And then?" Jason persisted, his gaze fixed on Mary's face.

Mary considered the question. "She seemed pleased when Mr. Carmichael paid her, and stowed the money in her reticule. He offered to find her a cab, on account of it being dark outside, but she said she'd find her own way home. She seemed unsteady on her feet," Mary added.

"Had she been drinking?"

"I'd be surprised if she hadn't."

"Why do you say that?" Daniel asked.

Mary gave Daniel a look so knowing, it nearly made him blush. "What do *you* think, Inspector?"

Daniel nodded, chastised. Few women would take off their clothes and allow perfect strangers access to their body while someone took photographs without some form of liquid courage.

"Who was the last person to see Eliza before she left?" he asked, eager to change the subject.

"Well, I suppose that would be me," Mary replied, her alabaster cheeks growing pink.

"Not Mr. Carmichael?"

Mary shook her head. "I had to see to eh…personal business, and there's nowhere inside the warehouse, so I went outside, behind the building."

"And you saw Eliza when you came out?" Daniel asked.

"No, I saw her on my way back. She was talking to someone. They seemed to be arguing."

"Was it a man?" Jason asked eagerly.

"More of a lad, really," Mary replied.

"You mean he was young?" Daniel asked.

"I suppose," Mary said uncertainly.

"Mary, what is it about the person you saw that gave you pause?" Jason asked, smiling at Mary in an encouraging manner.

"I only saw him for a moment, but there was something not quite right about him."

"Not quite right how?" Jason leaned forward in his eagerness to hear the answer.

"It was the way he moved. Unnatural-like."

"Did you hear his voice?" Daniel asked, leaning forward as well. Mary had seen what had to be Eliza's killer. She had to tell them something more if they were to make use of her testimony.

"I couldn't hear what they were saying. They were at the corner of High Wapping Street."

"Did you think the argument had the potential to turn violent?" Jason asked.

"I really couldn't say, sir. People argue all the time, don't they, but they don't go around killing each other."

"Sometimes they do," Daniel replied. "What time was it when you saw them. Do you know?"

"About five," Mary said.

"Which way did they go?" Jason asked.

"Toward the river," Mary replied confidently.

"And then?" Daniel asked.

"I went back inside to fetch my things. Then Mr. Tristan locked up, and we left. His carriage was waiting for us at the corner. I didn't see Eliza or the other person again."

"Because they weren't there?"

"Because it was dark, and the fog was rolling in," Mary explained. "Thick as pea soup, it was."

"Did you hear anything, Mary? A scream? A splash?" Daniel asked.

"I heard some men go by. They sounded drunk. I think they were sailors."

"Is Mr. Carmichael good to the girls?" Jason asked, clearly surprising Mary with the change of topic.

"Yes, sir, he is. Mr. Carmichael is not like the others."

"How do you mean?" Daniel asked.

"He lets the girls keep half of what they earn, and provides anything they need: gowns, shoes, even medicines if they're ill. He looks after them. He says loyalty is a much greater motivator than fear."

"I'm not sure he's right about that," Daniel muttered, but he no longer cared about Tristan Carmichael. If Mary had seen Eliza walk away with someone, then Tristan Carmichael couldn't have killed her and stowed her body in a boat. Unless Mary was lying for him. She was understandably loyal to the man.

"Mary, do you help other models at the studio?" Jason asked.

"Sometimes," Mary replied cautiously.

"And do they ever seem dazed?"

Mary averted her gaze. "I really couldn't say, my lord."

"What's the name of the photographer who was there the day Eliza Bennington was murdered?" Daniel asked.

"I don't know his name, sir," Mary replied, but it was obvious from her demeanor that she wasn't telling the truth.

"Should we go back to Mr. Carmichael and ask him instead?" Daniel pressed.

"I think you had better, Inspector."

"Thank you, Mary."

"I do hope you find whoever did this," Mary said, clearly relieved that she was off the hook. "Mr. Tristan takes me to the warehouse all the time, and I go for walks. It's nice to have a bit of freedom from my chores. But now I'll be too frightened to go out on my own."

"If it's any consolation, I don't think Eliza was killed by a random person. This was someone who knew her, and she knew them," Jason replied.

"How can you tell?"

"Because the person who killed her laid out her body with care, making sure she looked beautiful in death," Jason explained.

"Perhaps he's just not right in the head," Mary said, her young face full of doubt.

"Perhaps you're right," Daniel agreed. "Don't stray too far from the warehouse, and make sure to be back well before dark."

Mary nodded, clearly seeing the wisdom of this advice. "Are we done, then?" she asked. "It's only that I have a lot to do before the gentlemen start to arrive."

"We're done."

Mary jumped to her feet and was out the door before they could even say goodbye.

Chapter 21

It was nearly dark out, the first stars of the evening twinkling through the smoke rising from the forest of chimneys outlined against the purpling sky. The street was deserted, the windows casting slanted rectangles of light onto the ground below. The nearest hansom stand was near the opera house, so Daniel and Jason headed in that direction.

"Do you think Mary is protecting Tristan Carmichael?" Daniel asked.

Jason's gaze was thoughtful. "I'm not sure. On the face of it, Tristan Carmichael had nothing to gain by killing Eliza Bennington. He stood to profit off her, and if Mary can be believed, they had parted on amicable terms. But the fact that Eliza seemed dazed is concerning."

"Do you think she was intoxicated when she left the warehouse?"

"Or drugged," Jason replied. "And if that's the case, it's entirely possible that she did not consent to whatever took place during that session. We know that Eliza Bennington had posed for risqué photographs for money, but there's no evidence that she had acquiesced to performing sexual acts in the past. The images were artistic rather than pornographic in nature. Based on the postmortem, she had intercourse shortly before she died, which may have been rape, given the bruising and tearing to the genitalia and the fact that two men were present at the shoot."

Daniel gaped at Jason. "Are you suggesting that Tristan Carmichael drugged the woman and then had his flunkeys rape her on camera?"

"It's possible. Which would also explain why he sent Mary for a walk and then had her help Eliza get dressed. Eliza wasn't up to dressing herself."

"But why kill her?"

"Perhaps Eliza Bennington had threatened Carmichael in some way, but I can't see that any threat she made could have harmed Tristan Carmichael or his business interests. If anything, the exposure would hurt Eliza much more, since her own involvement would come to light. Or perhaps," Jason mused, "Carmichael had nothing whatsoever to do with the murder and Mary was telling the truth. She seems an observant girl, which is why I didn't believe her when she said she couldn't say if the other women seemed dazed or what the name of the photographer is. I think she'd been given clear instructions as to what she could and could not say and quickly realized that she'd strayed into dangerous territory when she admitted to Eliza appearing dazed."

Daniel exhaled loudly in his exasperation. "For all we know, everything Mary told us was a lie intended to protect the man who keeps her. The odd person she saw Eliza Bennington with might be nothing more than a figment of her imagination."

"Also possible," Jason agreed.

"If we take Mary at her word, which I am hesitant to do, then Eliza Bennington had finished the photography session, collected her pay, said goodnight to Carmichael, and headed out into the night. She would have been eager to get home before her husband, I should think, if only to wash away traces of other men, if she was even coherent enough to understand what had taken place."

"Whoever killed her took not only her clothes and shoes but her reticule, which only serves to reinforce my belief that the assault was not random. The killer must have known Eliza was carrying a great deal of money on her person or he wouldn't have bothered to rob her."

"But who would know that Eliza had been paid except for those present at that studio?" Daniel asked.

"I doubt Tristan Carmichael will give us the names of the participants, but perhaps Mr. Gillespie knows more than he initially let on," Jason suggested.

"We'll have to ask him. But in the meantime, we must focus on the people who stood to gain from Eliza's death, namely Alan Bennington and Lorna Simpson. Either of them could have slipped out for an hour or two without anyone noticing. And Lorna's son might have had a motive as well, and he's young enough to fit Mary's description," Daniel added.

"Would Eliza have known Lorna's son, do you think?"

"I highly doubt it. Why?"

"According to Mary, Tristan Carmichael was still at the warehouse after Eliza departed, and there were other people about, laborers and sailors. If a stranger accosted her, especially one she found threatening, she could have called for help or tried to run back to the safety of the warehouse. But Mary said they walked off together."

"Perhaps Eliza didn't feel threatened, or was too stupefied to recognize the danger," Daniel said. "Do you think the killer was not right in the head, as Mary suggested? That would certainly explain the whimsical display of the victim."

"It would, but why would a random assailant bother?" Jason replied, his dark brows knitting as he considered the possibility. "Surely the objective would be to get away as quickly as possible rather than linger. But, as you say, if the individual were mad, there's no telling what deranged notion their mind might have conceived of."

"We appear to be going in circles," Daniel said.

Jason nodded and pulled out his watch, peering at the face that was just barely illuminated by the light spilling from a nearby window. "It's half past four," he said.

"So it is."

"How late are newspaper offices open?"

"Until five or six. Why?"

"I think we need to issue an appeal for information. An advertisement in the *London Daily Post* or the *Daily Telegraph* would probably work best, since the *Illustrated Police News* is published weekly. According to both Mary Smith and Tristan Carmichael, Eliza Bennington left the warehouse around five. It would have been dark, and a thick fog was rolling in off the river, but there would still be plenty of people in the vicinity since the workday doesn't end until five at the earliest. Someone had to have seen or heard something."

"And you think they'd be willing to come forward?" Daniel asked, skeptical.

"If we offer a reward, they will."

"I doubt Ransome will agree to that. Besides, by the time I get back to the Yard and consult with him, it will be too late. It's probably too late already. The layout for tomorrow's papers must be complete."

"It might be possible to add something," Jason said. "And if we're too late, we can take out an advertisement in the next day's edition. I'll cover the reward. How much should we offer?"

"A crown, say?" Daniel speculated. "And the reward will only be paid out if the story corroborates what we know so far."

"I agree."

They quickened their steps and climbed into an empty hansom as soon as they arrived at the opera house, instructing the cabbie to take them to Fleet Street.

It was too late to place an advertisement in *The Daily Telegraph*, but the *London Daily Post* was willing to make an exception in exchange for an exclusive once the case was solved. Daniel had no wish to speak to the press, but John Ransome, who adored any kind of publicity and saw it as a means to elevate the reputation of the Police Service and his own role in it, would be thrilled to take the interview, especially if the outcome of the case was sensational.

The appeal would run in the morning edition, so it was reasonable to expect that they might get a response by lunchtime. Having concluded their business, Daniel and Jason stepped out into the crowded street, careful not to get jostled by passersby eager to get home, their tired faces briefly illuminated by the mellow light of a nearby gas lamp, their mufflers wound tight against the evening's damp chill.

Daniel was more than ready to return home as well but knew he wouldn't be able to rest until he put his questions to Lorna Simpson and accounted for the whereabouts of her son on the night of the murder.

"I'm going back to Blackfriars to speak to Mrs. Simpson," Daniel announced.

"I'm sorry, but I won't be able to accompany you. I must get home," Jason replied.

"Are you available tomorrow?"

"I have early morning surgery. Cancer of the stomach," Jason said softly. "The patient is only twenty-three."

"Does the poor bugger have a chance?"

"A very slim one, but to do nothing means certain death. And soon. I will remove the tumor and hope that the cancer has not metastasized. At best, the surgery will buy him a few years. At worst, a few extra months. Or weeks," he added sadly.

Daniel sighed. "Why do some people get these awful illnesses while others live to a ripe old age?"

"There are many factors, one of them being family history. Many illnesses are hereditary, and others are a result of living conditions, diet, as well as a person's occupation."

"What about your patient?" Daniel asked, genuinely curious. He welcomed the opportunity to speak about something other than this confounded case that was proving a sight more complicated than he could have anticipated. He had yet to form a comprehensive theory that encompassed all the clues they had collected and was bitterly disappointed with the lack of result.

"It's difficult to say," Jason replied tiredly. "The patient was orphaned at a young age, so we don't know what his parents were afflicted with. He's employed as a clerk at the Old Bailey, so the occupation is definitely not to blame. He does not drink to excess, nor does he eat poorly. Just bad luck, I suppose."

"Is he married?"

"Yes, and has two very young children. It is my hope that I'll be able to grant him a few more years with his family." Jason sighed.

"What about madness?" Daniel asked. "Do you think there's a cure, or at least something that might stave off the onset of the symptoms in an individual that's likely to be afflicted?"

"The brain is an unexplored country," Jason replied, "but I do believe that certain circumstances might bring about a crisis that will rob the individual of whatever tenuous hold they have on reality. Tragedy being one of them. Poverty another."

"Madness is not limited to the poor. And Eliza Bennington was not raised in poverty."

"Are you suggesting that she may have been mad?"

"What would induce a genteel young woman, the daughter of a vicar, to violate the very essence of respectability and stoop to associating with the likes of Tristan Carmichael?" Daniel asked.

"I really couldn't say," Jason replied. "The obvious answer is that she may have wished to hurt her cheating husband or earn enough money to leave him, but without having known the victim, it would be irresponsible to jump to such a conclusion."

Daniel paused to consider Jason's reply, then shook his head in disagreement. "I can't imagine that any woman of our acquaintance would choose the same path to vengeance. Can you?"

"It's impossible to predict what someone will do under extreme stress or if threatened with ruin."

"I can't help but feel pity for her," Daniel confessed, even though most men of his generation would opine that Eliza Bennington had brought about her own downfall.

"So do I, but all we can do at this stage is bring her killer to justice. So, what's your plan for tomorrow?" Jason asked as they neared a cab stand.

"There isn't much I can do until the advertisement is printed and the alleged witnesses come in to give their statements. But I will devote the morning to scouring the area near the warehouse for any signs of the murder weapon and the victim's clothes and reticule. The odds are against me, I'm afraid, but it would be negligent not to try now that we know approximately where the victim was last seen."

Jason's face expressed his skepticism. To find a length of pipe or a cudgel used to strike Eliza would be like looking for a needle in a haystack, and whoever had undressed her had most likely sold her clothes, since the items were of fine quality and would fetch a good price. If they were clever, they would take the clothes to a shop on the other side of town to ensure that no connection was made between the sale and the murder.

"I must also speak to Norm Gillespie and Eric Dawson," Daniel said warily. "They might know who Carmichael employs in his studio."

"Why don't you let me take care of Eric Dawson?" Jason suggested.

"With pleasure. I'll speak to Mr. Gillespie."

"May I call on you tomorrow evening?"

"Of course."

"Till tomorrow, then," Jason said.

"Good luck with the surgery."

"It's not luck I require, but skill," Jason replied, sounding uncharacteristically pessimistic.

He tipped his hat and climbed into the waiting cab that soon disappeared into the traffic moving slowly down Fleet Street.

Chapter 22

Daniel headed to John Carpenter Street but paused across from Lorna Simpson's building before going in. He could see her through the net curtain, seated at the sewing machine, head bent over her work. He crossed the street and knocked on the door, wondering if Elizabeth Coulter would be the one to answer it again. It was Lorna herself that came to the door, her expression transforming from one of expectation to wariness when she recognized Daniel.

"What is it you want, Inspector?" She made no move to step aside or invite him in, blocking the doorway with her body instead, as if she could keep him out both physically and emotionally.

"I want to know why you failed to mention you have a son," Daniel said, watching Lorna Simpson's face intently for any minute change in expression.

Her eyes widened in surprise, but she recovered in record time and stepped aside at last. "I think you had better come in. This is not a conversation to be had on the doorstep."

Daniel followed her into her apartment and watched as she shut the door. Since Mrs. Simpson did not offer to take his coat, Daniel simply unbuttoned it and sat on the settee, settling his bowler on his thigh. Lorna Simpson sat across from him. She looked worn out, and her shoulders slumped with fatigue, but it was the expression in her eyes that was arresting.

"I didn't mention George because I was afraid," she said at last.

"Afraid of what?"

She sighed heavily. "My husband was a violent man, Inspector. Oh, he could be witty and charming when he was sober, and it was that charm that won me over when I was hardly more than fourteen, but after a few pints, he was a different man. George

162

was nine when my husband's ship sank, and God forgive me, I was relieved to be free of him. I feared the influence he'd have on our boy once George was old enough to accompany his father to places where a woman is not welcome, at least not as a patron."

Lorna Simpson's gaze slid away from Daniel, her attention fixing on the flickering streetlamp just beyond the window. "I did my best to raise my son to be a decent man, but..." Her voice trailed off, and Daniel saw her eyes glisten with tears. "He's his father's son."

Daniel was about to ask if George Simpson was known to the police but swallowed back the question for fear of interrupting Lorna Simpson's confession. His instinct to remain silent paid off, since she continued to speak, her voice flat, her gaze still on the lamp as if she were mesmerized by the flickering light.

"George wanted to go to sea, like his father, and would have had Alan not stepped in. Alan helped me to secure an apprenticeship for George with the Thames Iron Works. Of course, George had no inkling that Alan was involved, or he would have refused on principle, but I was able to convince him he'd have a more secure future working for a shipbuilding firm. He likes the work, and he's good at it, but his temper sometimes gets the better of him. And he likes his drink," Lorna added miserably.

"Exactly how old is George?" Daniel asked.

"Fourteen."

"Does he resent your relationship with Alan Bennington?"

Lorna chuckled mirthlessly. "That's an understatement if I ever heard one."

"Where is George now?"

They were clearly alone, and Daniel saw no evidence of another person residing at the house. Surely, as an apprentice, George would still be living with his mother and would be back in time for supper. Now that he'd thought of food, Daniel realized he

163

didn't smell anything cooking. Did Lorna Simpson rely on the kindness of her neighbors for sustenance?

"George moved out just before Christmas. Said I was stifling him." Lorna's voice was barely audible, but her pain was there for Daniel to see. She clearly felt she'd failed with her son, and it was too late to mend the fences between them.

"So where does he live?"

"At the Golden Goose public house in Nightingale Lane."

"How can he afford it?" Daniel asked.

Lorna sighed, and her shoulders dropped a fraction lower, as if she were folding in on herself. "The publican is my late husband's brother, Charlie Simpson. He doesn't have a family of his own. Never could settle down with just one woman," she explained bitterly. "Charlie stepped in after my husband died. Said a boy needed a father. I didn't want him anywhere near my son, but I could hardly bar him from seeing his nephew."

"And is George fond of his uncle?"

"George idolizes Charlie and helps out in the bar most nights."

"Nightingale Lane is not far from where Eliza Bennington was murdered," Daniel said, and saw Lorna Simpson wince.

"What reason would George have to harm Eliza Bennington?" she cried.

"Perhaps he wanted to stitch up your lover. Or maybe he thought if free, Alan Bennington would marry you," Daniel suggested.

Lorna scoffed. "George couldn't be bothered about me, Inspector Haze. Maybe that's why I'm glad about the coming baby. I'll have another chance at a family, and maybe this time I'll get it right."

"Does George know about the child?"

Lorna nodded. "I told him the last time I saw him."

"And how did he take the news?"

"He seemed surprised that someone my age could be with child. To him, I'm as old as the hills."

Daniel noticed that Lorna had failed to answer his real question and tried again. "How did he feel about you having a child out of wedlock?"

"Given that I haven't seen him since, I think it's safe to say he wasn't too pleased," Lorna replied sarcastically, but Daniel could see the hurt beneath the bluster.

"And how long has it been since you've seen your son?"

"Nearly a month now."

Daniel stood. "I'll have to speak to George, Mrs. Simpson."

"He's angry with me, Inspector, but he would never intentionally hurt anyone," Lorna exclaimed.

"What about unintentionally?" Daniel asked, silencing Lorna with the unexpected question. The fear in her eyes was a testament to the fact that she hadn't considered that possibility and was now genuinely frightened. And with good reason.

It was entirely possible that what had been meant to be a conversation between George Simpson and Eliza Bennington, perhaps to warn her of her husband's infidelity, had taken an ugly turn, an incident that would very neatly tie in with what Mary Smith had described. Unprepared and his anger provoked, George would have reached for whatever weapon was to hand, such as a rock, and bashed the unsuspecting woman on the back of the head, possibly when she had turned away from him.

"Goodnight, Mrs. Simpson," Daniel said as he pushed to his feet. "I will not arrest your son without evidence," he added, seeing the terror in her face.

Lorna nodded and walked him to the door, shutting it quietly behind him.

Daniel sucked in a deep breath of frigid air that was redolent with coal smoke and the tang of brine from the river. All he really wanted was to go home, have a hot meal, and spend the rest of the evening by a warm fire, preferably with Rebecca, but it would be negligent not to speak to George Simpson before his mother had a chance to warn him of Daniel's suspicions. George could concoct a story, ensure he had an alibi for the time of the murder, or flee if he was guilty.

Finding a hansom, Daniel directed the driver to take him to the Golden Goose public house and asked him to wait. If Daniel were to arrest George Simpson, it would be helpful to have a cab waiting rather than wander the streets in search of transport on a cold, dark night in an area where people had an inherent mistrust of the police and might not respect his authority.

Leaning back in the cab, Daniel listened to the soothing clip-clop of the horse's hooves on the cobbles and wished Jason were by his side.

Chapter 23

The Golden Goose had to date back to Tudor times, with its dark beams, mullioned windows, and flagstone floor. The walls might have been white once, but now they were a dirty gray, years of smoke, damp, and spilled ale having left their marks on every surface. The tables were scarred, the benches wobbly, and the crowd rough. There were several groups of sailors, one bunch rowdier than the last, working men who'd stopped in for a pint before heading home, and half a dozen serving wenches, who, given their gaudy attire and bawdy comments, were offering considerably more than ale.

Daniel walked up to the bar and ordered a pint. He didn't really want it, but not to order anything would raise suspicions, more so because his genteel attire was already the subject of unwelcome attention from the publican and the patrons closest to him, who were studying him with ill-concealed hostility. He didn't belong in a place like this, and everyone knew it, especially him.

The man behind the bar was around forty, with thick dark hair, coal-black eyes, and a sinewy neck set on wide shoulders. His thickly muscled arms strained against the fabric of his shirt as he pulled pints and set them on the counter. The boy who helped him shared his dark coloring but bore an unmistakable resemblance to Lorna Simpson. His face was narrow and boyish, but he had the solid body of a man, long hours at the iron works having made him strong and fit.

Daniel took a pull of his ale and studied the pair as discreetly as possible given the obvious scrutiny he was under. He didn't think it would be wise to advertise his credentials and demand to speak to George, not if he wanted to walk out of the tavern with all his organs intact and limbs still attached. He would have to return with reinforcements, or better yet speak to the boy while he was at the shipbuilding yard, surrounded by coworkers rather than his brute of an uncle and tavern regulars.

Daniel was about to take his leave when something caught his eye. Like his uncle, George wasn't wearing a coat, only a linen shirt and a gaudy yellow waistcoat beneath an apron tied around his waist to protect his clothing. His hair fell into his eyes, and he lifted his hand to brush it away, his attention on one of the girls, who winked at him seductively as she passed by. When George raised his arm, his rolled-up sleeve slid down to his elbow, revealing a tattoo of a mermaid on his forearm. The mermaid had bright red hair and large breasts tipped with pointy nipples.

Daniel associated tattoos with sailors and convicts, but George's father had been a sailor, so perhaps this was a tribute to a man taken too soon. Or maybe the bare-breasted nymph had nothing to do with the elder Simpson and everything to do with George's taste in women and some teenage fantasy.

Leaving his half-full tankard on the counter, Daniel put on his hat, gave a stiff nod in response to the barman's quizzical gaze, and left the Golden Goose, glad he'd asked the cabby to wait. It would cost extra, but the ability to leave immediately was priceless.

Chapter 24

Daniel was relieved when Rebecca joined him for dinner after putting Charlotte to bed. It had been days since they'd had a proper conversation, and Daniel was eager to spend a quiet hour with her. He was even more pleased when Grace brought in a platter of mutton chops accompanied by roasted potatoes, buttered carrots and peas, and mint jelly after clearing away the soup plates.

"You look tired, Inspector," Rebecca said, her eyes warm with concern. "Perhaps you're pushing yourself too hard."

"I am tired," Daniel admitted, "but I'm happy to be back to work. A life of leisure wouldn't suit me," he quipped.

Rebecca averted her gaze, and Daniel felt a cretin for saying something so unkind. She had no choice but to earn her daily bread and would probably like nothing more than to have a well-to-do husband to look after her. Some foolhardy part of him wanted to reassure her that she wouldn't have to continue working for much longer and that he was seriously considering a future together, but this was neither the time nor the place to declare himself. He cared for Rebecca, found her devastatingly lovely, and could easily envision sharing a life with her, but he suddenly realized that he wasn't ready to make a lifelong commitment, not after what had happened last December. He'd had nothing but time to lie abed and think about all the mistakes he'd made, all the possibilities he'd squandered, and the betrayal he'd faced from the one person he was meant to trust most. He was still hurting and grieving, and it would not only be highly disrespectful to Sarah but utterly foolish to marry again so soon and pin all his hopes for the future on someone he barely knew.

Rebecca was a witty conversationalist, could effortlessly charm both him and Charlotte out of a sullen mood if required, and brought the sort of light into the house that had been missing since before Sarah died, but when it came down to it, Daniel knew little of her past. She didn't like talking about what had been a difficult time in her life, and Daniel didn't press her out of respect for her feelings. He knew she had been orphaned at eighteen and had been forced to seek a position as a governess to support herself. Rebecca had an impeccable character reference from her previous employer and had instantly disarmed Daniel when she came for an interview, and he, unable to talk about his own tragedy, had been happy to forge ahead without constantly looking back at the heartbreak they'd left behind.

"How was your day?" Daniel asked, eager to change the subject.

"Uneventful," Rebecca replied, but something in her gaze told him different.

"Did you and Charlotte go out?"

"Yes. We took a walk in the park and fed the ducks. You know how she loves that."

Daniel nodded, smiling. He'd take Charlotte to the park himself as soon as this case was closed and he could take the morning off to devote to her.

"There was a boy with a paper kite," Rebecca said. "Charlotte was transfixed. She especially liked the tail, since it was made of colorful ribbons."

"I will make her a kite," Daniel promised. "And the three of us can fly it together."

"I think she'd like that," Rebecca said, offering him an unguarded smile for the first time since they had sat down to dinner.

Grace was just about to clear away the plates and bring in the pudding when Daniel heard Charlotte calling from upstairs. Rebecca dropped her napkin and made to rise, but Daniel gestured for her to remain seated.

"I'll go," he said. "I have barely seen Charlotte these past few days."

"I'll hold the pudding," Grace offered helpfully.

"Thank you, Grace," Daniel said, and left the dining room.

Charlotte was sitting up in bed, clutching the blue velveteen rabbit she always took to bed with her. Her eyes were huge and frightened. Daniel sat on the side of the bed and reached out to stroke her hair.

"What is it, darling? Did you have a bad dream?"

Charlotte nodded. "Mama," she said miserably, and Daniel's vision blurred with tears. Charlotte had asked for Sarah constantly just after she died, but in recent months, she'd rarely mentioned her, and Daniel had hoped that she was beginning to get over the loss, but the pain in the child's eyes told a different story.

"Mama is looking down on you, thinking what a good girl you are," he said, knowing how woefully inadequate that sounded.

Charlotte reached out, and Daniel took her in his arms and held her close. She rested her head on his chest, her curls fragrant with lemon verbena soap and her own childish smell. They sat like that for a few minutes, each one lost in their grief and pain, then Charlotte raised her face to look at him.

"Would you like me to make you a kite?" Daniel asked, desperate to cheer her up.

Charlotte nodded. "Green, with a red tail," she said.

"All right. Maybe you can help me. And then we can go to the park and fly it together: you, me, and Miss Grainger."

"But not her friend," Charlotte said, thrusting out her little chin determinedly.

"What friend?" Daniel asked.

"He came to the park," Charlotte complained, clearly put out that their outing had been interrupted.

"How long did he stay?"

Charlotte shrugged. She was too young to have any concept of time.

"Did he walk you home?"

"No."

Daniel nodded. Rebecca must have run into an acquaintance while walking in the park. "Don't worry," he said softly. "It will be just us and our amazing new kite."

Charlotte smiled then. "Make the kite tomorrow?" she asked eagerly.

"I have to go to work tomorrow, but you and Miss Grainger can buy the paper and string, and we will work on it this week. I promise."

Charlotte looked dubious but accepted his promise and lay back down, her arm tightly wrapped around the rabbit. Her eyes were already fluttering with fatigue, so Daniel leaned down and kissed her forehead. "Sweet dreams," he said, and hoped they would be.

When he returned to the dining room, Rebecca was gone and there was only one place setting, the plate and cup looking unbearably lonely at the head of the long table.

"Shall I serve the pudding now, Inspector?" Grace asked, appearing in the doorway as if by magic.

"Let's save it for tomorrow, shall we?" Daniel suggested.

"As you say, sir."

Daniel checked the parlor, but Rebecca wasn't there. She must have gone up to her room while he was with Charlotte. Daniel poured himself a large brandy and settled before the fire, feeling pleasantly somnolent from the warmth and the good meal. As he stared into the flames from beneath lowered lids, he wondered who Rebecca's friend was and if the meeting had been accidental or prearranged.

Chapter 25

Having deftly parried Katherine's questions about the case all evening, Jason retired early, using the early morning surgery as an excuse. In truth, he simply had no wish to talk about Eliza Bennington. Katherine wasn't best pleased with him, he knew that, and had decided to read for a while in the parlor before coming to bed. She hated to be treated like some feebleminded female who needed to be protected from the world around her, and Jason would never dare belittle her, but this case disturbed him, and he needed to clear his mind before the surgery tomorrow. But try as he might, he couldn't get to sleep and was still wide awake when Katherine slid into bed beside him.

"Are you worried about the surgery?" she asked as she propped her head on her hand and looked down at him.

"Yes," Jason lied.

"Anything I can do to help?"

Jason smiled at her in the dark. "Distract me."

"All right. Tell me about the case."

"That's not quite what I meant."

"I know, but you've been unusually evasive these past few days, and now it's all I can think about."

"Katie, I'm only trying to spare you the unpleasantness."

"You don't need to wrap me in cotton wool, you know," she said defensively. "I won't break."

"I know."

"Then talk to me."

"Why are you so determined to hear about this case?" Jason asked, stalling for time.

"Because it troubles me."

"Why?"

Katherine sighed and looked away, her gaze traveling toward the window. Jason didn't like to sleep with the curtains drawn, and moonlight streamed through the panes, casting a silvery pool onto the floor below.

"This woman was not so different from me. She was the daughter of a vicar who married the man of her dreams despite her father's objections. By all accounts, they were happy. So, what went wrong?"

Jason sighed. He had no choice but to tell Katherine the truth, since he didn't want her to draw parallels between her life and that of Eliza Bennington. Katherine was an intelligent, level-headed woman, but somewhere beneath the matter-of-fact façade lurked an unloved little girl who'd been nothing more than an unpaid maidservant to a father who never considered her feelings or thought she deserved a life of her own.

Katherine had once confided to Jason that she didn't believe she deserved the happiness she had been able to snatch from the jaws of spinsterhood, and like Icarus, she had flown too close to the sun when she not only married for love but ascended to the title of Lady Redmond in the process. She still felt uncomfortable with her elevated station and devoted her time to helping those less fortunate.

Jason reached out and cupped Katherine's cheek. "Katie, Eliza was the daughter of a vicar and married the man of her choice, but that's where the similarities end. A marriage that's based on love doesn't always remain sacrosanct. People are often responsible for destroying their own happiness, and the vows they made bind them only as long as they're willing to uphold them."

"Did Eliza destroy her happiness by posing for those photographs?"

"I think that marriage was broken long before Eliza made that decision."

"How so?" Katherine asked, her eyes shining in the moonlight, her mouth drawn in a determined line.

"Her husband was having a relationship with another woman, and he's expecting a child by her."

Katherine's mouth opened in a moue of understanding. "Did he kill her?"

"There's no evidence to suggest that."

Jason pulled Katherine toward him until she was lying on top of him, her hair cascading around his face in silken waves and blocking out the moonlight. He kissed her gently, then brushed her hair aside so that he could see her face.

"Katie, I will never take what we have for granted, and no loving God would punish a woman for being happy in her role as wife and mother. What happened to Eliza Bennington has no bearing on our life or our future."

"I know, sweetheart. It's just that sometimes I can't believe how blessed I am," Katherine whispered. "I keep thinking it will all be snatched away one day."

"When I stood up in church and said, 'Till death do us part,' I meant every word, and I plan to hang around for a few years yet, so stop worrying and kiss me."

Katherine took his face in her hands and looked deep into his eyes. There was no need to say anything more. It was all there in her gaze.

Chapter 26

Tuesday, February 16

Daniel's day began with a visit to Scotland Yard to inform Superintendent Ransome and Sergeant Meadows of the notice he'd placed in the paper. He also planned to request that one of the constables accompany him first to Thames Iron Works and then to Wapping. Having felt uncomfortably exposed at the Golden Goose last night, Daniel even considered asking John Ransome for permission to arm himself with one of the Beaumont-Adams revolvers kept in the firearms cabinet, then decided against it. In broad daylight, his concerns seemed unfounded, the fear no doubt brought on by the events of a few months ago. It was only natural that he should feel vulnerable, but it'd be wise to keep his qualms to himself.

John Ransome fixed Daniel with an unflinching stare, his expression bullish as he surveyed Daniel across the expanse of his desk.

"Who put up the reward, Haze?" he asked, immediately going to the crux of the matter.

"Jason Redmond."

"Lord Redmond is not a member of the Police Service."

"No, but a private citizen can offer a reward if he so wishes. It's not illegal."

"This is an official Scotland Yard investigation."

"That's quickly going nowhere," Daniel countered.

"Surely you have a theory," Ransome said, watching Daniel intently.

"A theory is just that until there's evidence to support it."

Ransome nodded. "If Lord Redmond willingly put up the reward, then all we can do is offer our heartfelt thanks and hope for a favorable result."

Daniel decided not to point out that Ransome should have offered to reimburse Jason for the expenditure, since Ransome clearly had no intention of doing that. He guarded the budget jealously and never spent an extra farthing on anything that wasn't strictly necessary. The men took turns buying tea and supplying biscuits for the common room, but they drew the line at springing for coal, which was why the building was always cold and damp.

"Right," Ransome said now that the matter of the reward had been resolved to his satisfaction. "Do you have any other leads to follow, or must we rely on the advertisement for fresh tips?"

"George Simpson—the son of Bennington's pregnant lover—has a mermaid tattoo on his forearm," Daniel said.

Ransome's eyebrows rose a fraction. "Is that so? Have you questioned him?"

"I'm bound for the Thames Iron Works in Blackwall, where he's apprenticed, sir." Daniel was relieved that Ransome didn't inquire as to why he hadn't interviewed George Simpson last night.

"Take my carriage," Ransome offered in an uncharacteristic show of support. Blackwall was quite a ways, and it would take Daniel the best part of the morning to get there, interview George Simpson, and then examine the area of Wapping nearest to Tristan Carmichael's warehouse that might be the scene of the murder.

"Thank you, sir."

Ransome nodded. "I will have Sergeant Meadows take a statement from anyone whose account of events sounds legitimate, and then you can speak to them in your own time."

"Yes, sir."

"Bring George Simpson in if you think he's even remotely connected to the murder."

"I will, sir. I'd like Constable Collins to accompany me," Daniel ventured.

Ransome's eyebrows lifted again. "Are you expecting trouble?"

"No, sir, but I intend to search the area around Carmichael's warehouse after I've finished with the interview."

Ransome nodded. "Think there's anything to find after all this time?"

"I really couldn't say, but the rain's held off, so…" Daniel knew it was a long shot, but it would be negligent not to at least have a gander now that they had narrowed down the field somewhat.

"Yes, I take your point, Haze. Constable Collins can be a tad excitable at times, but he's like a bloodhound, that one. If there's anything to find—" Ransome smiled indulgently. He liked to give the constables a chance to learn through experience, and with Constable Collins being the youngest of the lot, Ransome made it a point to encourage his efforts.

"Thank you, sir."

"Off with you," Ransome said, with something like a smile playing about his lips. "It's good to have you back, Haze," he added before turning his attention to a letter on his desk.

Daniel nodded, a lump in his throat at the unexpected warmth he'd heard in the superintendent's voice, and went to find Constable Collins.

It took well over an hour to reach Leamouth Wharf, home of the Thames Ironworks, the superintendent's carriage crawling a good part of the way behind delivery wagons, a particularly slow omnibus, and numerous broughams and curricles belonging to individuals who were either early risers or were just returning home after a night spent dancing, gaming, or wenching. The scenery changed dramatically as they neared the East End, the elegant structures and parks of the city center giving way to rundown warehouses, seedy taverns, and rough-looking men and women who went about their business with a grim determination that gave them an almost feral quality.

Ragged children darted to and fro, the younger ones playing in the street, the older ones looking for ways to earn their daily bread by either thieving, running errands, or selling their bodies to anyone willing to part with a coin. Daniel had seen it all before, but it never failed to affect him, a stark reminder of how harsh life could be for those who didn't have the education or the skill to earn a decent living. For a brief moment, he missed the bucolic peace of Birch Hill and longed for the simple life he'd enjoyed in Essex before moving his family to London and setting off the chain of events that would end in Sarah's death.

Daniel was glad when they finally arrived at their destination. Climbing out of the brougham, he craned his neck to take in the iron-sided behemoth that towered above the building, its black hull even more menacing in the gloom of the February morning. The shipbuilding yard was massive, the area a warren of cranes, ladders, rails, and scaffolding that encircled the unfinished ships like body armor. Countless men, all in shirtsleeves despite the cold and wearing caps pulled low over their eyes, went about their assigned tasks, their attention focused on the job. Inside the enormous workshop, the noise was deafening, the heat from the blazing furnaces permeating the vast space. The sound of hammering enveloped Daniel and seemed to reverberate through his entire being, his heart hammering in tune with the blows. The screech of metal, massive hooks, and turning gears filled his senses and made him feel disorientated.

"Let's find a foreman," Daniel said to Constable Collins, who followed him like a shadow, his mouth open in astonishment as he took in his surroundings.

It took some considerable time to locate the man they were searching for, since every query had to be repeated numerous times to be heard over the din of hammers on iron. At last, they were directed to a small office, and once the door closed firmly behind them, Daniel could finally manage to formulate a coherent thought.

"Alfred Folsom," the man introduced himself. He was a bear of a man with wooly whiskers and a thick beard, both liberally streaked with gray. His paunch strained against a black waistcoat, and his sleeves were rolled up to reveal hairy forearms. Mr. Folsom held out a meaty hand that smelled of machine oil and was covered in soot, and Daniel had no choice but to shake it.

"Inspector Haze and Constable Collins of Scotland Yard."

Alfred Folsom appeared mildly surprised, but his demeanor was not hostile.

"Are you George Simpson's foreman?" Daniel asked, just to be sure he had the right man.

"I am. What's he done?" Mr. Folsom asked warily.

"We don't know that he's done anything, but his name has come up in relation to an ongoing investigation," Daniel replied, hoping that was vague enough to elicit answers but not put the man on his guard. "What can you tell us about George?"

Folsom shrugged, his expression noncommittal. "Hard worker. Quick to learn. But I think he has other aspirations."

"How do you mean?"

"His uncle owns a tavern in Wapping. The Golden Goose. And that's exactly what young George imagines it to be. He hopes to take over one day and enjoy some of those golden eggs for himself." Alfred Folsom chuckled at his own witticism.

"Is that likely to happen?" Daniel asked.

"You'd have to ask his uncle that."

"Can you tell me where George Simpson was last Wednesday, around five o'clock?"

Folsom made a show of thinking, which wasn't unreasonable since nearly a week had passed since the murder. "I reckon he was still here," he said at last. "Would have left around half past five, closer to six. We're on a tight schedule, Inspector, and he had a job to finish."

"That's a rare beauty you have out there," Constable Collins said as he gestured toward the iron-clad monster they'd seen earlier, clearly visible through the wide opening in the outer wall.

"Oh, yes. She's nearly ready. The *HMS Vigil*," Folsom said proudly. "An iron-hulled armored frigate. Four hundred feet long, and nearly eleven thousand tons displacement."

Daniel had no idea what that meant, nor could he comprehend how something that looked so heavy could stay afloat without going straight to the bottom of the sea, but he wasn't here for a shipbuilding lesson. "I'd like to speak to George Simpson now," he said.

"All right, but I would prefer to remain, if you've no objection, Inspector. George has yet to reach his majority, and I feel he should have someone who has his best interests at heart present during the interview."

Daniel was about to protest but changed his mind. Unless Alfred Folsom actively prevented George Simpson from answering his questions, there was no harm in him staying.

"As you wish, Mr. Folsom," Daniel said amicably.

Folsom nodded and walked to the door, where he called to someone to fetch George Simpson forthwith. The lad was brought to the office a short time later. He looked fearful, his gaze immediately straying to the foreman, who nodded to him in a reassuring manner that seemed to soothe the boy.

"These gentlemen here would like to ask you a few questions, George. Just answer to the best of your ability, and then you can return to work."

"All right," George muttered.

There was only one chair in the office, so everyone remained standing, with George closest to the door. He looked so shifty, Daniel thought he might make a break for it should Daniel go after him too hard.

George fixed his dark gaze on Daniel, clearly trying to place him. "Ye was at the Golden Goose last night," he said at last. "I saw ye."

"That's right. I wanted a word, but it was too loud," Daniel replied.

George gave him a look that implied that Daniel was a terrible liar, his lip curling with derision. "Uncle Charlie don't care for rozzers in 'is place o' business," he snarled. "Would 'ave tossed ye out on yer ear."

Daniel had no doubt that was true and didn't bother to explain himself. "Where were you last Wednesday?" he asked instead, ignoring the boy's mistrust.

"'Ere. Where else would I be?" His cockney accent was very different from his mother's more cultured speech, and Daniel wondered if that was intentional, a way to fit in with his uncle's patrons and perhaps with the men on the shop floor. Or perhaps to please an uncle who had no son of his own and just might make George the sole beneficiary of his estate.

"What time did you leave?" Daniel continued.

George shrugged. "I dunno. Round 'alf five mebbe."

"And where did you go?"

"'Ome."

"What time did you get home?"

George shrugged. "'Bout six, I reckon. Mebbe a bit after."

"Can anyone verify that?" Daniel pressed.

"Me uncle can. 'E were there, behind the bar when I got back. Why?" George asked, his gaze narrowing. "What am I meant to 'ave done, *Inspector*?" He uttered Daniel's title with derision, but Daniel could see the worry behind the insolent gaze. George Simpson wasn't nearly as unconcerned as he pretended to be.

"Do you know anyone called Eliza Bennington?"

"The mermaid?" George asked, grinning now. "Neh, but I wish I 'ad. Lovely, she were."

"Someone murdered her, George," Daniel said with more anger than he'd intended.

"What's that to do with me?"

"Eliza Bennington was the wife of Alan Bennington."

George looked blank. "Who's 'e when 'e's at 'ome?"

"He's your mother's fancy man," Constable Collins cut in, unable to remain quiet any longer. Daniel didn't appreciate the interruption, but the fact remained a fact whether he or Constable Collins had stated it.

"I don't see me mother," George replied.

"Why not?" Daniel asked.

"We don't get on. I prefer me Uncle Charlie."

"Why?"

"Cause 'e treats me wif respect," George said, puffing out his chest. "Me mam treats me like a child. She were the same with me da. Treated 'im like 'e were daft."

"Do you remember your father?" Daniel asked. He was surprised that George would feel a sense of offense on his father's behalf so many years after his death, but he supposed there wasn't much children forgot, especially if they needed a reason to blame someone for their current circumstances.

George nodded. "'E were a right clever cove, me da. I miss 'im." George's eyes took on a faraway look, as if he were gazing into a past where he had been part of a happy family, his recollections clearly clouded by the innocence of a child.

"Do you like mermaids, George?" Daniel asked.

"Wha'?"

"You have a mermaid tattoo on your arm. I noticed it last night."

George looked sheepish. "Me mates talked me into it when we got pissed one night. We all got one."

"Everyone got a tattoo of a mermaid?" Daniel asked.

George shook his head. "Neh. Me mate Gary got 'imself an anchor, and Stevie got a warship. Always wanted to join the Navy, Stevie 'as, but 'is da won't 'ave it." George fixed Alfred Folsom with a pointed look, and the older man stared back.

"Stevie's my boy," he said, turning to Daniel.

No wonder the foreman had asked to stay for the interview. He felt protective of George Simpson on account of his friendship with his son and hoped to intervene if Daniel decided to arrest him.

"So, why did you settle on a mermaid, George?" Daniel asked, going for a tone of mild curiosity rather than accusation. "That must have hurt." The tattoo he'd seen was intricate, not just a crude outline of a woman. The fish scales of the tail had been expertly shaded in, as was the mane of hair that fell about the mermaid's shoulders.

"It weren't too bad," George said, grinning for the first time. "And I were three sheets to the wind, so I didn't much care."

"But why a mermaid?" Daniel asked again.

"'Cause that's the closest I can get to a naked woman on my wage," George replied saucily.

That wasn't strictly true, since the cost of the tattoo could have easily paid for a few minutes with a dockside streetwalker several times over, but Daniel decided not to point that out. George was lucky that whoever had inked him was a true artist or he could have ended up with a hideous hag that he'd be stuck with till the end of his days.

"She is pretty, is all," George said wistfully. "Got noffin' to do with that Eliza. I never met 'er, or 'er 'usband. I ain't been to see me mam in weeks. I told ye, we don't see eye to eye."

"Would you be upset if your mother remarried?" Daniel asked.

"Why should I be?" George asked defensively. "A woman needs a man about, and if she found a cove as can stand 'er nagging, I says good for 'er. Not like I mean to look after 'er for the rest of me life."

Daniel hated to admit defeat, but George Simpson sounded genuine. He was nothing more than a defiant youth who didn't appreciate being treated like a child by his mother when he went out every day to do a man's job and then spent his evenings in a tavern, surrounded by the sort of male camaraderie he was sure to relish and an uncle who saw him as an extension of the brother he'd lost. If Daniel had imagined that George would kill to defend his mother's honor, he'd been on the wrong track.

"Thank you. You may return to work, George," Daniel said.

George stole a peek at Alfred Folsom, who gave him an encouraging nod. "Go on, son. If we're done here," Folsom said, glaring at Daniel from beneath bushy brows. They'd wasted enough of his time, the look implied.

"We are. Thank you, Mr. Folsom."

"Mind how you go," Folsom said once they stepped outside the office.

Daniel was immediately accosted by the cacophony of noise and infernal heat that had so disconcerted him earlier. This place was like a steppingstone to hell, he decided as he hurried toward the exit and walked toward the carriage that was some considerable distance away.

"Where to now, guv?" Constable Collins asked once they were safely inside.

"Oliver's Wharf," Daniel replied. "And let's hope we get there before the heavens open up."

Chapter 27

The last few days had been uncharacteristically dry, but now the sky was pewter, the clouds heavy and gray, like the thick, dirty coats of sheep before they were shorn. The cloud cover seemed to press in, creating a pressure in Daniel's head that made his temples pound like a drum. Or maybe it was some sort of delayed reaction to the deafening noise of the shipbuilding yard, the metallic clanging still ringing in his ears.

Daniel experienced a wave of crippling pessimism as he gazed upon the filthy stretch of riverbank. It had been days since Eliza's body was discovered. What could he hope to find when he didn't even know what he was looking for? And how would it look if he failed to solve the crime?

Everyone had heard of Eliza Bennington by now, and today's advertisement was a humiliating admission of incompetence. After days of investigating the murder, he was—for lack of a better word—clueless, forced to appeal to the public for information. Londoners turned to the police in time of need, but they were quick to turn on those who helped them, calling the policemen defamatory names, and taking potshots at their competence. Daniel's name would be synonymous with failure, at least until the next big story broke and some poor sod who'd managed to blunder even worse eclipsed Daniel's inadequacy.

"You all right, guv?" Constable Collins asked, looking at Daniel with concern.

"Yes. Why?"

"It's just that you look a bit peaky," the young man replied. "The smell of the place is enough to give anyone a turn," he added, scrunching his nose in disgust.

One benefit of rain was that it cleared away the refuse that washed up on the banks, pulling it back into the current and carrying it out to sea. After days of dry weather, the smell was stronger than usual, but that hadn't been the cause of Daniel's foul mood. He shook his head in irritation, disgusted with himself for allowing his doubts to dictate his mood. He had a job to do, so appeasing his vanity would have to wait.

Daniel instructed Constable Collins to blow his whistle should he come upon what might be the crime scene and set off in the direction Mary had indicated, starting with the warehouse and going to the left. He peered at the ground, appraising every stick and stone. It was then that he noticed a furrow in the dried mud leading away from Wapping Old Stairs toward the bank. The furrow ended abruptly at the tideline, but it was indicative of something sizeable being dragged toward the shore. Daniel began to descend the steep steps slowly, his gaze glued to the worn stone beneath his feet. He was on the sixth step down when he noticed a rock the size of his fist pushed into the corner of the step and up against the side wall. The side of the rock was crusted with what looked like blood, and about three steps down, there was a brown smear on the stair wall.

Daniel grinned, his earlier self-flagellation forgotten. There was no way to know for certain that the blood was Eliza's, but the evidence did fit with Mary's account. If Eliza and the individual Mary had seen had gone toward the river, they would have come to the top of Old Wapping Stairs. The stairs would have been shrouded in darkness at that time of the evening, and no one would notice a woman get hit on the head if they happened to be nearby. The fog had a way of muffling sound, so even if she had cried out, she likely wouldn't have been heard. The attacker had then tossed the rock away and continued to guide Eliza down the steps. Stunned, Eliza might have leaned against the wall for support, resting her head against the stones and leaving a bloodstain level with her head.

Perhaps she'd made it down a few more steps on her own or had collapsed when she lost consciousness, at which point her assailant would have hauled her toward the water's edge. If he did drag her, that would indicate that he wasn't concerned with mucking up her clothes and shoes and had probably disposed of the items instead of selling them on. But robbery never had figured as the motive for this murder, so that last bit fit with the theory as well.

Whether the assailant had had a boat waiting or had made use of one that was already there was impossible to tell, but it was plausible that it had gone into the river at Wapping Old Stairs and drifted toward Westminster. Of course, if it had traveled uninterrupted from five in the evening, it would have been carried out to sea long before it was spotted by the ferryman at dawn, but if Eliza had been left in a boat that had been dragged onto the bank and only began to drift when the tide came in, then it was possible that she only got as far as Westminster Bridge in the time the boat was actually in the water. Perhaps it had even snagged on something and was eventually freed by the current, which would also account for the elapsed time, or maybe Eliza had come to at some point and tried to get back to shore, but with no oars, that would have been nearly impossible.

Picking up the rock on his way back up the steps, Daniel wrapped it in his handkerchief and was about to go find Constable Collins when the young man appeared at the top of the stairs and hurried down to join Daniel.

"Did you find something, guv?" the constable exclaimed.

"I think Eliza Bennington was attacked here, then dragged down to the river. I found a bloodied rock, and there's a runnel in the mud that leads to the tideline."

Constable Collins stood still, his gaze sliding toward the nearby Execution Dock. "Seems fitting somehow," he said, his young face creasing with sadness.

"You think Eliza Bennington was executed by her killer?"

Constable Collins nodded. Daniel didn't necessarily agree, but he had no wish to discourage the young man from speculating or voicing his opinion. Somewhere, a church clock struck the hour. Almost as if on cue, fat raindrops began to fall, splattering on the stone steps and pooling on the brim of Daniel's hat. Constable

Collins' helmet didn't have a brim, so the rain slid right down and dripped onto his chin and pelted his shoulders.

Galvanized into action, the two men hurried back to Ransome's carriage. The driver looked none too pleased as he sat hunched on the bench, peering from beneath the brim of his topper. He was getting wet, and he was probably hungry to boot.

Daniel spotted a woman of middle years who stood huddled in a doorway, her shoulders stooped beneath the weight of the heavy tray that hung by a leather strap around her neck. The appetizing aroma of her meat pies momentarily displaced the stink of bloaters, sold by a young boy who was calling out his wares in a high-pitched voice. Daniel was starving but in no mood to deal with either the bones or the smell of the smoked herring on his hands, so he bought three pies, one for each of the men, and handed one to the driver before climbing into the carriage.

The meat filling tasted borderline rancid, but Daniel was hungry and needed something to tide him over until he could have a proper meal. He only hoped the greasy pie wouldn't upset his stomach, which had been more delicate since his surgery.

Constable Collins finished his pie, licked his fingers, and settled deeper into the corner of the carriage, resting his head against the window. He was asleep in moments.

Chapter 28

If Daniel had hoped to find Sergeant Meadows busy taking statements, he was sorely disappointed. The sergeant sat behind the counter, enjoying a mug of tea and a ham sandwich, the vestibule empty of visitors.

"Any response to the advertisement?" Daniel asked, suddenly wondering if perhaps the newspaper had failed to print it.

Sergeant Meadows shook his head. "Sorry, Inspector, nothing yet. A few would-be witnesses tried it on, but they were after the reward. And there was one old man, said the dinghy was his."

"Did you take down his name?" Daniel asked.

Sergeant Meadows nodded. "I did, but he saw nothing. Found his boat gone when he came for it."

"Where did he leave it, and why?"

"By Wapping Old Stairs. Said he had a mighty thirst on him," Sergeant Meadows replied with a shake of his head.

Daniel felt a flutter of excitement. This tidbit fitted nicely with his theory. "Did he say what time he returned?"

"He couldn't recall. Reeked of spirits, he did. It's a wonder he roused himself enough to come in, but he was angling to get the reward. It would keep him in drink for days."

"Did he tie up the boat there often?"

"More often than not, I reckon. Wapping Old Stairs is near his favorite watering hole."

"I see," Daniel said, and headed for the office he shared with another detective, who was thankfully out. Daniel had no desire to discuss the case. What he needed was to think. He hung up his coat and hat and settled behind the desk, his gaze fixed on the dark green wall.

"Thought you might like some tea, guv," Constable Collins said as he walked into the office, carrying a steaming mug.

"Thank you, Constable," Daniel said, and accepted the tea gratefully. The chill of the river had settled in his bones, which invariably made him think of Eliza, lying there in that boat, naked except for a flimsy shawl, the fog wrapping her in its foul embrace. How long had she survived out there before perishing of exposure? Probably not very long, since the shawl had still been firmly wrapped around her legs. Had she woken, she would have disturbed the cocoon with her frantic thrashing.

Daniel finished the tea, then pushed to his feet, grabbed his coat and hat, and headed toward the exit. He wanted another word with Alan Bennington.

Alan Bennington looked awful. Dark circles shadowed his eyes, his hair was untidy, and he hadn't shaved in several days. The shop was empty of customers and very cold. Alan Bennington folded his arms defensively and stared at Daniel.

"What do you want this time?" Alan growled, but he sounded more desperate than truly angry.

"Exactly what time did you get home last Wednesday, Mr. Bennington?" Daniel asked.

"I already told you. I came home straight after work, as always."

"Can anyone verify that?"

Alan shrugged. "Nell was out, so I guess not, unless you check with that busybody Miss Bloom. She was always looking out the window, spying on her neighbors." He scoffed. "It doesn't matter how many times you interview me, Inspector. You'll find nothing because I've done nothing."

"You had a good reason to wish yourself rid of your wife," Daniel countered. "Not only had she shamed you, but your lover is expecting your child. If you have genuine feelings for her and were not just using her to stroke your ego, you are now free to make a life with her."

"I care for Lorna. I've never denied that. And I'm excited about impending fatherhood, but I didn't kill Eliza," Alan Bennington replied patiently. "I couldn't. It's not so easy to take a life."

"No, it isn't," Daniel agreed. "Do you think George could have done it?"

"George?" Alan asked, feigning ignorance.

"Yes, George Simpson. Lorna's son, the one you neglected to mention."

Alan's shoulders drooped. "What makes you think George could have had anything to do with Eliza's death?"

"He has a tattoo of a mermaid on his forearm."

"Does he really?" Alan replied, clearly surprised. He took a deep breath and met Daniel's gaze. "George is an ungrateful little weasel, but he had no reason to hurt Eliza."

"To free you to marry his mother, perhaps," Daniel suggested halfheartedly.

"George doesn't care about his mother. All he wants is the Golden Goose. Lorna was desperate to get George that apprenticeship at the Iron Works. She wanted him to learn a respectable trade so he could stand on his own two feet. And she wanted to get him away from his uncle, but instead, she seems to have driven him straight into Charlie's arms."

"Why was she so adamant to keep George away from his uncle?"

"Because he's a bad influence. But neither George nor Charlie Simpson had any good reason to kill Eliza. What could they possibly have to gain by her death?"

"Does anyone else stand to gain from her death, besides you?" Daniel inquired.

Alan shrugged. "I really don't know. Eliza came from a respectable family. She didn't have any close friends. And I can't think of anyone she even had a cross word with much less enraged enough to inspire a murderous rage."

"Your wife led a double life," Daniel pointed out.

Alan's eyes reflected his inner pain. "So it would seem, Inspector. I know you think I'm glad to be shot of her, but I did love her, desperately. I tried to make our marriage work, but after the first few months, something changed between us. We were never able to recapture the closeness we once shared."

Looking at the man before him, Daniel found it hard to imagine that he was faking his grief. He'd resented Eliza, possibly wished he'd never married her, but regretting one's marriage was a long way from deciding to commit murder. And surely Alan would have settled on a less flamboyant display. He was clever, well read, and the sort of man who could easily blend into the crowd and disappear if he'd wished to.

"Don't leave town," Daniel said, and turned to go.

"Where would I go?" Alan replied dejectedly, but Daniel didn't think he really expected an answer.

Chapter 29

Jason finally left the hospital after three o'clock. The surgery had lasted nearly two hours, and then he'd remained on hand to monitor the patient's post-operative condition. He had removed the tumor in its entirety and left enough of the stomach for the young man to live a relatively normal life should he recover, but at this stage, Jason wasn't about to make any predictions. As he had discovered in both the hospital in New York and the battlefields of the American Civil War, recovery often hinged on the individual, and although some patients had every reason to get better, they didn't, while others defied the odds and lived to fight another day. The human spirit was a force to be reckoned with, and the outcome often depended on whether the individual chose to persevere or give up.

Eager for some fresh air after hours indoors, Jason walked to Eric Dawson's studio. A young couple with a small child were just leaving, having had their portrait taken, and the photographer's attention was on the plate he had removed from the camera. He looked up, the smile of welcome freezing on his face when he recognized Jason.

"My lord," he said warily. "How may I be of assistance?"

"May we speak privately?" Jason asked. A young assistant was hovering in the doorway, and Jason had no desire to involve him in the conversation.

"Of course. We can speak in my office. Mr. Alder, please take over for me," he said to the young man, who seemed eager to be in charge, if only for a short while.

Eric Dawson shut the door behind them and invited Jason to take the guest chair. Once seated, he allowed his worry to show. "There's nothing more I can tell you about Eliza Bennington," he said. "I wish I did, but I honestly don't know anything."

"It's not Mrs. Bennington I've come to talk about," Jason replied.

"Then who?"

"Tristan Carmichael."

The color drained from Dawson's face. "I—I can't tell you anything about him either."

"Mr. Dawson, who does Tristan Carmichael employ to take photos at his studio in Oliver's Wharf?"

"I don't know."

"And if you did?"

"Lord Redmond, if you know anything about the Carmichaels, then you also know that tattling on them can be detrimental to one's health. I have a family—a wife and two young children."

"Yet you're not afraid to dabble in an illegal trade," Jason pointed out.

"An illegal trade that no one has the resources or the inclination to quell. A good portion of the subscribers on my list are magistrates, cabinet ministers, and military personnel. And even if the climate were to suddenly change and a reckoning was imminent, I'm but a tiny fish in a vast sea."

"And Tristan Carmichael is a whale," Jason finished for him.

Eric Dawson nodded. "I can't give up his employees. I took enough of a risk by telling you that Eliza was acquainted with him."

"Mr. Dawson, I will ask you another question, one I hope you can answer based on your knowledge of your competitors."

"All right," Dawson said, clearly rattled.

"Have you heard any talk of the models being drugged before the photo sessions?"

Jason could tell by the rapid shifting of Dawson's eyes that he had.

"I don't know anything for certain," the man replied, "but I have heard rumors. Carmichael also makes it a point to learn about the people who work for him, so if they ever try to cross him or just walk away, he has leverage against them."

"So a woman who thought she might pose for a few tasteful and well-paid shots might find herself involved in something altogether much more lurid but have no recourse, since Tristan Carmichael now has photographs that can ruin her."

"Precisely. Tristan Carmichael might seem charming and well-spoken, but he's a thug, my lord, and he means to run the East End. His organization has steadily been moving in and marking their ground, and anyone who tries to fight back finds himself wishing he hadn't."

Jason's gaze slid toward several portraits mounted on the wall. The quality of the work was excellent, the lighting just right. Jason had seen many a photograph where the subjects looked like corpses, their skin too light against the dark backdrops the photographers often used. In several photographs, the couples were even smiling or gazing at each other, their expressions a far cry from the stiff, formally posed portraits one often found in people's homes.

"I would like to have a family photograph taken," Jason said, taking the photographer by surprise.

"My lord?"

"If anyone asks why I was here, you can tell them truthfully that I came to finalize the details. When do you have an opening, Mr. Dawson? Morning would be best, since my daughter is still quite small and takes an afternoon nap."

Eric Dawson took out an appointment book and flipped through the pages. "How about eleven o'clock Tuesday next?"

"Yes, I think that would do very well. Until then, Mr. Dawson."

Eric Dawson dutifully scribbled in the name as Jason donned his hat, buttoned his coat, and left the office, nodding politely to the assistant, who had been gazing out the window at the purpling twilight beyond.

Chapter 30

It was just past four o'clock when Sergeant Meadows knocked lightly on the doorjamb, startling Daniel out of his reverie. "I think you should speak to this one, guv. He sounds like he could have seen something."

"Thank you, Sergeant," Daniel replied as he sprang to his feet.

At least twenty people had responded to the advertisement, but except for the old man who'd claimed the dinghy was his, no one knew anything more than what they'd read in the newspapers. A few had been surprisingly creative, but their statements were nothing more than a blatant attempt at claiming the reward.

Daniel had spoken to Norm Gillespie as well after he'd returned from Alan Bennington's shop. Mr. Gillespie had come by the Yard to drop off a folder containing crime scene photographs for another case, but the man told Daniel in no uncertain terms that he knew nothing of Tristan Carmichael's activities and had no wish to get involved lest he wind up the next body to be pulled out of the river. Not for the first time, Daniel reflected on the street appeal of organized crime and how quickly the Carmichaels, who'd been based solely in Essex for decades, had gained ground in London.

Daniel followed Sergeant Meadows to the interview room. A man of about sixty sat at the scarred wooden table, his hands piously folded before him. He was dressed like an undertaker, and his thinning gray hair was elaborately pomaded over his balding scalp. He wore gold-rimmed spectacles and a pencil moustache, and his nails and fingertips were discolored, a yellow tinge revealing his profession as someone who dealt with compounds, an apothecary perhaps.

"Good afternoon, sir. I'm Inspector Haze," Daniel said as he took a seat opposite.

"Phineas Potter. It's a pleasure to make your acquaintance, Inspector."

"Likewise," Daniel replied politely. "Sergeant Meadows tells me you have something to share with me."

"Indeed I do, my good man. I thought little of it at the time, but once I had heard what happened to that young woman and then saw the call for witnesses, I felt it my duty to come forward."

"And what exactly did you see, Mr. Potter?"

"I own a small warehouse near Oliver's Wharf," Mr. Potter said. "I deal mostly in spices. Saffron, cinnamon, and the like. I locked up at five and headed down the Wapping High Street. Normally, I walk, but I felt a bit under the weather and was eager to get home, so I was on my way to the hansom stand on the corner of Church Street when I saw her, Eliza Bennington. She was walking, or ambling, I should say, a few yards ahead of me. She was well dressed and appeared respectable, so I inquired if she was in need of assistance. She shook her head and waved me away."

"Do you think she was ill?" Daniel asked.

"It's difficult to say, Inspector. She appeared—" Mr. Potter paused as he searched for the correct term. "Befogged," he said at last.

"You mean she seemed confused?"

"Yes."

"Did she smell of spirits?" Daniel asked.

"Not that I noticed," Mr. Potter replied.

"Did you just leave her there?"

"As I said, I was feeling unwell and wanted to get home, but as I moved past, I saw a young man coming toward her. And he called to her by her name. Eliza. I couldn't help but turn around to see if he would help."

"And did he?" Daniel asked.

"He slid his arm through hers in a companionable sort of way, but she seemed taken aback, peering into the young man's face as if she were surprised to see him," Mr. Potter said.

"Did you happen to overhear an altercation between them?" Daniel was growing more hopeful. This was the second sighting of a young man with Eliza Bennington shortly before her death.

"I couldn't hear what they were saying, but I didn't get the impression that it was antagonistic in any way."

"Can you describe this young man, Mr. Potter?" Daniel asked, his pen at the ready.

Mr. Potter made a show of thinking. "He wasn't particularly tall. A bit stout. He wore a dark-colored coat and trousers and a cap pulled low over his eyes. He had a blue scarf, I think."

"How did you know he was young if his face was partially obscured?"

"I saw the lower half of his face, and it was smooth. No evening stubble." Mr. Potter's hand went to his own face, which was covered with the stubble of a man who'd been shaving for decades. "And his voice was that of a boy, not a man. I thought he might be fifteen or so."

"Was the young man carrying anything?" Daniel asked.

"No. His hands were in his pockets when I saw him."

"What about Eliza Bennington? Did she have anything with her?"

"She had a beaded reticule. The beads reflected the light from a passing hansom's lamps; that's the only reason I noticed it."

"Did you hear anything as you walked away, Mr. Potter? A scream, perhaps? A call for help?"

The man shook his head. "I didn't hear anything out of the ordinary, but then there was a good number of people about."

"Thank you. You were most helpful, sir." Daniel reached into his pocket and extracted the coins, but Mr. Potter waved them away.

"I don't require a reward, Inspector Haze. Just doing my civic duty," he said loftily. "I do hope you find whoever did this. It boggles the mind that a young woman can be murdered in full view of so many people."

"That it does," Daniel agreed.

He walked Phineas Potter out to the vestibule, where a young sailor, judging by his canvas trousers and pea coat, was just coming in. The man walked up to the counter and addressed Sergeant Meadows.

"I'm here about the advertisement. The one about Eliza Bennington's murder," he added.

Sergeant Meadows looked to Daniel to check if he wished to speak to the man in person or if the sergeant should just take a statement.

"Come this way, please," Daniel said. "I'm Inspector Haze, and I'm conducting the investigation into the murder of Mrs. Bennington."

"Oh, good," the man said, and followed Daniel to the interview room. "Then I have much to tell you."

Chapter 31

Daniel studied the sailor more closely as they settled in the interview room. He was tall and broad-shouldered and had the wiry build of someone who was naturally lean. His jet-black hair was cut short, and his light blue eyes contrasted sharply with a tanned, weather-beaten face. Daniel waited while the man removed his hat, laid it atop the table, and unbuttoned his pea coat to reveal a blue jacket with brass buttons underneath. He was not in the Royal Navy, so probably the Merchant Marine.

"Petty Officer Patrick McGuinness of the *Heron*," he introduced himself at last. "She's a merchant vessel," he added. "We docked last Tuesday." He had a lovely Irish lilt, the sort that made everything he said sound like some whimsical Celtic legend.

"Did you see Eliza Bennington on Wednesday evening, Mr. McGuinness?" Daniel asked.

The man nodded. "I spent the afternoon at the Admiral, drinking with some mates, but I left around five."

"Where were you headed?"

McGuinness smiled shyly. "I had an assignation with a young lady."

Daniel couldn't think of any respectable young lady who'd be prowling the Wapping docks after dark but kept his opinion to himself. "Where were you going to meet?"

"Her brother owns a tavern on the Wapping High Street. The Beacon. Do you know it?"

"I've seen it."

"The lassie was going to meet me outside, on account of her brother not being entirely supportive of her plans," Mr. McGuinness said with a grin. "I was passing the alley that leads to the Wapping Old Stairs when I heard something. I turned to look, and there was a lad leading a redheaded lass toward the stairs. She looked unsteady on her feet and seemed upset."

"You didn't think to help?" Daniel asked, more angrily than he should have. How was the man to know Eliza Bennington was about to be murdered?

"To be honest, Inspector, I assumed she was a drunken doxy, and the lad was hoping to get some on the cheap. And neither one would have appreciated the interference."

"Can you describe the man you saw?"

"Middling height. Barrel chested. Smooth, pale face," he said. His dark brows knitted as he seemed to recall something. "There was something about him, Inspector. Something that didn't square with the rest of him."

"What was it?" Daniel asked, intrigued.

"I can't rightly say, but I suppose if I had to put it into words, I'd say the features were too delicate, the face narrow. Like a little lad whose bollocks had yet to drop."

"So you think he was very young?"

"His face was youthful, aye, but his body was not that of a young lad."

"Did you see the color of his eyes? Or the hair?"

"No, but I did spot a flash of blue. I think he wore a blue kerchief round his neck." Patrick McGuinness shrugged. "It was dark, Inspector, and I only saw them for a moment. I honestly thought nothing of it until I saw the lass that was found floating on the river. I recognized her then."

Daniel took out the coins and slid them across the table. "Thank you, Mr. McGuinness."

The sailor picked up the coins and dropped them into his pocket. "I wish I could tell you more, Inspector. Do you think it was the lad that killed her?"

"I do," Daniel replied. "I really do."

Chapter 32

Jason was waiting for Daniel by the time he finally got home. Jason was in the parlor with Rebecca, the latter laughing merrily at something he'd just said, her cheeks a delicate pink, her eyes sparkling with good humor.

"Where's Charlotte?" Daniel demanded, rather ungraciously.

Rebecca's color heightened and she shot him an angry look. "She is with Grace. She wanted to help with dinner. I'll get her," she added when she must have noted the look on Daniel's face.

"Is something wrong?" Jason asked carefully once Daniel had removed his coat and hat and tossed them carelessly across a chair before pouring himself a large drink. Jason still had plenty, so Daniel didn't bother to offer him a top-up.

"Grace has enough to be getting on with," Daniel replied tersely.

"And Miss Grainger is taking advantage of your regard for her," Jason concluded.

Daniel gave a curt nod and sat down. "Something has shifted between us this past week, but whatever it is, I wasn't there when it happened."

"Have you spoken to her?"

"I don't feel I have the right to press her," Daniel replied.

"You do when it comes to her work."

"You are right. I will have a word with her tomorrow."

"What's wrong with tonight?" Jason asked.

"I'm too weary," Daniel admitted. "It's been rather a long day."

"Were you able to learn anything?"

Daniel took a sip of whisky and set the glass down. Otherwise, he'd gulp the whole thing down and pour himself another.

"Constable Collins and I interviewed George Simpson, who just happens to have a mermaid tattooed on his forearm, then traveled to Oliver's Wharf, it being the last known place Eliza Bennington was seen alive. I found a bloodstained rock on the Wapping Old Stairs and blood on the stone wall, and there's a runnel in the mud that leads to the tideline."

"Do you believe that's where she was killed?" Jason asked.

"Given that that's the precise location Eliza was last seen, I think that's very likely. An old drunkard came in to give a statement today. Said his boat had gone missing from that very location on the night of the murder."

"And George Simpson? Anything come of that?"

"Unless I missed something, George Simpson had no reason to kill Eliza Bennington, nor could he have if Eliza was murdered shortly after she was last seen. He left the shipyard around five, maybe even later, and it would have taken him at least a half hour to get to Oliver's Wharf, which would make it six o'clock at the very earliest by the time he was in the area. But several people saw Eliza in the company of a young man, and I can't for the life of me figure out who he might have been."

"And the advertisement? Any luck?" Jason asked.

"There were the usual fraudsters hoping to claim the reward and two credible witnesses who came in just as I was about to leave for the day. A Mr. Potter and a Mr. McGuinness. Both men saw what they believe to be Eliza Bennington around five o'clock on Wednesday in the vicinity of Wapping High Street and

Wapping Old Stairs. They both mentioned that she seemed unsteady on her feet. Mr. Potter described her as befogged, while Mr. McGuinness thought she was drunk."

"Yes, Mary Smith had thought so as well."

Daniel nodded. "According to Mr. Potter, who owns a warehouse in Oliver's Wharf and came across as sober and respectable, Eliza appeared to be ambling down the Wapping High Street until she met a young man who addressed her by name. He then steered her toward the stairs and presumably down to the river. Mr. McGuinness, a sailor, also saw Eliza with a young man heading toward the stairs. I think it's safe to say that young man was the last person to see her alive and probably her killer."

"What do we know about him?" Jason inquired.

"Not a lot. Both witnesses describe him as being of average height, stocky, and youthful in appearance. Mr. McGuiness did mention a blue kerchief the young man wore around his neck."

"What age do they put him at?"

"Mr. Potter thought he was around fifteen. He said there wasn't a trace of stubble, so this is a youth that hasn't started shaving regularly yet. Mr. McGuinness thought much the same. But both men described him as being stocky. Barrel-chested, according to Mr. Potter."

"Curious," Jason said.

"Which part?" Daniel asked. He knew he sounded surly, but this case as well as Rebecca's inexplicable behavior had put him in a sour mood.

"What reason would this young man have to kill Eliza Bennington?" Jason asked. He was clearly perplexed, his gaze thoughtful.

"I'll tell you what reason," Daniel replied, the idea having only just occurred to him. "The boy had seen photographs of her and somehow found out who she was. He then ambushed her on Oliver's Wharf. Eliza Bennington had clearly been unwell, an easy target. He saw his chance and went for it, acting on his basest impulses. He maneuvered her down the steps, struck her on the head with a rock he'd picked up, and forced himself on her as she lay unconscious. Perhaps he thought she was dead and thought it prudent to dispose of the body. He spotted the dinghy and made use of it."

"So you're suggesting that this killing was entirely opportunistic?" Jason mused.

"Maybe not entirely. He did seek her out, but then he made use of whatever he had to hand. He did not come prepared, or he would have stabbed or throttled her. Perhaps he only wanted to meet her or see if she would be willing to take his coin. When she refused, he became angry, his lust getting the better of him."

"And the display?" Jason asked, the glass poised halfway to his lips.

"Having admired Eliza, he decided to give her a final tribute, make her look beautiful in death. He dragged her toward the water, undressed her, loosened her hair, wrapped her lower half in what was probably her own shawl, since the kerchief would not have been big enough to cover her, and then laid her in the dinghy he found tied up to a post and pushed it out, probably hoping she'd be carried off by the current. And she was, but not far enough."

"And the flowers?"

"He might have bought the flowers to give to her and then used them to decorate her remains."

Jason nodded. "The theory makes sense, but there's something troubling me."

"What's that, then?" Daniel asked, rather pleased with himself for tying up the facts so neatly.

"Mary Smith said there was something odd about the young man. Same goes for Mr. Potter and Mr. McGuinness. They all said that they were surprised by his youthful face."

"Mr. McGuinness described it as narrow," Daniel said.

"Exactly," Jason said. "All three witnesses say the young man was stocky, but he had a thin face. As a rule, when a person is stout, their face tends to be fleshy as well. How is it that this young man had a thin, youthful face, and a stocky, barrel-chested body? It sounds odd."

"It does, but perhaps he was wearing a heavy jumper beneath his coat that made him look stouter than he really was."

"Yes, I suppose that's a possibility," Jason agreed. "Have you managed to speak to Mr. Gillespie?"

"He was no help," Daniel replied sourly.

"I paid a visit to Eric Dawson this afternoon," Jason said. "He claimed not to know the name of the photographers Tristan Carmichael uses, but he did admit that he'd heard rumors of women being drugged and forced to perform base acts and then threatened with exposure if they tried to complain. I think Eliza Bennington was still under the influence of whatever Carmichael had given her."

"What could he have given her?" Daniel asked.

"I doubt he'd use anything that might cause vomiting, or a stomach upset, but there are certain substances that produce hallucinations, delirium, or simply lower the individual's defenses. They're highly dangerous in large quantities, but if a small quantity was administered, particularly mixed with alcohol, it might serve to incapacitate the taker enough to disassociate themselves from whatever is happening and possibly not remember what had taken place once the effects wore off."

"And Carmichael would have access to such substances?"

"We know he has unlimited access to opium. Belladonna and morphine can be obtained at any chemist shop, and there are foreign solutions that can be brought in by anyone in his network. There's a plant that's native to the Americas called jimsonweed. The leaves and seeds are highly toxic and will cause hallucinations and a feeling of complete detachment from reality. When taken in small doses, it's relatively safe."

"How do you know?" Daniel asked, curious that Jason should be so well informed.

"I tried it once," Jason admitted. "A surgeon I met had offered to share. We had worked around the clock, operating on men who'd been torn to pieces by the enemy's cannon. We lost most of them," he said quietly. "And the ones who had survived would never be whole again, either physically or mentally. I suppose we just needed to escape from reality for an hour, and the jimsonweed worked a treat."

"Were you not afraid to ingest it?"

"At that point, the only thing I was afraid of was reality," Jason replied. "I think we need to search Carmichael's studio."

"And you think he'd simply invite us in and play the gracious host?"

"I never said it had to be with his permission."

"No," Daniel replied, his voice louder than he had intended. "If Tristan Carmichael is drugging women and forcing them to commit lude acts against their will, he must be stopped. We must go through the proper channels."

"In theory, I agree with you, but in reality, there's little you can do. For a start, you can't prove the women did not ingest whatever it was he gave them willingly, to calm their nerves. And Carmichael can just set up shop elsewhere. Distributing those photographs is like minting his own money. It's too profitable to simply stop."

"The Carmichaels break the law every day," Daniel said through clenched teeth.

"Then get him on something he can be charged with," Jason replied. "Even if we find a hallucinogenic substance, we can't prove that Tristan Carmichael is in any way responsible for Eliza Bennington's death."

"How is it that these ignorant thugs are so well versed in the vagaries of the law?" Daniel demanded, utterly exasperated.

"They have highly learned men advising them, men who benefit handsomely from the opium dens, the brothels, and the pornography people like Tristan Carmichael peddle to the public."

"Tomorrow, I will obtain a warrant and search Carmichael's warehouse. I might not find anything, but I want him to know that we're on to him and we will be coming for him."

"Are you sure that's wise?" Jason asked.

"About as wise as breaking in under the cover of darkness," Daniel replied.

"You have a point there," Jason agreed, and pushed to his feet. "I would like to come with you, if I may. I am the only one who can identify any substance found at the scene."

"Give me about an hour to convince Ransome and gather together some men. Shall we meet at the Yard at ten?"

"I will be there," Jason promised, and took his leave.

Chapter 33

Wednesday, February 17

Daniel hadn't expected Superintendent Ransome to wholeheartedly approve of a raid on Tristan Carmichael's warehouse, but he was still surprised by Ransome's outright refusal to investigate the man's activities.

"I can't allow it, Haze," he said after Daniel had presented his case, which he'd thought was convincing.

"If Carmichael is drugging women and using them at their most vulnerable to line his own pockets, is that not a crime, sir?"

"Wise up, Haze," Ransome said warily. "There are thousands of prostitutes in this city, ranging in age from mere children to women who are old enough to be your mother. Do you think this is the life they'd dreamed of when they sat at their mother's knee? And behind every one of those women is a man, making a profit off their vulnerability, or a madam who relies on men to keep her girls in line. What are we to do about it?"

"You might not know the identity of every man, but you know of the Carmichaels."

"I do, and it is my intention to stay clear."

"Sir?" Daniel exclaimed. "How can you turn a blind eye to this?"

"Daniel," Ransome said patiently, adopting a fatherly tone that was at odds with his demeanor. "Look around you. How many men do we have here? Two dozen? And a few hundred policemen across the other divisions? We are no match for the likes of Tristan Carmichael and his ilk. Highly organized criminals like the Carmichaels are taking over. They have networks consisting of hundreds of men, men who are committed and dangerous. These are not hungry boys that form into gangs and roam the streets, picking the pockets of the wealthy, or even the nimble-fingered chits of the Forty Elephants Gang, who rely on women's wiles to fleece their targets. These are soldiers in a war for control. They're armed, and they're not afraid to kill."

Ransome sighed resignedly. "I can't risk the well-being of my men for the sake of one woman, who, frankly, was nothing more than a trollop who got her just deserts. This was not a desperate woman whose very survival depended on earning a few bob that would pay for her next meal and a bed for the night. Eliza Bennington was a married woman, the daughter of a vicar, and the sister of a well-respected businessman. She was not desperate, nor was she friendless. She made her own bed, Haze," Ransome finished, glaring at Daniel like an avenging angel who'd just loosed his flaming arrow of judgment.

"Are you suggesting that Eliza Bennington doesn't deserve justice?" Daniel demanded.

"I'm suggesting that you conduct a thorough investigation without endangering the lives of your fellow policemen. How you do that is up to you. I give you free rein, Haze, because I know you're a damned good detective, but I will not be responsible for the kind of retribution that will rain on our heads should we disturb a hornet's nest. Understood?"

"Understood," Daniel replied, barely keeping his anger in check.

He was so upset, he grabbed his coat and hat and stormed out of the building, waiting for Jason outside, where he could cool his ire, both figuratively and literally, since it was cold and damp, the lowering sky growing darker by the minute. When Jason's brougham pulled up, Daniel climbed in and let out a frustrated sigh.

"Ransome refused, did he?" Jason asked conversationally.

Daniel gaped at him. "You knew he would?"

215

"I thought he might," Jason admitted with a careless shrug.

"He doesn't think the Metropolitan Police Service is a match for an army of thugs."

"He's probably right," Jason replied calmly. "Daniel, men who work for Tristan Carmichael are armed with pistols, knives, clubs, and fists, when all else fails. Young, inexperienced constables armed with little more than a stick are at a serious disadvantage. Ransome is charged with lowering the rate of crime in this city, but he's also responsible for the men who serve under him, and that includes you."

"I'm not afraid of Tristan Carmichael," Daniel cried.

"You should be," Jason replied. "He wouldn't think twice about sticking a knife between your ribs, and then where would you be?"

Daniel didn't need reminding that he was living with only one kidney after just such an outcome, but now that he was marginally calmer, he could admit to himself that Jason had the right of it. As did Ransome. They had to take on what they could and retreat and regroup when they came up against a situation in which they were bound to lose.

"What do you suggest?" Daniel asked, turning to face Jason.

"I suggest we have a quiet look and see if we can find any evidence that would implicate Carmichael in Eliza Bennington's murder. If not, we continue to investigate, although I must admit, the trail is growing colder by the minute, since we have no way to identify the young man who must have done the killing."

"That it is," Daniel agreed with a heartfelt sigh. "How do you propose to get into the warehouse?"

"Through the door," Jason replied. "You simply inform whoever is there that you must see the studio as part of the investigation. Tristan Carmichael has been cooperative so far, and

216

he doesn't know what we're looking for, so most likely, we'll be allowed inside, if only briefly."

"I do so admire your American optimism," Daniel said, smiling for the first time that morning. "I suppose it's worth a try."

"Good. I'll tell Joe to take us to Oliver's Wharf."

Daniel settled in for the ride once the conveyance began to move. He wasn't a materialistic person by nature, and his household was on the Spartan side, but he did wish he could afford his own carriage and driver. The convenience was unrivaled, and the speed of getting from place to place even greater than that of the infernal underground railway, which Daniel avoided like the proverbial plague, since he didn't relish being trapped in a dark, underground tunnel with nothing but a rickety wooden box to protect him in case of a collapse.

"Do you really think Carmichael would openly go to war with the police?" Daniel asked, his thoughts returning to the matter at hand.

"I do," Jason replied. "And I think he would win. The beauty of the British justice system is that a man is innocent until proven guilty, and Tristan Carmichael is not stupid enough to implicate himself in a crime. He has lieutenants to do that for him. And as long as the leaders of the network remain at liberty, there are always more men who're willing to take up arms in the name of shared profit."

"He freely admitted to producing and distributing pornographic images," Daniel argued. "That's a crime."

"Good luck getting a conviction, though," Jason replied. "Not only does Tristan Carmichael keep his own hands clean, but he has magistrates in his pocket who will fail to convict on evidence that's circumstantial at best. Having photographs taken for one's own pleasure is not a crime. If a greedy photographer happens to use the plates to print the images and sell them for his own profit, Tristan Carmichael cannot be held responsible."

"Do you honestly believe that?" Daniel screeched.

"Of course not, but that's how the case would be presented to the court. It would be up to opposing counsel to prove otherwise."

"So you mean he's untouchable?"

"As good as." Jason smiled bitterly. "As long as men like Tristan Carmichael have competent legal counsel, they will always walk away unscathed, leaving their flunkies to pay the price."

Daniel remained silent. What was there to say? Jason was right.

Chapter 34

Daniel was relieved when they were met by a single watchman rather than a gang of Carmichael's men. Whatever the warehouse was used for, there was nothing going on at the moment. The man who opened the door to them was sixty if a day, but he looked strong and wiry, his gaze narrowed in suspicion when Daniel identified himself and showed his warrant card.

"Ye ain't comin' in," the man, who'd said his name was Withers, stated flatly. "Mr. Carmichael won't like it."

"Mr. Carmichael has pledged his cooperation," Daniel replied. That was stretching the truth a bit, but Withers had no way of knowing that.

"Well, 'e ain't told me noffin 'bout it."

"Does he normally share his decisions with you?" Jason asked in a tone so high-handed, it nearly made Daniel laugh.

"Well, no," Withers dithered. "But ye can't come in all the same."

"Feel free to check with Mr. Carmichael, but he won't be pleased when he discovers you have tried to obstruct a police investigation," Jason said.

"Mr. Withers, we only need to take a quick look. No one is accusing Mr. Carmichael of anything," Daniel piped in when he saw the man waver in his resolve.

"Like I believes ye," Withers grumbled. "There ain't no such thing as an 'onest rozzer."

"That's rich coming from you," Jason said.

"I ain't put a foot wrong in all me life," Withers said, but his eyes were dancing with mirth. He probably had a list of crimes as long as his arm.

"Mr. Withers, we only need a few minutes," Jason cajoled. He reached into his pocket and drew out a shiny sovereign. "I'm happy to make it worth your while."

The man still looked uncertain, but the promise of easy money won out. He snatched the coin from Jason's hand and pocketed it. "Ye 'ave five minutes, and I's only letting ye in cause Mr. Carmichael 'as nothing to 'ide."

"That's all we need," Jason replied smugly.

The watchman led them to a good-sized room at the front of the warehouse that was obviously the studio. The walls were a dull gray, and there was no natural light, but there were several gas lamps affixed to the walls. Withers turned them on.

Inside, there were two separate areas divided by beautifully painted silk screens. The area at the front of the room contained a velvet reclining couch in deep purple velvet. There were two potted plants that had to be fake, since no living greenery would survive without sunlight, and two octagonal tables made of dark wood and topped with Oriental vases. A colorful carpet covered the floor, and a maroon curtain mounted on a rail above could be drawn to isolate that part of the room. The resulting photograph would depict a richly appointed room, not a staged area in a dockside warehouse.

The set-up at the back was quite different. Here, there was a wide bed with a brass bedstead. The screens gave the impression of patterned wallpaper, and there was a heavy velvet curtain that could be drawn around one part of the stage. When in use, this would appear to be a cozy boudoir, the setting not only intimate but also more erotic.

A scarred wooden sideboard stood along one side of the wall and wasn't part of the backdrop. On it were several bottles. Jason picked up a bottle containing a green liquid and opened the stopper. He sniffed experimentally, made a face, then returned the bottle to its place.

"What is that?" Daniel asked.

"Absinthe." Jason didn't seem inclined to explain, so Daniel didn't press him.

"What ye sayin', then?" Withers demanded, but Jason didn't bother to reply.

Jason examined the other two bottles, then casually wandered off while Daniel pulled open the cabinet doors. He found several boxes of photographs.

The first box contained at least twenty images. Daniel suddenly felt short of breath, heat rising not only in his cheeks but in his groin, which had begun straining against the linen of his drawers. He had never seen anything so intimate or so unsettling. When stripped down to the base act the images depicted, the people in the shots were no better than animals, coupling in front of prying eyes. The men seemed intent on their task, but the women appeared to be in a faint, their eyes closed, their limbs loose, their heads thrown back in what was meant to represent abandon. Now that Daniel knew what they were looking for, it was easy to see the women were under the influence of something other than unbridled desire.

He hastily returned the photographs to the box and turned his attention to the second container. This box contained images of nude women in seductive poses, but the women were clearly aware of what they were doing. They gazed into the camera with brazen defiance, some smiling as if they had been caught doing something naughty, others looking sultry and almost predatory. These photographs were no different from those given to them by Norm Gillespie at the start of the investigation. Each photograph was labeled with a code on the back. Perhaps they corresponded to the slide or perhaps to the individual depicted.

Daniel was about to return the stack to the box, but in his clumsy attempt to organize them, he dropped the entire pile on the floor. He sighed and bent down to pick up the lot, eager to be gone from this place. This studio unnerved him. He was snatching up the photographs one by one when one of the images caught his eye. In it was a young woman, no older than sixteen or seventeen.

She had fair curls that tumbled around her shoulders and light-colored eyes. Her bare breasts were full and lush, and her rounded hips were nothing short of voluptuous. Her gaze was shy, her smile pained. If Daniel had to guess, he'd say this young woman had not been a willing participant. It was a moment before he realized that he'd seen her before and was about to show the photograph to Jason, who was walking toward him, when Withers bore down on them.

"Off with ye," he cried, his forehead creased with worry. He may not be the sharpest knife in the drawer, but even he was clever enough to realize that he probably shouldn't have let them in. The sovereign he'd earned would be small recompense in the face of Tristan Carmichael's fury if he learned of Withers' transgression.

Daniel hastily replaced the images in the box and returned it to its rightful place before following Jason out the door, which slammed shut behind them, the key scraping in the lock as they approached the waiting carriage.

"Did you find anything of interest?" Daniel asked once the carriage began to move.

"There's nothing inside that warehouse to incriminate Tristan Carmichael," Jason replied. "The storerooms are full of chests of tea, bolts of lace and silk, and there are crates of ivory tusks. All profitable commodities, but not illegal to import, as far as I'm aware."

Daniel highly doubted that Tristan Carmichael was bringing these goods in legally and paying duties, but Carmichael's imports weren't the focus of his investigation. "What is absinthe?" he asked.

"It's a highly alcoholic spirit made of herbs. Anise, I think. Absinthe alone is probably enough to intoxicate the models, but if mixed with another substance, like opium, for instance, it would be sure to cause hallucinations and a complete break with reality until the effects began to wear off. But there's no concrete proof of anything, Daniel. Offering someone a drink is not illegal, and there's nothing to substantiate the claim that the content had been tampered with."

"Clever bastard," Daniel said through clenched teeth. He extracted the photograph of the fair-haired young woman from the pocket of his coat and passed it to Jason.

"Well done," Jason remarked with an amused smile. "That's Janet Reynolds, if I'm not mistaken."

Daniel nearly cringed at the praise. Taking the photo was unethical and technically a crime in itself, but this was the first tangible piece of evidence they had that linked Eliza Bennington, Janet Reynolds, and Tristan Carmichael.

"I think we have our young man," Jason said as he studied the image.

"You reckon?"

"If a woman dressed as a man, unless she bound her breasts, she would appear barrel-chested, especially a woman who's as well-endowed as Janet Reynolds obviously is," Jason said. "And that would explain the hairless, narrow face that didn't square with the body. And if Miss Bloom is to be believed, Janet Reynolds had been on the stage and would know about dressing in costumes and acting a part."

"But why would Janet Reynolds wish to kill Eliza? By all accounts, they were close," Daniel mused.

"Perhaps they weren't as close as Mrs. Reynolds would like us to believe."

"I think it's time we spoke to Janet Reynolds," Daniel said determinedly.

"No time like the present," Jason agreed.

Chapter 35

They arrived in Mornington Crescent just before one o'clock. A drenching downpour had left the streets running with murky water and reduced visibility to a few meters. Joe, who had to be soaked to the skin, pulled up the brougham as close to the door as possible, and Jason and Daniel dashed toward it, Daniel glad he'd had the forethought to bring an umbrella.

A maidservant they hadn't met on their previous visit looked at them with obvious disdain, probably assuming they were about to beg a donation for some worthy cause from Mr. Reynolds.

"I'm Inspector Haze of Scotland Yard, and this is Lord Redmond. We're here to see Mrs. Reynolds," Daniel informed her.

"Mr. and Mrs. Reynolds are not at home to visitors, sir."

"We're not visitors; we're with the police," Daniel replied in what he hoped was a patient but authoritative tone.

"But they're presently at luncheon, sir," the maidservant protested.

"Then we will wait for them to finish," Daniel said, and all but pushed past her into the foyer. He had no desire to keep arguing in the rain.

The maidservant glared at the puddle of water forming beneath the dripping umbrella and snatched it from Daniel's hand.

"Kindly inform your mistress she has visitors." Jason smiled at the woman, but his tone brooked no argument.

"Yes, sir," the woman replied sullenly, then rushed off.

Alastair Reynolds strode into the foyer not two minutes later, his expression one of intense irritation.

"What do you want with my wife?" he demanded.

"We'd like to ask her a few questions," Daniel replied politely.

"I forbid it," Reynolds replied.

"Mr. Reynolds, in case you forgot, we're conducting an investigation into the murder of your sister," Daniel reminded him. "Your wife might be in possession of vital evidence."

"My sister is dead, and your farce of an investigation will not bring her back. Leave my family alone and allow us to grieve in peace," Reynolds barked, his face growing puce with anger.

"I'm afraid we can't do that," Daniel replied stubbornly. "We can do this in a civilized and *discreet* manner," he said, stressing the promise of judiciousness, "or I can return with several constables, who will take both you and your wife into custody, in cuffs, if necessary."

"What is it you think Janet knows?" Alastair Reynolds demanded, working hard to get his anger in check and regain control of the situation.

"More than she previously told us."

Mr. Reynolds gave a curt nod. "I will sit in on the interview."

"You will not," Jason said, speaking for the first time. "You will allow Inspector Haze to do his job and respect the jurisdiction of the police."

"Or what?" Alastair Reynolds thundered.

"Or you will find yourself on the front page of several London publications. I can't imagine that would be good for business, Mr. Reynolds, or for the reputation of your family."

"You have no right," Reynolds forced through clenched teeth.

"The laws of this country say different," Jason snapped.

225

"What right have you to lecture me, you American upstart!"

"I'm not lecturing you, Mr. Reynolds. I'm simply stating the facts as I know them. Now, we've wasted enough time, don't you think? We speak to your wife here or there, in private or in public. Which will it be?"

Reynolds had no choice but to back down. "I will get Janet."

"A wise decision," Jason said. Daniel thought he was taunting the man just a little but was grateful to Jason for stepping in, since he really wasn't inclined to arrest Alastair Reynolds for obstruction.

Janet Reynolds looked put out when she entered the drawing room, her demeanor brisk. She did not instruct the maidservant to take Daniel and Jason's things, nor did she offer them a seat. Daniel had no intention of conducting the interview standing up, so he removed his wet coat and hat and made himself comfortable, settling next to Jason, who had already claimed the armchair closest to the fire.

"I really don't see what more I can tell you," Janet Reynolds said once Daniel had explained the reason for their visit. Her nostrils flared with exasperation, and her gaze kept straying toward the door, probably in the hope that her husband was hovering outside.

"Do you know Tristan Carmichael, Mrs. Reynolds?" Daniel asked. If he had hoped to catch her off guard, he'd succeeded.

Janet Reynolds raised her head defiantly, jutting out her chin, but her shoulders stiffened, and she clasped her hands in her lap as though to keep them from shaking.

"I do not," she replied.

"Are you certain?" Jason asked softly.

"I am."

"He seems to know you."

The woman's bottom lip began to tremble ever so slightly, but she instantly got hold of herself. "I don't know what you mean."

Jason looked to Daniel, but Daniel decided to try a different tack. "Where are you originally from, Mrs. Reynolds?"

Clearly taken aback by the change of topic, Janet Reynolds relaxed somewhat. "Chelmsford."

"What a coincidence. I was born and bred in Essex as well," Daniel said. "And what year did you arrive in London?"

"Eighteen sixty-two," Janet replied. "What does this have to do with Eliza's death?"

"Just establishing the facts," Daniel said as he jotted down the information in his notebook. "Did you come alone?"

A brief flare of panic entered Janet's eyes, but she quickly collected herself and fixed Daniel with a challenging stare.

"Mrs. Reynolds, did you come to London alone?" Daniel asked again.

"Yes. My father died, leaving me nothing but debts. The bailiffs took everything, even my personal possessions. I was left with nothing but the clothes I stood up in."

"So you decided to try your luck in London?" Jason asked. Janet Reynolds nodded. "And you went on the stage."

The woman's eyes narrowed, and bright spots of color bloomed in her cheeks. "That venomous old shrew told you, didn't she?"

"Which shrew are you referring to?" Jason asked.

"Orchid Bloom. Except her real name is Dorcas Butte. She was in demand for a short while, then became a dresser. She nosed for scandal the way a French pig roots for truffles, and she used it to her own advantage."

"Were you acquainted, or did you know her only by reputation?" Daniel asked.

"We were. When she saw me with Eliza, she recognized me," Janet said angrily.

"Was she blackmailing you, Mrs. Reynolds?"

Janet nodded. "She said she'd tell Alastair that I had been on the stage unless I paid her every month."

"How much did she ask for?" Jason asked.

"Twenty-five shillings per week," Janet replied. "I think she enjoyed the power more than the money. She has little use for it these days."

"And how long have you been paying her?" Daniel asked.

"Two years now. I handed over most of my allowance to that wicked old woman." Janet gazed from Daniel to Jason and back again. "Please, don't tell my husband. It was a long time ago."

"Mrs. Reynolds, how did you meet your husband?"

"Through a mutual acquaintance."

Several questions floated to the top of Daniel's mind, but he dismissed them for the moment. Janet Reynolds had clearly been clever enough to devise a way to meet a respectable man and dupe him into marriage, but unless Eliza Bennington had been blackmailing her as well, it probably wasn't relevant to the murder.

"And Tristan Carmichael? Where does he fit into this?" Jason asked.

The woman looked like she was going to be sick. She seemed to be searching for an acceptable answer but realized that the game was up. They were onto her, and she was only staving off the inevitable.

"I knew him from Chelmsford," she choked out.

"What was your relationship, exactly?"

Janet let out a shuddering sigh. "My father borrowed money from Lance Carmichael." Silent tears slid down her cheeks, the expression in her eyes that of a wounded animal that knew it would die in its trap. "I was expected to repay it after his death."

"Was that when you agreed to pose for his photographs?" Jason asked gently.

"I never agreed," Janet hissed. "I wasn't given much of a choice. It was either pay back the debt or work it off in one of their brothels. Tristan took pity on me and suggested a compromise. I got to keep my virtue, but I had to sell my soul."

"Was that why you came to London? To escape?"

"There was no escape. He would always know where to find me. He makes it his business to keep tabs on those he owns."

"How did Eliza come into it?" Jason asked.

Janet was the picture of confusion. "Eliza? How do you mean?"

"Where were you last Wednesday, around five o'clock, Mrs. Reynolds?" Daniel asked, the hope that he had this murder solved slipping away as he looked at the woman's uncomprehending expression.

"I was here. Alastair was away, in Manchester. I wasn't feeling well, so I took supper on a tray in my room. Gladys can vouch for me." Janet Reynolds speared Daniel with an accusing stare. "You think I killed Eliza?"

"Did you?" Jason countered.

"What possible reason would I have to kill my sister-in-law?"

"She had been posing for Tristan Carmichael as well," Daniel said, and watched shock settle over Janet's face.

"Eliza was involved with Tristan Carmichael?" Her astonishment seemed genuine, but Daniel wasn't inclined to believe her.

"She was. She had been at his studio at Oliver's Wharf on the night she was killed," he explained.

"Which only goes to show that she was no threat to me," Janet exclaimed. "She had her own secrets."

"Why would Eliza feel the need to compromise herself in such a way?" Jason asked.

"I can only assume it's because she wanted to get away. And hurt Alan. Eliza found out he was keeping a mistress. She was devastated. She spoke of going to America."

"When was this?"

"A few weeks ago. She said it in passing."

"What exactly did she say?" Daniel asked.

"Eliza said she wished she could go to America and start over in a place where no one knows her. I didn't think anything of it. Eliza often talked about the things she wished she could do."

"Like what?" Jason asked.

"Like explore the Colosseum in Rome or visit the Egyptian pyramids. It's not as if she was ever going to go, but she liked to dream of freedom. We all do," Janet added miserably. She turned to Daniel again, her gaze pleading. "Inspector, please don't tell

Alastair about my past. I only did what I did to survive. I have a husband and a child. Surely I deserve a chance to be happy."

Daniel looked into Janet's tear-filled eyes and nodded. "You have my word, Mrs. Reynolds. There's no need for him to know."

"Oh, thank you," Janet said on a breath of relief. "Thank you, Inspector Haze."

Feeling like an utter fool, Daniel stood, took his things, and walked to the door. The rain had stopped, and a watery sunshine streamed through the half-moon window above the front door, but Daniel felt anything but sunny. If Janet Reynolds didn't kill Eliza Bennington, then who did?

Chapter 36

"We need to speak to Miss Bloom," Daniel said as soon as they were back in the carriage. "I think she knows more than she told us."

"You think she knows what Eliza Bennington was involved in?" Jason asked.

"Perhaps she was blackmailing her as well. I don't think she would have followed Eliza herself, but she could have easily put her maidservant up to it, or even found a street child who was happy to earn a few pence."

Jason didn't seem overly impressed with this theory and countered with one of his own. "Eliza Bennington could have been blackmailing her sister-in-law."

"To what end?" Daniel asked, taken aback.

"Perhaps she really did mean to go to America and needed the money. Since everyone connected to this case seems to be lying, the warm friendship between Eliza and Janet might be nothing more than a fabrication," Jason replied.

"Every clue seems to lead to a dead end," Daniel grumbled.

It was difficult not to become dispirited in the face of such circumvention, and he feared this case would go unsolved if they failed to find that one loose thread that when pulled could finally unravel this tightly woven conspiracy.

"I think we're hovering at the edge of a solution," Jason said stubbornly. "We have several important pieces of information. We just need to arrange them in a way that forms a cohesive narrative. Perhaps Miss Bloom, or Miss Butte," Jason added with a chuckle, "can furnish us with that one piece that will tie it all together."

Jason casually glanced out the window as they pulled into Frances Street, his brows knitting in puzzlement as he leaned closer to the window to get a better look. "What the...?" he muttered.

Daniel peered over his shoulder but couldn't see anything from his vantage point until the conveyance was almost level with Miss Bloom's front steps. An undertaker's van was parked out front, two men dressed entirely in black and carrying a canvas stretcher heading toward the steps. Jason jumped out of the carriage as soon as it came to a stop and hurried after them, with Daniel bringing up the rear.

"What happened?" Jason demanded of Miss Bloom's maidservant, who stood off to the side, wringing her hands as the undertakers continued up the stairs, presumably to Miss Bloom's bedroom.

The woman looked up at Jason, and her bottom lip began to quiver. Her eyes were red-rimmed, and her apron looked less than fresh, as if she had been using it to dab at her runny nose.

"Miss Bloom passed on, sir," the woman whispered.

"When?" Jason asked.

"Last night. When I came to wake her this morning, she..." The servant began to cry in earnest.

"What's your name, miss?" Daniel asked.

"Polly. Polly Akers, sir," she wailed.

"Who sent for the undertakers, Miss Akers?"

"I did. Miss Bloom left express instructions and a burial fund, should anything happen to her."

"Did she think something would?" Jason asked.

"Not that I know of, but she had no family to see to the arrangements."

"Why don't you make yourself a cup of tea and wait in the kitchen," Jason suggested kindly, and headed up the stairs, closely followed by Daniel. They arrived at the bedroom door just as the undertakers were about to transfer Miss Bloom's body onto the stretcher.

"Wait," Jason said, his authoritative demeanor forcing the men to pause. "I need to examine the body."

"And who might you be?" the older of the two undertakers demanded.

"I'm a surgeon, and this is Inspector Haze of Scotland Yard."

Daniel held up his warrant card, which the older man peered at pointedly before nodding to his assistant to step aside. He clearly had no wish to tangle with the police.

"All right, but be quick about it," he grumbled. "We're expected back with the body."

"If you would kindly wait outside," Jason said to the undertakers, and shut the door as soon as they departed.

Daniel remained by the door as he watched Jason go about the examination. He pulled up the eyelids and stared into Miss Bloom's glassy pupils, looked inside the mouth, and sniffed audibly. He then examined the hands, the feet, and the abdomen, and searched for any marks or bruises on the cold, gray skin of the deceased. Daniel looked away when Jason moved on to the more intimate areas of the body, not so much out of respect for the late Miss Bloom but because he couldn't bear to watch.

"How long has she been dead?" he asked once Jason pulled down the nightgown Miss Bloom was still wearing.

"Twelve to fourteen hours, at a guess."

Jason poured some water into the bowl on the makeshift washstand in the corner and washed his hands thoroughly, using the cake of lavender soap he found on a matching soap dish.

"Anything suspicious?" Daniel asked.

"Nothing obvious," Jason replied.

"Might she have died of natural causes?"

"She might have," Jason conceded, but he didn't sound convinced.

"Will you perform a postmortem?"

"I may need to, but let me speak to Miss Akers first." Jason opened the door, motioning for the undertakers to come inside. "This woman is not to be buried until you have express permission from Scotland Yard," he told the older man.

"What's this about, then?" the man demanded.

"There might be some question as to how she died," Daniel said.

"Ye mean she were murdered?" the younger man said, his eyes widening in shock.

"She may have been," Jason said.

"She don't look like she died by violence."

"No, she doesn't, but that doesn't mean someone didn't help her along," Jason replied patiently.

"Poison, ye mean?" the man asked, giving Jason a knowing look.

"Ever thought of applying to the Police Service? You just might have what it takes to become a detective." Jason might have been joking, but the young man puffed out his chest with pride, his eyes glowing with the praise.

"Ye reckon? That would be something. Me a police detective."

"Shut your gob and grab the other side," the older man said, clearly tired of the exchange. "We've got work to be getting on with."

The younger man grabbed Miss Bloom by the ankles, and the two men lowered her onto the waiting stretcher. They then maneuvered it through the door and down the stairs. Once they were gone, Jason invited Polly Akers to join them in the parlor. He and Daniel sat down, but Polly remained standing, her fingers pleating the fabric of her snotty apron.

"What did Miss Bloom do yesterday, Polly? Don't leave anything out, no matter how insignificant," Jason invited.

The woman's feathery eyebrows knitted with concentration. "Well, she woke at her usual time, took breakfast, then went out for her morning constitutional, as she were wont to do."

"Did she go alone?"

"Yes."

"Where did she normally walk?"

"She liked to walk by the river."

"How was she when she returned?" Jason asked.

"She were fine, sir. In good spirits. She asked for tea and then attended to her correspondence until luncheon."

"And then?"

"She lunched at one and then retreated to her favorite chair by the window with a novel."

Jason nodded. There was no need to ask why Miss Bloom preferred the chair by the window. It offered an excellent view of the entire street so that she could note all the comings and goings of her neighbors.

"Did Miss Bloom go out again, or receive any visitors?" Jason prodded.

"Yes, sir," Polly said, her lip curling slightly in what could only be derision. "She saw Mr. Bennington arriving at home just after three and decided to call on him. She thought there might be some new development in the case that resulted in him closing the shop early."

"What time did she leave the house?"

"'Round four. She hoped she'd be invited to stay for tea."

"And was she?" Daniel asked.

"Yes. She said Mr. Bennington didn't have any teacakes, but he had offered her the most divine chocolates. Miss Bloom always was partial to sweets."

"How did she seem when she returned?" Jason asked.

"She seemed fine, sir. Happy, even, as if she'd learned something interesting. She didn't tell me what they talked about," Polly hastened to add.

"And then?" Daniel asked.

"And then she said she were feeling tired and wished to retire early."

"Did she have anything to eat later in the evening?" Jason asked.

"No. She said she weren't hungry."

"Was that usual?"

"It wasn't *un*usual. If she didn't eat her supper, I just saved it for the next day's luncheon. I helped her to bed, drew the curtains, wished her goodnight, and shut the door."

"Did you hear anything after that?" Jason asked.

"Like what?" Polly asked, staring at him round-eyed.

"Like retching. Did you take out the chamber pot this morning?"

"It were empty, sir."

Jason sighed with impatience. "Thank you, Polly. You were very helpful."

"Was I?" Polly asked, clearly pleased to have been thanked for her contribution.

"You were," Jason assured her. "What will you do now that your mistress is gone?"

"I don't rightly know, sir. I suppose I'll wait until the funeral, then start looking for a new situation."

"Did Miss Bloom own this house?"

"No, sir, but the rent's paid up till the end of the month."

"Good luck to you, then," Jason said.

"What are you thinking, Jason?" Daniel asked as soon as Polly left the room.

"I'm thinking we need to find those chocolates. It's too much of a coincidence that Miss Bloom died after calling on Alan Bennington."

Daniel nodded in agreement. "Perhaps Miss Bloom knew more then she let on and tried to sell the information to Alan Bennington."

"And he just happened to have slow-acting poison on hand?" Jason shook his head. "If Alan Bennington is in any way responsible for the death of Miss Bloom, it had to have been planned."

"But how could he know that Miss Bloom would call on him?" Daniel mused.

"Oh, he knew," Jason replied. "It wasn't a matter of if, but of when."

Daniel pushed to his feet. "Let's go have a word with Mr. Bennington, then."

Daniel copied the name and address of the undertakers from the instructions Miss Bloom had left for Polly, then they headed across the street.

"The master's not here," Nell said when she opened the door to them. "He went to the shop."

"May we come in for a moment?" Daniel asked.

Nell reluctantly stepped aside, and the two men entered the foyer.

"Did Mr. Bennington come home early yesterday?" Daniel inquired.

Nell gaped at him as if he were clairvoyant. "Yes, he did. He seemed in very low spirits," she added sympathetically.

"Nell, were you here when Miss Bloom came by yesterday?" Jason asked.

"Yes, sir."

"Did you make the tea?"

"Yes, sir."

"And the chocolates. Where had they come from?"

"The master bought them before the mistress—" Nell stumbled on her words, her young face pinched with grief. "Well, there was nothing to offer Miss Bloom, so he asked me to set out the box."

"Was the box still full?" Jason asked.

"Yes, sir."

"How many chocolates did Miss Bloom have?"

Nell shrugged. "I don't know, sir. The box was half empty when I cleared away the tea things."

"Did Mr. Bennington have any chocolates?" Jason asked.

"I don't know, sir. I left the room after I brought in the tea tray."

"Where is the box of chocolates now?"

"It's in the kitchen."

"Can you please get it," Jason said.

Nell retreated to the kitchen but returned empty-handed. "It's not there," she said, looking perplexed. "There were at least four pieces left. I think maybe the master ate them last night."

"Nell, where's the rubbish?" Daniel asked.

Nell took them through to the kitchen and pointed to a covered bucket in the corner.

"Do you have a newspaper?" Jason asked.

Nell shook her head. "Not today's edition. Mr. Bennington usually buys a paper on the way to the shop."

"Any newspaper," Jason clarified.

Nell brought a newspaper that was a few days old, and Jason spread it on the kitchen floor before dumping the contents of the bucket onto it. The box of chocolates was securely wrapped in several sheets of brown paper, as if someone hadn't wanted anyone to notice it. Jason unwrapped it and lifted the top. Four pieces lay nestled inside the box. Two spaces were empty. Jason set the box aside, folded the newspaper around the trash, and stuffed the lot back into the bucket, leaving the floor clean. Nell's look of gratitude wasn't lost on Daniel.

"Thank you, Nell," Jason said, and headed for the door.

"What do you mean to do?" Daniel asked once they were outside.

"I will take the remaining pieces to the hospital chemist. He might be able to help me figure out if the chocolates had been tampered with."

"I'll come with you," Daniel said. "But first, let's stop by the Yard. I need to update Ransome and ask him to authorize a postmortem on Miss Bloom. The undertakers will not release the body unless I present them with an official request."

"Why not?" Jason asked.

"Since there's no family to give their permission, they are responsible for Miss Bloom's earthly remains. If they were at liberty to hand over bodies, the anatomists would be lining up at the back door."

Given the demand for bodies by the medical schools and private anatomists, the remains of the dead had to be guarded, even well after death. Many families took turns watching a fresh grave to prevent their loved ones from being dug up in the middle of the night and sold to men of science. They only gave up on their vigil once the body was sufficiently decomposed to render it safe from the resurrection men.

"Haze, Lord Redmond, my office please," Superintendent Ransome called as soon as the two men walked through the door.

Jason and Daniel dropped off their things in Daniel's office and hastened to comply with Ransome's request.

Chapter 37

John Ransome leaned back in his chair, his gaze wary. "So, you don't believe Miss Bloom died of natural causes," he said, directing the statement to Jason.

"It's too coincidental that she died after paying a call on Alan Bennington."

"But what reason would Alan Bennington have to kill Miss Bloom?"

"She may have been blackmailing him as well," Daniel cut in, and was rewarded with a reproachful stare from the superintendent.

"With what?"

"Perhaps she found out what his wife was getting up to," Daniel replied.

"Alan Bennington has a mistress who's expecting his child. If he wished to be rid of his wife, all he had to do was use the photographs against her. No judge would deny him a divorce," Ransome pointed out. "Were I to find myself in his position, I would thank Miss Bloom for providing me with ammunition against the woman."

"Perhaps he didn't wish the world to know the truth of his marriage," Daniel replied. "Imagine the scandal. The case would almost certainly get into the papers."

"If Miss Bloom was a blackmailer, she may have been blackmailing any number of people, which widens the net," John Ransome pointed out.

"According to Miss Akers, her mistress saw only Alan Bennington yesterday."

"Miss Akers also said that Miss Bloom went for a walk. Perhaps she encountered someone else who had a score to settle."

"Miss Bloom went for a walk in the morning," Jason cut in. "In order for her to die that night, the poison would have to have been extremely slow-acting."

"Would not most poisons kill her within a short time of ingesting them?" Ransome asked.

"Yes, they would."

"So there is a chance that she died of natural causes. She might have suffered a heart attack, or an apoplexy. Is that not so?" Ransome demanded, his attention on Jason.

"Yes, that is a definite possibility."

Ransome sighed. He looked tired and irritable. "Gentlemen, because of the newspaper coverage of this case, I'm under intense scrutiny, from both the public and my superiors. We need to wrap up this case, and focusing on a woman of advancing years who may or may not have been poisoned is a waste of time and resources. To date, no one has mentioned Miss Bloom in connection with Eliza Bennington's murder. Miss Bloom was not the one to strike her over the head or lay her body in that boat. Find the person who did," he said decisively. "And Haze—"

John Ransome never got a chance to finish the sentence because Sergeant Meadows erupted into the office, the door slamming against the wall in his agitation.

"What is the meaning of this, Sergeant?" Ransome bellowed, but the sergeant's pleading gaze was fixed on Jason.

"Lord Redmond, Constable Napier has taken ill," he cried. "Please, come quickly."

Jason sprang to his feet and dashed after Sergeant Meadows, who left without so much as apologizing to his superior.

They found Constable Napier in the back room, where the men ate their sandwiches and brewed tea on the potbellied stove in the corner. The young man was sprawled in his chair, his head thrown back, his eyes closed, his long legs stretched out before him. He was deathly pale, and a sheen of sweat had broken out on his forehead.

"Constable," Jason called to him as he gently slapped the side of his face to rouse him. "Clive," he called more insistently. "Clive, can you hear me?"

Constable Napier muttered something incomprehensible, and then his head lolled to the side.

"Oh, Lord," Sergeant Meadows moaned. "He's given up the ghost."

"He hasn't," Jason replied gently.

Sergeant Meadows practically quivered with relief. "Will he be all right, then?"

Jason replied with a question of his own. "Sergeant, what did Constable Napier eat?"

"I don't know. I wasn't here. Constable Collins came in to make tea and found him."

"He ate the chocolates," Constable Collins said. He had materialized in the doorway, the box they'd taken from Alan Bennington's residence in his hands, now empty. "He saw the box on Inspector Haze's desk and helped himself. Clive could never resist a sweet," he added. His gaze was anxious as it slid to his friend.

"I need a bucket," Jason said.

A bucket was instantly produced, and Jason pushed Constable Napier forward and shoved the bucket between his feet. Jason pushed his fingers into the constable's mouth until he began to gag, and then a stream of vomit erupted from his pale lips, his eyes opening, his gaze glazed with incomprehension. Jason held the young man's head over the bucket, speaking to him gently.

"You'll be fine, Clive. Just get it all out." He then turned to Constable Collins. "Get him some water, Constable."

Once Constable Napier finished vomiting, he looked up at Jason with heavy-lidded eyes. "I'm sorry," he muttered. "I was just so hungry."

"It's all right. You'll be just fine," Jason assured him. "Drink all the water and just sit quietly for a while."

"I have my duties," Constable Napier protested, but Jason patted him on the shoulder.

"Your duties can wait. We must make sure there are no lasting ill effects."

"Yes, sir," the young man replied, his frightened gaze on John Ransome, who'd appeared in the doorway and was glowering viciously at everyone in the room, but especially Daniel.

"I'm sorry, sir," Constable Napier moaned, his cheeks turning a mottled red.

"It's all right, Constable. I'm just glad you're well, even if you did eat the evidence that Inspector Haze had so carelessly left lying around without warning anyone of the danger. But I suppose we need no further proof that Miss Bloom was poisoned."

"How could I have known?" Daniel began, outraged by the accusation, but Ransome held up his hand, a ghost of a smile tugging at his mouth. "Haze, you really should know by now that anything edible has a way of disappearing around here, especially sweets."

He turned to Sergeant Meadows and Constable Collins. "Arrest Alan Bennington, if he hasn't fled by now," he added with disgust. "Lord Redmond, if you would remain on hand to make sure Constable Napier doesn't relapse."

"Of course." Jason smiled encouragingly at Clive Napier, who still looked shamefaced and a bit green around the gills.

He and Daniel sat with Constable Napier for a half hour, then retreated to a nearby chophouse, since they were both ravenously hungry and the constables had yet to return with the suspect. Once orders were placed for beefsteak served with fried potatoes and buttered peas, Daniel asked the question that had been niggling at him since he'd seen the sorry state Constable Napier had been in.

"It took hours for the poison to affect Miss Bloom, but Constable Napier couldn't have eaten the chocolates more than a few minutes before he was taken ill. Why would that be?"

Jason took a sip of his wine and set the glass down. "There are several reasons. The box originally contained six chocolates. Four were left, so Miss Bloom had only consumed two, half the amount Constable Napier ate. Miss Bloom had undigested food in her stomach left over from the luncheon she'd taken a few hours before. By his own admission, Constable Napier was famished, so much so that he took chocolates off your desk without permission. There was nothing in his stomach to dilute the poison save the tea he'd drunk with the chocolates. Constable Napier is also thin and wiry, whereas Miss Bloom was rather stout. It takes a higher dose to poison a corpulent person."

Daniel nodded. The reasons Jason listed made perfect sense. "Can you identify the poison that was used?"

Jason shook his head. "Even if we still had the chocolates, it's not possible to break down the compounds in order to isolate the poison, but I can make an educated guess based on what I've seen. Neither victim seemed to experience vomiting, diarrhea, or severe confusion. Clive Napier appeared to be falling into a deep sleep, and Miss Bloom said she wished to retire early. The only two slow-acting agents I can think of are ricin and morphine. Ricin causes violent stomach pains, but morphine, when administered in large doses, will send the victim into a deep sleep that will eventually result in death."

"How difficult would it be to find this out without arousing suspicion?" Daniel asked.

"Alan Bennington owns a bookshop. There must be medical volumes on his shelves, as well as books on botany and chemistry. He would have had plenty of time to research if he meant to poison someone."

Daniel waited until the waiter placed their meals before them and left before continuing with his train of thought. "We have fairly conclusive evidence that Alan Bennington murdered Miss Bloom, but that still doesn't bring us any closer to figuring out who killed his wife. If he could poison Miss Bloom, he could just as easily have poisoned Eliza. Why bother with all the rest of it?"

Jason appeared to be deep in thought, then set down his knife and fork, as if something monumental had just occurred to him.

"Alan Bennington would be glad to be rid of the wife who had not only deeply humiliated him but failed to produce children. Janet Reynolds would be equally glad to be rid of Miss Bloom, who'd been blackmailing her for years. What if they made a pact to help each other?"

Daniel shook his head in disbelief. "That would be an idea of staggering genius, since the police would be hard pressed to figure out the motive for the murders."

"Precisely," Jason said, picking up his utensils again. "Think about it. We have eyewitness accounts of a young man leading Eliza Bennington down to the riverbank. The young man was described as being stout but having a thin, youthful face. A woman with a generous bosom, like Janet Reynolds, would look barrel-chested if dressed as a man, but her smooth face would look boyish from a distance. Mary Smith thought the young man was someone known to Eliza, but she had seemed surprised."

"It would be surprising indeed to come upon one's sister-in-law dressed as a man," Daniel replied.

"So, Janet kills Eliza, setting Alan Bennington free. Perhaps he would have waited until the case was closed to deal with Miss Bloom, but Janet, in her obvious distress, revealed to us that Miss Bloom was blackmailing her, so it became imperative to silence her in case she spilled any incriminating secrets. We may never have even known she was dead if we hadn't decided to speak to her again," Jason stressed.

"The perfect murder," Daniel mused, "performed by two people who both had something valuable to gain but wouldn't be connected to the crimes since neither had an obvious motive."

"Had Clive Napier not eaten the chocolates, God Bless his guileless little heart, we'd have no concrete evidence that Miss Bloom was poisoned and no obvious link to Alan Bennington."

"Unless we tested the chocolates on an animal, but I'd hate to do that," Daniel said. "It's not uncommon, but it does seem awfully cruel."

Jason nodded his agreement.

"I think it's time we brought Janet Reynolds in," Daniel said as he pushed away his empty plate. "If we allow Alan Bennington to think that Janet Reynolds has confessed to the scheme, and let Janet Reynolds think Alan Bennington has betrayed her, we just might get a confession."

"Would a confession obtained by misleading the suspect be admissible in court?" Jason asked.

"Implying that I know more than I do is hardly a crime," Daniel replied. "I would be remiss in my duties if I didn't test my theories."

"Then I think it's time we spoke to them both. Separately."

"This promises to be a long night," Daniel said, but he felt energized for the first time in days and was relieved that Jason would be by his side. "Ready?" he asked once he thought Jason was finished with his meal.

"As I'll ever be," Jason replied with a conspiratorial grin.

Chapter 38

Even though Alan Bennington was anxiously pacing in one of the cells, Daniel and Jason decided to wait until Janet Reynolds was brought in and interview her first. The more information they had to work with, the better chance of extracting at least one confession, and Janet Reynolds seemed like the easier one to break. The arrival of Mrs. Reynolds was marked by a commotion in the vestibule, her husband's voice booming over the whimpering of his wife.

"What is the meaning of this?" he thundered as soon as Daniel and Jason joined the melee. "How dare you drag my wife out of her home in full view of the neighbors and haul her here like a common criminal when she's done nothing wrong," he cried.

"If we got it wrong, Mrs. Reynolds will be released with our apologies," Daniel replied calmly.

"I don't need your damned apology," Reynolds exclaimed. "On what grounds have you arrested her?"

"We believe she had a hand in your sister's murder," Jason said.

"Poppycock! Utter poppycock! Janet and Eliza were like sisters. You are trying to cover up your incompetence by targeting an innocent woman. I will not stand for this. I am going to involve my solicitor."

"That is your right," Daniel replied. The more Alastair Reynolds raged, the more convinced he felt that they were on the right track.

"You'll be hearing from me!" Alastair Reynolds stormed from the building, leaving his mewling wife to gape after him.

"Please, step this way, Mrs. Reynolds," Daniel invited.

There seemed little need to cuff the woman, so they waited until she removed her coat and hat and took a seat at the table, her demeanor that of a frightened rabbit.

"Why did you bring me here, Inspector?" she asked, her voice so low that Daniel could barely hear her.

Daniel glanced at Jason, urging him to take this question.

"Mrs. Reynolds, Miss Orchid Bloom, or Dorcas Butte, as she was known to you, died last night after taking tea with Alan Bennington. We were able to ascertain that her death was caused by poisoned chocolates that were offered to her by Mr. Bennington."

Janet Reynolds looked perplexed. "But I don't understand," she muttered. "What's that to do with me?"

"Miss Bloom was blackmailing you. Alan Bennington had a wife he wished to rid himself of. Both individuals died within a week of each other," Daniel explained.

"So?" Janet Reynolds looked more defiant than she had only a moment ago, no doubt assuming that was all the proof they had.

"You and Alan Bennington made a pact to rid each other of people who had become a liability," Jason said. "In fact, both Miss Bloom and Eliza Bennington were a danger to you, were they not?"

"That's an absurd suggestion."

"Is it?" Daniel asked. "We have proof of your involvement with Tristan Carmichael. If Eliza had discovered that you have a history with a man who's supplying London with illicit images, you'd have much to lose."

"That would be the pot calling the kettle black, wouldn't it?" Janet Reynolds scoffed.

"Not really. According to you, Eliza Bennington was looking for a way out. Once she had earned enough money, she would have gone to America, or abroad. But she would still be in possession of certain knowledge, which would mean you could never feel truly safe, not as long as you were married to her brother." Daniel paused for effect. "Meanwhile, Alan Bennington wished to be with his lover but couldn't marry her, stuck as he was with a wife who couldn't give him children and made him feel inadequate. Suddenly, you're both free of the people who so oppressed you."

Janet looked away, fixing her gaze on the window, where night had settled on London.

"Mrs. Reynolds," Daniel tried again. "You have a child to think of."

"A child I would lose if the truth ever came out," the woman retorted. "Do you have any idea what it's like to live in constant fear of losing everything you hold dear, either of you?"

Daniel swallowed the lump that had formed in his throat. He'd already lost two of the people he held dear, his wife to suicide and his young son to a terrible accident, and Jason had lost much as well, but they were not the ones suspected of murder.

"The truth of your past need never leave this room," Daniel said. "But you must tell us what happened."

For the first time, Janet looked truly frightened. "And if I tell you, will I go free?"

"That depends on the level of your involvement."

Janet sighed deeply and nodded, her shoulders sagging with the weight of defeat. She was intelligent enough to understand that she wouldn't simply walk away from the accusation, but she might still hope to shift most of the blame onto someone else and mitigate her guilt.

"I met Alan when I first arrived in London. He was an actor and went by the name Sebastian Rydell on the stage. Alan put in a good word for me when I tried out for the chorus. I had big dreams," Janet said with a wry smile. "I thought I could become a star and have my pick of wealthy men. But even though I eventually tried out for a few parts, I was told I had neither the looks nor the talent to become the next big thing. 'Forgettable' was the word the director used to describe me."

She sighed and continued. "Alan and I were lovers, but our relationship was a casual one. No words of love were ever spoken between us, and neither had very much to offer the other. That was when we hatched a plan to get ahead in the world. Alan would help me meet a suitable gentleman, and I would help him make an advantageous match in return. We never aimed very high because there was always the threat of discovery if we tried to marry into a distinguished family. We simply wanted a comfortable, secure life."

Janet suddenly looked much older than a woman in her mid-twenties. "Alan posed as a family friend and escorted me to all the venues where a young lady might meet a gentleman. We went to music recitals, exhibitions, gardens, and the British Museum. That's where I met Alastair," she said with a wistful smile.

"It was so easy. I made sure to drop a glove as I passed by him. He picked it up and ran after me, by which time Alan had melted away, leaving me to converse with the gentleman. The first few times Alastair and I met in public, but once I knew he was smitten, it was time to move to the next phase. Besides, there were several other contenders by that stage, and I had to convince them I was a respectable young lady worthy of becoming their wife. Alan and I found furnished rooms near Leicester Square and hired a maidservant and an elderly lady to act as chaperone. We could only afford to keep the pretense up for a month, but that was all it took. I had three offers of marriage, but it was Alastair I really liked. We were married within a fortnight since neither of us wanted a big wedding."

Janet smiled dolefully as she recalled that time. "And then it was time to help Alan."

"Did your husband not realize that he'd already met Alan?" Jason asked.

Janet shook her head. "Alastair tends to look through people rather than at them, so he rarely recalls people he's met in passing, and Alan always made himself scarce when Alastair called. By the time I introduced Alan to Eliza, Alastair had completely forgotten that they'd met a year before, especially since I told him that Mr. Rydell had gone abroad. I never expected Eliza to take an interest in Alan, but she did. And she was not only beautiful but would receive a sizeable portion. Alan was thrilled and quickly ended things with Nancy Pruitt."

"How did he come by the shop?" Daniel asked.

Janet looked uncomfortable. "Alan often went to the shop to read, since he couldn't afford to keep buying books. He's a voracious reader, Alan," she added. "He befriended the old man who owned it, Mr. Lemuel Franken, and often took over while Mr. Franken went home to take a rest. When he died, Alan destroyed the will and made a new will in his favor, forging Mr. Franken's signature. He had no family to speak of, and the cousin from York who tried to claim the estate had no proof that the shop was left to him."

"What happened to Eliza's money?" Jason asked the question that was on Daniel's mind. Alan Bennington was hardly living the high life.

"Alan had debts, and he has no head for numbers," Janet said. "And then the blackmail began."

"Was Alan Bennington paying off Miss Bloom?" Daniel asked.

Janet nodded. "My husband is rather tight-fisted, so I could ill afford to pay the woman every month. Not without asking

Alastair for money. Alan helped me and would have continued to do so if it wasn't for the photographs."

"Photographs of you?"

"Photographs of Eliza. Like most shopkeepers in the Strand, Alan was selling pornography under the table. Eventually, he came face to face with a photograph of his own wife. They had already grown apart, but now Alan felt betrayed and humiliated. He may have gone on like that if Lorna hadn't told him she was with child. Alan had always longed for children, you see," Janet said, her eyes warm. "As did I. I suppose people who grow up as we did, with little love, always long for a large, close family."

"So that was the last straw?" Jason asked.

"Yes. Alan wanted to be rid of Eliza, and I needed to free myself from Dorcas Butte."

"So you figured out how to free yourselves in a way that would not lead the police to your door," Daniel concluded.

"I didn't want to kill Eliza," Janet wailed, wringing her hands in agitation. "I really didn't. She would have been happy to leave and start a new life elsewhere, but Alan said that as long as Eliza was alive, she was his wife before God and the law, and he couldn't marry Lorna and be a father to his child. He said he would tell Alastair about my past if I didn't do my part. And he needed to make sure she was found so that there would be no doubt." Janet angrily wiped away the tears that had started to fall. "He wanted me to leave her naked. He said that if she liked taking off her clothes that much, then that's the way she should be remembered."

"So what did you do?" Jason asked.

"I knew Eliza went out on Wednesdays, and I had a good idea of where she went. I had followed her a few times to Eric Dawson's studio. I waited until Alastair was away in Manchester, dressed in his old clothes, and followed Eliza. Except this time, she went to Oliver's Wharf. I didn't think I could go through with it. Eliza was my friend, and I cared about her, but when I saw Tristan

255

Carmichael, I knew I had no choice. My past would come to haunt me otherwise, and I would never be free."

Janet drew a deep breath and continued. "After Eliza left the studio, I approached her on Wapping High Street. She seemed out of sorts, dazed and confused, and it took her a moment to recognize me. She became frightened and tried to walk away, so I took her by the arm and led her toward Wapping Old Stairs, where it was dark and far away enough from the street not to be seen. I was going to get her down to the riverbank and use the shawl I'd worn under my coat to strangle her, but she was carrying on, so I picked up a rock and bashed her on the back of the head. She was stunned but still alive, so I got her down the steps. That's when I saw the dinghy."

"What was the significance of the dinghy?" Jason asked.

"Eliza loved mermaids. She thought they were beautiful and mystical and synonymous with freedom. So I had an idea. I removed her clothes and stuffed them into my pack, then laid her out in the dinghy. But I couldn't bear to leave her naked. It seemed so cruel, and I had no wish for Alastair and my father-in-law to be shamed. So I took the shawl and wrapped it around her hips and legs to give her some modesty and make her look like a mermaid. There was a bunch of flowers someone had thrown away, and I took the flowers and spread them over Eliza. I wanted to give her something beautiful in death. It was a form of atonement," Janet said.

"And then you pushed the dinghy into the water, knowing Eliza would die out there in her own good time," Jason said angrily.

"I never pushed it into the water. I just left her there. I knew she didn't have long." Janet shuddered, as if she were recalling that awful moment. "It was either Eliza or my own life, and my family."

"So then, as soon as Alan Bennington was free, he carried out his end of the bargain?" Daniel asked.

"He was going to wait a few weeks, but I'd let it slip when you questioned me that Dorcas was blackmailing me, and Alan was afraid you'd arrest her, and she'd spill all our secrets. So he poisoned Dorcas Butte with morphine-laced chocolates."

Janet gazed at Daniel, her eyes swimming with tears. "Please, Inspector Haze, have mercy on me. I never wanted any of this. I had been under duress for years, and I was frightened of losing my family. Please, recommend leniency," she pleaded.

"It's not up to me to decide what happens to you, Mrs. Reynolds, but I will mark it in my report that you have confessed, and you claim to have been coerced."

"But I was coerced," she cried.

"Let's just see what Mr. Bennington has to say, shall we?" Daniel said.

Janet slid lower in her chair, a faraway look entering her eyes. "It's all over," she whispered. "Alastair will never forgive me, even if I don't get the noose."

"I can't speak for your husband, Mrs. Reynolds, but you will be charged with the murder of Eliza Bennington and transported to prison to await trial."

Janet Reynolds nodded. "Please, can I have some paper, ink, and a pen? I would like to write a letter to my son."

"Of course," Daniel said. "I will have the items brought to your cell."

Chapter 39

Alan Bennington was just about spitting nails by the time he was brought up. "This is harassment is what it is!" he cried. "Surely there's a law against interrogating a man daily in relation to the same crime."

"There isn't," Daniel said. "And we're here to talk about a different crime. Sit down, Mr. Bennington."

Alan slumped into the chair, his angry gaze fixed on Daniel. "So, what is it this time?"

"Oh, I think you know," Daniel replied coyly.

"Do I?"

"Miss Bloom was found dead this morning."

"My condolences," Alan Bennington spat.

"You killed her," Jason interjected.

"Where's your proof, Lord Redmond?"

Daniel noticed that Alan Bennington didn't bother to claim innocence. He was more interested in how much evidence they really had, which in itself was almost an admission of guilt.

"We have all the proof we need," Jason replied calmly.

"Along with a signed confession from Janet Reynolds. So, it seems you knew all about your wife's activities," Daniel said. He'd hoped to rile Alan Bennington into an outburst, but Alan wasn't so easily manipulated.

"No comment," he snapped.

"What happened to all your wife's money, Mr. Bennington? Did you truly spend it, or did you stash it somewhere, just in case?" Jason asked.

"No comment."

"You are too clever by half to have burned through it already."

Alan Bennington did not reply, but the smugness in his gaze was answer enough. He wasn't nearly as hapless as everyone had inferred.

"Mr. Bennington, we know you conspired with Janet Reynolds to murder Eliza Bennington and Orchid Bloom, and we have enough evidence to charge you," Daniel stated.

Alan rested his cuffed hands on the table, the chain between the cuffs rattling against the wood, and bowed his head. His shoulders slumped in defeat, and Daniel felt a momentary sense of satisfaction at having solved this most complicated of cases. He would never have cracked it without Jason's help, and he had turned to Jason to make a comment to that effect when Alan Bennington lunged out of the chair, his eyes blazing, his teeth bared in a ferocious grimace of fury.

Jason sprang to his feet in alarm, but Daniel wasn't as quick. Alan Bennington was behind him in an instant, the chain between the cuffs encircling Daniel's throat, the back of his head pressed against Alan Bennington's chest, the beating of the man's heart thudding in Daniel's ears. He gasped for breath as the iron links pushed painfully against his Adam's apple, choking him as Alan tightened his grip. Daniel clawed at the chain but couldn't get his fingers between the iron and the tender skin of his throat.

Dark spots appeared before Daniel's eyes, there was a tingling sensation in his extremities, and his heart galloped as his chest constricted with terror. All he could think of was Charlotte, her little face floating before Daniel's bulging eyes as he mourned all the things he would miss if he were to die. Was he about to die? Was this how it was all going to end?

And then suddenly it was all over. The chain loosened as Alan Bennington crumpled atop Daniel, pinning him to the table with his weight. Daniel was about to throw him off but realized that the chain was still around his neck, and he would flip backward if Alan went over.

Setting the chair he'd used to strike the man back in place, Jason quickly freed Daniel and pushed the limp form of Alan Bennington into the chair before giving Daniel his full attention. "Are you okay?" he asked.

Daniel nodded and coughed, then rubbed his throat to ease the ache that had settled there. He could still feel the pressure of the links and was sure they were imprinted on his skin. The bruises would remain long after Alan Bennington had been sent down to await trial.

"I'm okay," he croaked, using Jason's odd expression back to him. "I'm more than okay." He got to his feet and hobbled to the door. "Constable Napier," he called out, "please take Mr. Bennington back to the cells. And bring some writing implements to Mrs. Reynolds. She wishes to write a letter."

"Mr. Reynolds is in the foyer, sir, with his solicitor," Constable Napier said as he surveyed the scene before him. He didn't ask why the suspect was unconscious or why blood was seeping from the back of his head. Just as he made no comment about Daniel's disheveled state or the livid red marks that must have shown on his throat.

Daniel nodded and returned to his seat, his knees suddenly buckling beneath him. "I'll speak to them shortly," he muttered, and laid his head down on the table, hoping the dizziness and colorful stars that floated before his eyes would dissipate if he closed his eyes for a spell.

Chapter 40

It was close to midnight by the time Jason got home. He was exhausted but knew he wouldn't be able to sleep, so he went down to the kitchen. He'd have a cup of warm milk and see if he could find anything in the larder to tide him over till breakfast. He wasn't surprised to find Mrs. Dodson sitting at the worn pine table, a cup of tea in her work-roughened hands.

"Hard day?" she asked, taking in Jason's crumpled appearance.

He nodded, unable to speak.

"Would you like a cup of tea?"

"A glass of warm milk, I think," Jason replied as he dropped wearily onto the bench. "And if there are any leftovers..."

"Would you like me to heat up your supper?"

"No. Maybe just some bread and cheese," Jason said. He couldn't stomach anything heavier than that at the moment.

"Of course."

Mrs. Dodson filled a pan with milk and set it to warm, then went about organizing Jason's meal while he sat at the table, staring numbly at the darkness beyond the window. Their relief at finally solving the case had been short-lived. It was during the heated exchange with Mr. Hoyt, the Reynolds' solicitor, that Constable Napier had come banging on the door, calling for help.

"What happened?" Daniel had demanded.

"Your lordship, come quick," Constable Napier cried, his face pale and his gaze dazed for the second time that day. "Hurry, please!"

Jason raced after the young constable, his feet barely touching the steps that led to the cells below. He could hear Alan

Bennington's desperate cries, but no sound came from Janet Reynolds' cell. Jason saw it before he even reached the door, thick crimson liquid slowly spreading across the floor, seeping into the crevices between the flagstones, and glistening darkly as it began to congeal.

"No!" he cried when he saw Janet Reynolds.

She lay on the narrow bunk, her eyes closed, her face bone white. Blood dripped from the mangled wrist that hung limply off the side, the pale green silk of her fashionable dress soaked in blood just above her abdomen as if she'd been disemboweled.

"Mrs. Reynolds," Jason called to her. "Janet," he whispered as he bent over her and placed two fingers on her neck.

The pulse was faint, but she was still alive. Jason pulled out his handkerchief and bandaged the left wrist before accepting the constable's handkerchief to bind the other. The thin fabric instantly sponged up the blood, the white cotton turning nearly black.

"Janet," Jason tried again. "Please, stay with me."

Janet Reynolds' lips were bloodless, her voice barely audible, but Jason heard the words clearly enough. "Let me go."

Jason turned to find Alastair Reynolds standing in the doorway, Daniel behind him. Mr. Reynolds looked shaken, but there was a hard set to his mouth, and the tendons in his throat stood out against the stiff collar of his shirt as he tried to swallow back his tears and his anger.

"Say you forgive me, Alastair," Janet Reynolds pleaded in a whisper, but her husband shook his head, unable to give her absolution.

"You destroyed us, Janet," he said softly, his eyes bright with unshed tears. "You destroyed us," he said again, then turned on his heel and left.

"Can you save her?" Daniel asked as he carefully stepped into the cell, making sure not to step in the quickly spreading blood.

"She's lost a lot of blood."

"How?" Daniel asked, looking around for a razor or a knife.

"She used the nib of the pen," Jason replied.

The poor woman must have been desperate, since it would have taken several attempts to open her veins with the metal tip of the pen. It would have been painful, her suffering prolonged. She had really wanted this, and there was nothing he could do to tether her to this world, not that there was any point. Janet Reynolds was guilty of murder, and the sentence would be death. Whether she died now, by her own hand, or in a few months, the end result would be the same—a young life corrupted by poverty, fear, and anger, then snuffed out in payment for the one she'd stolen from another young woman, who'd been just as angry and just as frightened.

"Is there anything I can do?" Daniel asked.

"No. Go home, Daniel. You look worn out."

"I am," Daniel admitted, but he didn't leave. Instead, he brought in a chair and sat down next to the cot, his hand on Janet Reynolds' shoulder.

It took her nearly an hour to die, and then the constables moved her to the mortuary Jason used for postmortems and cleaned up the cell. There was nothing more either Jason or Daniel could do, but they couldn't seem to find the strength to leave, so they joined John Ransome in his office for a quiet drink, which turned into four, yet none of them were intoxicated when they finally left the building close to eleven o'clock. Watching a young woman die slowly had a sobering effect on one's senses.

Mrs. Dodson set a cheese sandwich and a cup of warm milk before Jason and resumed her seat. "Do you want to talk about it?" she asked in her unassuming, motherly way.

"No. But I would love it if you stayed with me for a little while."

"I had better freshen my tea, then," Mrs. Dodson replied, and refilled her cup from the cozy-covered earthenware teapot.

They sat in silence until Katherine's shadow fell over the table as she materialized in the doorway. She didn't say anything, just sat down next to Jason and rested her head on his shoulder.

Mrs. Dodson finished her tea and pushed to her feet. "Tomorrow is another day, Captain," she said, addressing him by his rank rather than his title, probably to remind him that in any battle, there were always casualties. "You have lives to save and cases to solve."

Jason nodded and stood, taking Katherine's hand in his and pulling her toward the door. All he wanted was to lose himself in her and forget this miserable day and the lives they had inadvertently ruined, most notably that of the little boy who'd never see his mother again and the child yet to be born who'd likely never meet its father.

Chapter 41

It took Daniel a while to get home, since he'd opted to walk. It was a cold, quiet night, just what he needed to clear his head and calm his aching heart. He knew he wasn't responsible for what had happened. Janet Reynolds and Alan Bennington had sealed their fate the moment they had conspired to murder two people, but it was easier to cope when he didn't have to witness the direct result of his efforts.

Daniel sighed heavily as he let himself into the house and hung up his coat and hat on the coatrack in the tiny foyer. He was surprised to see light glowing through the parlor door and looked in to find Rebecca sitting by the fire, the shawl he'd given her around her shoulders. She looked up but didn't smile. Her gaze was serious, her lips pursed.

"Are you all right?" Daniel asked as he entered the room. He hoped she wouldn't notice the livid bruises on his neck in the light of the dying fire, but Rebecca wasn't really looking at him, at least not in the way that would allow her to really see.

"Can we talk, Daniel?" she asked.

"Of course."

Daniel sank into his favorite chair, wishing only that he could go upstairs and get to bed. Whatever Rebecca wanted to talk about wouldn't bode well for him, and he wasn't sure he had the mental capacity to deal with it just then. He would have preferred to get back to whatever this was in the morning, but he could hardly refuse her a few minutes of his time.

Rebecca stared at the smoldering coals, her shoulders tense, her hands pale in her lap.

"What is it?" Daniel asked, unable to bear the suspense any longer.

"I am giving my notice. I am to be married."

Of all the things Daniel had been expecting, this wasn't one of them, and he sucked in his breath, feeling as if he'd been punched in the gut.

"Who to?"

"Leon Stanley. He was a friend of my father's."

"Have you been seeing him all this time?" Daniel asked, unable to work out how he could have missed something so vital.

Rebecca shook her head. "Leon went out to Argentina about six years ago. He owns a cattle ranch, and he also makes wine," she added dreamily. "He came back to London on business two weeks ago and asked to see me."

"If he was a friend of your father's—"

"Yes, Daniel, he's considerably older. But he's a good man, and he can offer me a safe, comfortable life."

"In Argentina," Daniel said flatly.

"He showed me a photograph of the house. It's quite beautiful. Leon says it's warm and sunny nearly all the time."

Daniel pushed to his feet. "Well, I wish you much joy of each other. How long do I have to find a replacement?"

"A month. Leon would have liked to depart for Argentina in a fortnight, but I don't want to leave you in the lurch."

Daniel gaped at her. "You don't want to leave me in the lurch?" he repeated, incredulous.

"Daniel," Rebecca began, but he raised his hand to silence her.

"I accept your resignation, Miss Grainger. I will place an advertisement for a new nursemaid in the morning. With any luck, I will find a replacement before the week is out."

"Daniel, please!" Rebecca cried.

"What do you expect me to say?" He didn't wish to sound angry, but he was. And hurt.

"Daniel, I really care for you."

"Really? You could have fooled me."

Rebecca got to her feet and came to stand before him, her face raised so she could look at him. "When you were attacked, I was terrified. I thought you were going to die. I realized then that I love you, but I cannot agree to a life as a policeman's wife. It's too frightening. Too uncertain. Leon can offer me security, both financial and emotional."

"Then take it," Daniel replied. "Go to Argentina and be happy, Rebecca. Charlotte and I will get along without you. If we can live without Sarah, we can certainly live without you."

"There's no need to be cruel," Rebecca replied.

"The truth is often cruel. Goodnight, Miss Grainger."

"Goodnight, Inspector Haze."

Daniel trudged up the stairs, shut the door to his bedroom, tore off his clothes, and got into bed. He thought he wouldn't be able to sleep, but he was so weary, his body succumbed to sleep before he had a chance to really mourn everything that had been lost this day.

Epilogue

March 1869

Daniel settled before the fire and opened the book he'd meant to start weeks ago. This was his first Saturday off since he'd returned to work, and he meant to enjoy it, even if Rebecca Grainger was still in residence until the new nursemaid arrived on Wednesday. Rebecca would be leaving on Thursday and moving into a hotel from which she would be married on Saturday. The newlyweds would then sail for Argentina the following Monday. At this point, Daniel wanted nothing more than to see the back of her, since the atmosphere in the house was tense and uncomfortable as they had been avoiding each other. It was easier during the week when Daniel was at work, and then Rebecca would retire to her room as soon as he arrived and take her supper on a tray. Even Grace had been subdued, sensing the tension and choosing to stay as far away from it as possible and finding solace in Charlotte, who only vaguely understood that things were about to change yet again.

Daniel glanced at the clock. It was past noon, and Rebecca and Charlotte should have been back from their walk by now. Charlotte would be ready for her luncheon and afternoon nap, and it seemed to have grown darker outside, the heavens threatening to open at any minute. Daniel hoped they wouldn't get soaked. He had just finished the first chapter when there was a loud knock on the door. Hoping it was Rebecca, Daniel went to answer the door and was surprised to find Sergeant Meadows on the doorstep.

"Sergeant, what's happened?" he asked.

Sergeant Meadows normally wouldn't be the one sent to fetch him if he was needed. Such tasks were relegated to the constables. Sergeant Meadows looked nervous and held his helmet against his side as if it were likely to abscond. "Inspector Haze, I'm afraid I have some rather distressing news."

The sergeant stepped from foot to foot, his gaze fixed on Daniel's shoulder rather than his face.

"Well, what is it, man?" Daniel demanded. The sergeant was making him nervous.

"A woman was found dead in St. John's churchyard. A passerby identified her as your daughter's nursemaid, Miss Grainger."

"Where's my daughter?" Daniel cried, his heart slamming urgently in his chest.

Sergeant Meadows looked like he was about to cry. "I don't know, sir. There was no sign of the child when we arrived."

Daniel felt as if time had suddenly stopped, and all the color had been leached from the world. He thought he was going to be sick and grabbed on to the doorpost, but then suddenly, there was Jason, jumping out of the brougham and hurrying toward them.

"Daniel, we'll find her," he said, but all Daniel saw was the movement of his lips. The roaring in his head prevented him for hearing anything but his own erratic heartbeat.

"We'll find her," Jason repeated, but Daniel simply staggered away. This was one case he couldn't afford not to solve, because this time, it was personal.

The End

Please turn the page for an excerpt from

Murder Among the Dead

A Redmond and Haze Mystery Book 12

An Excerpt from Murder Among the Dead

Prologue

The silence was almost eerie, even the birds preferring to keep away from the neglected graveyard. Both ancient and more recent tombstones lined the narrow paths, some inscriptions still sharp, others nearly obliterated by time. The sky had darkened, and rain seemed imminent, but the crisp air held the promise of a bracing walk.

Reverend Brompton ambled along the overgrown path, enjoying the solitude that so often eluded him in his line of work. The burial ground was no longer in use, so there was little chance of being disturbed, although the occasional trespasser did cross his path. Some people were as drawn to graveyards as others were to public houses or dens of ill repute. They found some strange sensual pleasure in being surrounded by the dead, and some actually believed that the veil between the worlds could be drawn aside long enough to speak to the departed. The reverend thought this was utter poppycock and would say as much to anyone who asked, but thankfully, none of his parishioners were foolish enough to seek such heathen pursuits.

The reverend's footsteps inevitably turned toward Ezekiel. It was distinctly unministerial to name a headstone, but the Reverend Brompton thought the marble angel truly beautiful and the meaning of the name, "God is Strong," undeniably appropriate to its purpose. As he drew closer, he saw her. She rested on the marble slab at Ezekiel's feet, her skirts spread out around her, her fair hair framing her pale face, and her hands folded on her breast as if she were praying. The woman's gaze was turned up to the sky, but Ezekiel's shadow fell upon her face, making her features difficult to make out.

Outraged by such blatant disrespect for the dead, the Reverend Brompton hastened toward the woman, about to chastise her in the strongest of terms for her transgression when he realized that she hadn't moved the entire time he'd had her in his sights. His footsteps slowing of their own accord, the reverend drew in a shaky breath as he realized the beautiful young woman gazing up at Ezekiel with such adoration was actually quite dead.

Chapter 1

Saturday, March 6, 1869

The rain was relentless, an icy deluge that pounded the gravestones and soaked into the thirsty earth. Only the funeral of a loved one would bring anyone to a burial ground on a day like today, but there was no funeral, only death. Lord Jason Redmond stood very still, his gaze fixed on the young woman laid out on a marble slab. Her hands were folded on her chest as if in prayer, her eyes open, the unseeing gaze fixed on the human-sized angel that loomed above her, its wings folded, its head bowed. Rainwater ran down the angel's marble cheeks and dripped onto the woman's face, as if the angel were weeping at the senseless loss. No wound was visible, and the water that sluiced off the slab and into the ground at Jason's feet bore no traces of blood, but there was no doubt that the young woman had been murdered.

As a surgeon and a veteran of the American Civil War, Jason had seen death in all its forms, but it still held the power to shock him, especially when the victim was someone he had known. Rebecca Grainger had been Jason's goddaughter's nursemaid and the woman Inspector Daniel Haze had believed might snatch him from the bottomless chasm of melancholy his wife's sudden death had plunged him into nearly a year ago.

Only a short while ago, Daniel and Rebecca had taken the first tentative steps toward becoming a family, but things had changed after Daniel was brutally attacked while investigating a murder. His fragile relationship with Rebecca had fractured, the lady turning cold once she understood the danger and uncertainty of being a policeman's wife. After weeks of nursing Daniel through his recovery, Rebecca gave her notice. A few more days and she would have married another man and set off on a voyage to her husband's ranch in Argentina. Instead of preparing for her upcoming wedding, she lay dead on the cold stone, the only witness to her death the indifferent angel that would keep its secrets long after they were all dead and gone.

Jason tore his gaze from Rebecca's sightless stare to check on the rain-drenched constables who were combing the graveyard for Charlotte. Inspector Haze's small daughter had been with her nursemaid at the time of the attack, presumably on their way home. The policemen had expected to find Charlotte right away, hiding behind one of the ancient stones, frightened, confused, and chilled to the bone in her sodden coat and hat, but with every passing minute, the possibility of finding the child became more remote. Charlotte was nowhere to be found.

The constables periodically called out her name, urging her to show herself, but if Charlotte was within hearing distance, she would have made her presence known—especially since her father had yelled himself hoarse searching the graveyard for her. He now stood stock-still beneath an ancient yew, his eyes wide with terror behind his fogged spectacles as he grappled with the tragedy that had struck so unexpectedly on a peaceful afternoon.

Leaving Rebecca's remains to the police photographer, who had just set up his tripod and was complaining bitterly about the rain, Jason strode over to join Daniel beneath the yew. Daniel barely seemed to register Jason's presence. His shoulders were hunched, his hands balled into fists, and his head tucked into his muffler. The tweed of his coat was drenched, and rainwater dripped from the brim of his bowler hat, but Daniel didn't seem to notice, his gaze fixed on the tall helmets of the constables as they moved between the weathered headstones.

"Daniel," Jason began, but Daniel shook his head, as if to dispel his stupor.

"She's not here, Jason," he said quietly. "She's not here. What if she's dead?" Daniel's voice broke on the final word, and he finally turned to Jason, his face bone white.

"No, Daniel," Jason retorted vehemently. "If Charlotte were dead, she'd be here. Whoever has done this would have no reason to take her away." Jason couldn't bring himself to refer to Charlotte as a body and resolutely spoke of her in the present tense, even though he couldn't be sure of anything. "Charlotte was either taken or she's hiding."

"She's not hiding," Daniel replied woodenly. "If she were, we would have located her by now."

"Daniel, you must pull yourself together," Jason said, his tone brooking no argument. "If you are not up to the task of investigating what happened, then Superintendent Ransome will assign another detective to the case, and then you will have no say in the investigation. You must put your personal feelings aside if you hope to find Charlotte."

"I don't know that I can, Jason," Daniel replied, his voice barely above a whisper. "I've been standing here for a quarter of an hour, and I can't seem to find the strength to move or the presence of mind to formulate a plan. My thoughts are fragmented, and my heart is shattered."

Daniel's gaze slid toward the body of Rebecca Grainger, his eyes misting with tears of shock and grief. Mr. Gillespie had finished and was packing away his tripod and camera, and two constables stood at the ready, a canvas stretcher held between them. They would transport Rebecca's remains to the waiting police wagon and convey them to the mortuary at Scotland Yard.

"Buck up, cowboy," Jason said, knowing the odd expression would force Daniel to focus on him. Daniel found most of Jason's American sayings baffling, but this one was sure to top the list.

"What?" Daniel echoed, staring at Jason in obvious incomprehension.

"It's a call to rally," Jason explained. "We must interview the vicar who found the body right away, while the details are still fresh in his mind. Then I will perform the autopsy. We need to establish the cause of death."

"Jason, I don't think I can formulate a coherent question, much less hunt for clues or draw possible connections. I am numb with shock."

Jason nodded. "Leave it to me. Come, Daniel. Let's get you inside. You're soaked through."

"Really? I haven't noticed," Daniel said as he reluctantly left his spot under the tree and followed Jason toward the porch of St. John's Wood Church.

Chapter 2

Jason was glad to get out of the rain, but the interior of the church, although dry, was no warmer than the outside, nor was it brighter. No candles were lit so early in the day, and the light that filtered through the high windows did little to dispel the gloom that nearly swallowed the nave. Their footsteps echoed on the flagstone floor as they strode toward the hunched, black-clad figure in a front pew.

The Reverend Brompton was a thickset man of about sixty-five with a ruddy complexion and thinning white hair. His dark eyes peered out from pockets of wrinkled flesh, and his jowls rested on his stiff clerical collar. He turned toward Jason and Daniel as they approached, his expression transforming to one of hope.

"Did you find the child?" he asked.

Jason shook his head. "Not yet. May we ask you a few questions, Reverend?"

"Of course. Anything I can do to help."

Daniel sank into the pew across from the vicar and bowed his head. Jason thought he might be praying for Charlotte's safe return and had no wish to disturb him, so he sat down next to the reverend to ensure he didn't tower over the man as he addressed him.

"Please, tell me precisely what happened this afternoon," Jason invited.

"I stepped out at eleven. I like to take a walk before luncheon, you see, just to clear my head and cast my thoughts over the week's sermon. I always keep to the same schedule. I'm a creature of habit," the vicar said. "I take my midday meal precisely at twelve at the chophouse in Wellington Road. They do an excellent oyster stew. And the roast beef is always most tender," he blathered on. "It wasn't raining when I set off, but the sky had already turned dark. I didn't think I'd be able to stay out there for long and hoped I'd get at least a half hour in."

"The body," Jason prompted.

"Ah, yes. Do forgive me. Finding that young woman was something of a shock. I see the dearly departed all the time in my line of work, but I hadn't expected to find her there. She looked so peaceful, as if she were praying. At first, I thought it was a prank, you see," he said, looking to Jason for understanding. "Some strange new ritual perhaps to commune with the dead. There are all these spiritualists about these days, aren't there? They have no respect for the Lord or the teachings of the Bible and seem to think it's perfectly acceptable to try to summon the dead. It's disgraceful," the Reverend Brompton said more forcefully. "I do not condone these practices and say so from the pulpit."

"The young woman," Jason prompted again.

"Ah, yes. I'm sorry. I digress," the reverend said contritely. "I walked toward her, in something of a huff, I might add. I was going to tell her that the burial ground was closed, and she was trespassing. Besides, she'd catch her death lying there, on that cold marble slab." The vicar seemed to realize the absurdity of what he was saying and hurried to finish. "It was then that I realized she wasn't moving."

"Did you see anyone when you stepped outside?"

The vicar shook his head. "I'm afraid I didn't."

"And you saw no sign of the child?" Jason pressed.

"I'm afraid not. When I realized the young woman was dead, I immediately went to summon a constable. It took some considerable time to locate one."

"What did you do then, Reverend?"

"I came back here to wait for reinforcements. I gave my account to Constable Napier of Scotland Yard when he arrived. It was the constable who told me about the missing child."

"Had you ever seen the victim before?"

The reverend considered the question. "She wasn't a member of my congregation, but I have seen her in the street. I believe she lived nearby."

"Yes, she did," Jason confirmed.

The vicar looked at Jason, his gaze pleading. "May I go now? I'm rather hungry, you see. I don't normally take a large breakfast as it gives me terrible indigestion, and it's well past one o'clock."

"Yes, of course," Jason replied as courteously as he could. "Thank you for your assistance, Reverend."

"Damn fool," Daniel hissed as they left the church. "All he cares about is his bloated belly. I reckon he can afford to miss a meal or two."

Jason didn't think a reply was warranted. His mind was on Rebecca Grainger and the final moments of her life. He had yet to perform an autopsy, but there were certain things he had been able to ascertain just by looking at Rebecca's remains. She had not been shot or stabbed, and her clothes didn't appear to have been disturbed, but he had noticed that the skin of her throat, which was partially hidden by the high collar of her gown, was reddened, and the white of the left eye was tinged red as a result of a broken blood vessel. Jason had not looked inside Rebecca's mouth, but her lips had been slightly parted, the tongue visible and unnaturally swollen. All initial signs pointed to strangulation, which would mean that Rebecca had faced her killer and had known she was about to die.

She must have been terrified and had perhaps begged for her life and that of Charlotte. Had she warned Charlotte to run and hide, or had the child listened to her instincts and tried to get

278

away? Had she succeeded and was even now hiding somewhere, waiting until she felt it was safe to come out? Or was there a darker explanation for her continued absence? Normally, Jason would share his thoughts with Daniel, eager to test his theory, but given Daniel's relationship to the victim, it was wiser to keep his counsel for the time being. There was one logical step, however, that Jason could propose that would help divert Daniel's attention from his fears and allow him to focus on finding Charlotte, as well as Rebecca's killer.

"We should speak to Rebecca's fiancé," Jason said. "Will you question him on your own, or would you prefer that I accompany you after I complete the postmortem?"

Daniel stared at Jason for a moment, as if he didn't quite comprehend what Jason was asking of him, but then his gaze sharpened, and an expression of determination replaced one of helplessness. "By the time you've completed the postmortem, the scoundrel might have fled."

"I agree it would be unwise to wait," Jason said, pleased by the reaction his suggestion had elicited. "Do you think Mr. Stanley could be responsible?"

"I don't know," Daniel replied tersely. "I've never met the man."

"Now would be a good time to make his acquaintance," Jason said, wondering if Daniel was in the right frame of mind to question a suspect and if perhaps it would be prudent to send someone else. "Perhaps you should ask Sergeant Meadows to accompany you. He's still in the burial ground."

If Daniel had realized that Jason had assumed unauthorized command, he didn't bother to comment. He seemed grateful to have been given an important task. "Yes. I will," he said with a nod. "I can use the support, to be honest."

"Sergeant Meadows is a competent policeman," Jason said.

"He is," Daniel agreed. "I'll see you back at the Yard."

"We will find her, Daniel," Jason said softly, reaching out to touch Daniel's arm in a gesture of support. "We will get Charlotte back."

"You don't know that, Jason," Daniel replied, and his eyes misted with tears. "It may already be too late."

"No. I refuse to believe that," Jason said stubbornly. "Until we know for certain, we keep looking."

"Thank you. If not for you—"

Daniel didn't bother to finish the sentence before turning on his heel and heading down the path, Jason following closely behind. The rain had stopped, but the sky was still a menacing gray, the clouds low and dense. Having summoned Sergeant Meadows, Daniel walked off without a word of farewell, leaving Jason to return to the carriage that would take him to Scotland Yard. Jason dreaded the task ahead, but he owed it to Daniel to be the one to perform the postmortem and treat Rebecca's remains with the respect they deserved before she was laid to rest.

Chapter 3

Daniel huddled deeper into his damp coat and strode purposefully away from the church, Sergeant Meadows at his heels. The police wagon had already departed, removing the mortal remains of the woman Daniel had cared deeply about, possibly even loved, and leaving behind two constables to continue the search for Charlotte. Daniel's chest was constricted with agitation, the pressure like iron bands encircling his ribcage. His breath came in short gasps, and his stomach threatened to turn itself inside out, but he refused to give in to physical discomfort. His every thought was for the wellbeing of his little girl, and although he wished he could remain and join in the search, as an experienced detective, he realized that his purpose would be best served elsewhere.

Daniel spotted an empty hansom heading toward the cab stand on Wellington Road and hailed the driver. As soon as Sergeant Meadows settled in beside him, Daniel called out, "Charing Cross Hotel. And be quick about it. We're about police business."

"As ye say, guv," the driver replied in a gruff tone, seeming utterly unimpressed with Daniel's declaration.

The length of the journey depended on the volume of Saturday afternoon traffic rather than the driver's personal commitment to complying with the request. If a delivery wagon or an omnibus happened to obstruct his path, there wasn't much he could do about it, and all three of them knew it. Daniel sighed irritably and settled back against the cracked leather seat, staring balefully at the street beyond the cab.

The traffic became heavier as they neared Charing Cross. Hackneys, sleek private carriages, and delivery wagons jostled for space, and the level of noise seemed to escalate with every passing minute, the vendors and newsboys screaming themselves hoarse as they hawked their wares to the travelers streaming in and out of the station. Daniel tried to block out the cacophony and focus on the questions he intended to ask, but all he could see was Charlotte's sweet face, her large dark eyes pleading with him to find her, and soon.

Removing his spectacles, Daniel rubbed his eyes and pinched the bridge of his nose, but the headache that had been building since Sergeant Meadows arrived on his doorstep with the dreadful news that Rebecca's body had been discovered finally exploded, blurring his vision, and forcing him to grit his teeth.

Ignoring the pain, Daniel cleaned his glasses thoroughly, then alighted from the cab when it finally drew up before the hotel. The Charing Cross Hotel, one of the hotels recently constructed to provide affordable lodging near Charing Cross station, had been built in the Franco-Italian style and harbored aspirations of grandeur not entirely in concert with its location, but if not a desirable address, at least it had convenience to recommend it. On any other day, Daniel might have taken a moment to appreciate the ornate architecture and learn something of the many luxuries offered by this modern establishment, but today, he hardly noticed his surroundings.

He strode past the uniformed doorman, heading directly for the reception desk, which was manned by two somber-looking young men. They were both helping newly arrived guests, who seemed to have an inordinate number of questions that prevented Daniel from gaining access to one of the clerks. A large clock mounted on the wall behind the desk cruelly reminded Daniel just how much time had passed since he'd last seen Charlotte, when she had stood in the foyer as Rebecca buttoned her coat and tied the ribbons of her hat beneath her chin, then smiled and waved to Daniel, calling cheerfully, "See you later, Papa."

At last, the matronly woman who'd been hogging the clerk's attention had moved away, and Daniel approached the desk.

"What room is Leon Stanley in?" he demanded.

"Is Mr. Stanley expecting you, sir?" the clerk asked, his gaze sliding anxiously toward Sergeant Meadows, who was in uniform but had removed his helmet upon entering the foyer.

Daniel whipped out his warrant card, and the clerk immediately held up a placating hand, not wishing to draw any more attention to the presence of the police.

"Four hundred fifteen, Inspector. That's on the fourth floor. Is something amiss?" he asked.

"We need to speak to him urgently," Daniel replied, but his attention was no longer on the young man behind the desk. Daniel pushed past an adolescent bellboy struggling with two large cases and hurried toward the stairs, taking the steps two at a time, Sergeant Meadows behind him, his helmet under his arm.

The two men mounted the stairs to the fourth floor and paused before approaching Leon Stanley's room. The corridor was quiet, only one maidservant cleaning a chamber that looked to have been recently vacated. She paid them no mind and went about her duties, leaving the door ajar so that anyone who passed by would notice her economical industry.

At room 415, Daniel knocked and listened intently. He wasn't at all sure what he would do if Leon Stanley weren't in. There was movement inside the room, and then footsteps approached the door, and it opened.

"Mr. Stanley?" Daniel inquired before asking to come inside.

"Yes. And you are?" he asked, his attention turning to Sergeant Meadows.

"Inspector Haze and Sergeant Meadows of Scotland Yard."

"You're Rebecca's employer," Leon Stanley said, his brow creasing with confusion. "Why are you here?"

"May we come in, Mr. Stanley? This is not a conversation to be held in the corridor," Daniel replied, and stepped forward.

Leon Stanley had no choice but to step back, allowing the two men to enter. Sergeant Meadows shut the door behind them, while Daniel took a moment to study Leon Stanley in the light streaming through the window. The man was around forty, possibly a few years younger, with neatly oiled auburn hair, dark blue eyes, and a carefully brushed moustache. He wore well-cut black trousers, a crisp white shirt, and a waistcoat of dark blue and silver silk with a matching puff tie. His shoes were polished to a shine, and a coat made of black broadcloth lay slung over a chair, as if the man had taken it off upon entering the room.

"Do sit down, gentlemen." Leon Stanley indicated the two chairs that stood on either side of a small round table.

Daniel unbuttoned his coat as he sat down, then took off his hat and settled it on his thigh, while Sergeant Meadows remained standing.

"Please, take a seat, Mr. Stanley," Daniel said, his gaze never leaving the man's face.

Although Leon Stanley was clearly surprised by the unannounced visit and was probably more than irritated by the unwelcome intrusion, he did not seem frightened nor behave in a way that would speak to his guilt. He sat down across from Daniel and laid his hands on the table, interlacing his fingers.

"Inspector Haze, I cannot account for your presence here. The only thing that comes to mind is that something has happened to Rebecca. Please, won't you allay my fears?" Leon Stanley's gaze was so anxious that Daniel actually felt pity for the man.

"Mr. Stanley, I'm terribly sorry to tell you that Rebecca's body was found in St. John's Wood burial ground this morning. We have reason to believe she was murdered."

"What? Are you certain it's her?"

"I'm certain. I saw her myself. I'm very sorry," Daniel said again.

Leon Stanley erupted out of his seat, nearly knocking Sergeant Meadows sideways, and began to pace the room. After prowling for a few moments, he stopped before the window and stared out at the bleak afternoon. "No," he moaned miserably. "No." Daniel realized he was crying.

When he finally turned, Leon Stanley looked as if he had aged several years. His shoulders were stooped, and his mouth quivered as he tried to hold back the tears that glistened on his cheeks. "Why? Who would do such a thing? Rebecca was..." His voice trailed off as he fumbled for his handkerchief and dabbed at his eyes. "She was an angel," he whispered. "She was my angel."

As much as Daniel wanted to disbelieve the show of grief, his instinct told him it was genuine, and Leon Stanley had had no idea what had happened to his beloved.

"Mr. Stanley, Rebecca and Charlotte were out for a walk when—" Daniel was about to say that Rebecca had been accosted and dragged into the burial ground, but he didn't know that was the way it had happened and chose to keep to the facts. "Rebecca was with Charlotte," he said, his voice hoarse with feeling. "We don't know what occurred."

"Oh, I'm so sorry. I pray Charlotte was not harmed."

"We haven't been able to locate her."

"I don't understand," Leon Stanley said, and sank onto the bed so heavily, the mattress springs groaned in protest. "I just don't understand. Rebecca and I were to be married next week. We were—" He buried his face in his hands, and his shoulders heaved with sobs. "I—I'm sorry," he muttered. "I'm just..."

He went silent, unable to finish. Daniel sat still, giving the man a few moments to compose himself.

"Mr. Stanley," Daniel said at last. "I need to ask you a few questions. Time is of the essence."

"Yes, of course," Stanley said as he wiped his eyes and blew his nose, seemingly ready to talk. "Forgive me. I'm in shock. Anything I can do to help, just ask." He wiped his eyes again and fixed his gaze on Daniel.

"Is there anyone you know of who might have wanted to harm Rebecca Grainger?"

"Aside from you?"

"Why would I wish to hurt Miss Grainger?" Daniel asked, stunned by the accusation.

"Rebecca led me to believe that you had feelings for her and were deeply upset by her decision to marry me," Leon Stanley replied. Daniel saw no malice in his gaze, only earnestness.

"Miss Grainger and I had a complicated relationship, Mr. Stanley, but that hardly suggests that I wished to harm her."

Leon Stanley turned to Sergeant Meadows, and Daniel noticed a change in his demeanor. He still looked bereft, his eyes reddened from crying, but his shoulders were drawn back and his chin now jutted forward, his expression more aggressive. "Is it appropriate for a detective who was involved with the victim to be investigating the crime, Sergeant?" he demanded.

"There are no rules against it," Sergeant Meadows replied.

Daniel had no idea if that were the case, since he'd never come up against such a situation before, but he had no intention of surrendering this case without a fight. "Mr. Stanley, I ask again. Was there anyone who might have wished to hurt Rebecca?"

"I don't know. She never really talked about her life," Stanley said. "I got the impression the past few years had not been happy ones."

"Rebecca told me you were a friend of her father's," Daniel tried again.

"Yes, I knew Rebecca's father some years ago, before I left England for good."

"In what capacity did you know him?"

Leon Stanley looked distinctly uncomfortable. "How much do you know of Rebecca's family, Inspector Haze?"

"Clearly not enough," Daniel replied.

"Rebecca's father was a fence."

Daniel felt as if he'd just taken a punch to the gut. Rebecca had told him that her father was a shopkeeper, but she had neglected to mention that he'd fenced stolen goods.

"I was led to believe he died some years ago, leaving Rebecca to fend for herself," Daniel said.

Leon Stanley nodded. "Yes, he died when Rebecca was seventeen. Stabbed in the gut over a silver snuffbox at his shop in Seven Dials."

"Oddly, she had never mentioned her father's criminal past," Daniel said angrily.

His innards were twisting into a knot, his heart rate accelerating by the moment. He had entrusted his child to a woman he had believed to be of good character, and now he was discovering that he hadn't known anything of Rebecca Grainger's true nature.

"We don't choose our parents, Inspector, any more than we choose our social class when we're born, but Rebecca was a good woman," Leon Stanley said quietly, as if reading Daniel's mind. "She was honorable, and kind, and I won't hear a bad word said against her. She did everything in her power to elevate herself from the gutter into which she'd been tossed by her father."

"Forgive me," Daniel muttered. "I did not mean to impugn her character."

"Rebecca didn't deserve the upbringing she had, but Edgar Levinson got what was coming to him."

"Levinson?"

"Grainger was the name Rebecca took when she went into service," Leon Stanley replied rather smugly. Despite his grief, he seemed to derive satisfaction from how little Daniel actually knew of the woman he thought he'd loved.

"And how is it that you came to be acquainted with a fence, Mr. Stanley?" Daniel asked.

If he had hoped to frighten Leon Stanley with the possibility of an arrest, the threat was lost on the man. Stanley shrugged. "We'd had some dealings in the past, but I left that life behind a long time ago. I'm proud of the man I have become, and Rebecca would not have spared me a second glance if I were engaged in anything even remotely unethical."

"And would you have told her if you were?" Daniel asked.

Leon Stanley met Daniel's gaze squarely. "I would. I was completely honest with her. I'm thirty-eight years old, Inspector. What I want…wanted," Leon Stanley amended, "was a good woman by my side and a chance at a family. That's why I had traveled to England, to find a wife. There are many beautiful women in Argentina, but they're not the sort of companion an Englishman wants to take to wife. They're all Papist, for one thing, and I wanted my wife to share my beliefs."

"How did you find Rebecca?" Daniel asked.

"How do you mean?"

"Well, if she had changed her name when she went into service, how did you know where to look for her? Had you kept in contact all these years?"

"No. Rebecca wanted nothing more to do with that sort of life after her father was murdered. They didn't just kill the man, they eviscerated him and then sacked his shop. Took everything of value and destroyed the rest. Rebecca was left with nothing."

"How did she survive? It's not an easy thing to find a position as a nursemaid without a character." Of course, one could always forge a character reference and hope that the prospective employers never bothered to check with one's previous employer. Rebecca's references had been impeccable, but were they pure fiction?

Leon Stanley looked uncomfortable, as if he were betraying a confidence, but his desire to bring Rebecca's killer to justice seemed to prevail. "I called on her grandfather," Stanley said.

"Her grandfather? Rebecca told me she had no living kin," Daniel replied, trying in vain to suppress his anger.

Leon Stanley smiled wryly. "She didn't pull the name Grainger out of thin air, Inspector. It was her mother's name. There was bad blood between Rebecca's mother and her family, I reckon on account of her having married so far beneath her station, but Rebecca did have a living grandfather, and it was to him that she'd turned in her desperation."

"And did he welcome her, this grandfather?"

Leon Stanley shook his head. "He did at first, but in the end, they fell out. Rebecca's grandfather wouldn't receive me, but I was able to learn where to find Rebecca. The housekeeper told me."

"And does the grandfather have a name?" Daniel inquired.

"Abel Grainger. Lives in Brook Street."

"Brook Street, you say?"

Brook Street was a desirable address, its affluence reflected in rising real estate value. If Abel Grainger lived there, he had to be relatively well off. Surely he could have supported his granddaughter instead of allowing her to go into service, but there was clearly more to the story.

"Nineteen, Brook Street. It'll break his heart to learn what has happened to Rebecca," Leon Stanley said. "But he deserves to know."

"Mr. Grainger will be informed." *And thoroughly questioned*, Daniel added silently. "Surely, given Rebecca's past associations, there must have been someone who'd held a grudge against her, or her father," Daniel tried again.

"I don't believe so. Rebecca earned her living honestly and devoted herself to the children in her charge. She loved Charlotte, Inspector. She told me so on more than one occasion," Leon Stanley said. "And she loved me," he added in a whisper, as if he still couldn't believe that what had happened was real and permanent.

"And what about you, Mr. Stanley?" Daniel pressed. "Might someone have wished to retaliate against you?"

Leon Stanley looked momentarily stunned but then nodded in understanding. "Inspector Haze, this is the first time I've been back to England in nearly seven years. Whatever debts I once had were settled long ago, and if they weren't, I could now easily afford to repay them. No one would have any reason to hurt Rebecca to get to me, nor would they bother with taking her charge. What use is a little girl to them? My past associates have children aplenty."

The man sighed deeply, his gaze straying to the leaden sky beyond the window. "I know you need to ask your questions, Inspector, and I have answered them to the best of my ability, but may I now be left in peace to grieve the life I have so suddenly lost?"

Daniel nodded. He felt compassion for the man despite the resentment that had been bubbling away in him since Rebecca had informed him that she would be marrying the man.

"Please accept my condolences, Mr. Stanley," Daniel said, rising to his feet. He didn't think Leon Stanley had anything more to tell them. "I will ask you not to leave London until the case is closed."

"May I bury her, Inspector Haze?" Leon Stanley asked. He was clearly broken by Rebecca's death and was groping for something to hold on to, even if it was the organizing of a funeral.

"I expect we'll be able to release the body in a few days, Mr. Stanley, at which point you can proceed with a funeral. If Mr. Grainger has no objection. Since you were not married, he's legally her next of kin."

Stanley nodded. "I'm sure we can come to some arrangement. Please, keep me apprised of any developments."

"I will," Daniel promised, even though he wasn't at all sure he ever wanted to see the man again.

"Where to, sir?" Sergeant Meadows asked once they had descended the stairs and were back in the reception area.

Daniel glanced at the clock. "You may return to the Yard, Sergeant. There's something I must do."

"Are you sure you'll be all right, sir?" Sergeant Meadows asked, eyeing him with concern.

"Yes," Daniel promised. "I will see you there in about an hour."

"Very well, sir." Sergeant Meadows donned his helmet and departed, leaving Daniel in the crowded foyer.

"Do you need a cab, sir?" the doorman asked when Daniel stepped outside.

"Yes, I do."

The doorman lifted his hand, and a hansom pulled away from the line waiting just down the street and stopped at the door.

291

"Where to?" the driver asked.

Daniel almost gave the cabbie his home address in the hope that Charlotte would be there when he returned, sitting in her chair in the kitchen while Grace went about preparing dinner, but Charlotte would not be at home. Daniel knew that, just as he knew that this case would not be solved quickly.

"Nineteen, Brook Street," he said instead and slumped against the seat. He felt as if every ounce of strength had been sapped from his body, and he wanted nothing more than to curl into a ball and howl until his fear and grief abated, but this was only the beginning, and he couldn't give in to weakness. He'd howl later. Right now, he had Rebecca's grandfather to interview, and he wanted to speak to Mr. Grainger on his own.

Made in United States
Troutdale, OR
09/23/2023

13141963R00181